Dead

KATHERINE GARBERA

MILLS & BOON
Pure reading pleasure™

This edition published in Great Britain December 2008
by Harlequin Mills & Boon Limited,
Eton House, 18-24 Paradise Road, Richmond, Surrey TW9 1SR

First published in 2005 by Harlequin Enterprises Ltd under the title
The Amazon Strain

© Katherine Garbera 2005

ISBN: 978 0 263 86019 1

46-1208

Harlequin Mills & Boon policy is to use papers that are natural, renewable and recyclable products and made from wood grown in sustainable forests. The logging and manufacturing processes conform to the legal environmental regulations of the country of origin.

Printed and bound in Spain
by Litografia Rosés S.A., Barcelona

ABOUT THE AUTHOR

Katherine Garbera has had fun working as a production page, lifeguard, secretary and VIP tour guide, but those occupations pale when compared to creating worlds where women save the day and wounded hearts are healed. Writing romantic suspense novels is the perfect job for her. She's always had a vivid imagination and believes strongly in happily-ever-after. She's married to the man she met in Walt Disney World's Fantasyland. They live in Central Florida with their two children. Readers can visit her on the web at www.katherinegarbera.com.

This book is dedicated to my sisters,
Linda Beardsley and Donna Sutermeister, who
shared many journeys all over the world from
our backyard – too bad that tunnel to
China never paid off! Thanks for the good
times and great memories!

Acknowledgements

Thanks to Dr John Walden, who was so
generous with his time and knowledge
of the Amazon. Any mistakes are my own.

Thanks also to Dr Michael Miller, who
answered my questions on infectious
diseases and virology. Again, any mistakes
are my own.

Special thanks to Eve Gaddy, Nancy Robards
Thompson and Beverly Brandt, who
were my cheerleaders!
And to Matt who is always so supportive and
believes in me when I start to doubt.

Chapter 1

Dr. Jane Miller, virus hunter.

The words echoed in her head as she exited the elevator in the bowels of the Centers for Disease Control headquarters in Atlanta, Georgia. Entering the deepest part of the building always made her feel like some sort of superspy. Maybe it was the fact that security was as tight here as it was at the White House.

Whatever the reason, she always heard the 007 theme in the back of her head as she moved through the hallways. She passed by labs that worked with lower-level infections, such as a new strand of the flu, before reaching steel-reinforced doors with a sophisticated security scanner. The security guard smiled at her. He'd worked at the lab for about a year now.

"Good evening, Dr. Miller."

"Hello, Stan."

He had a nice face. He was a doting grandfather who'd embodied all the things she'd always kind of longed for when she thought of family, but had never found. "Working late again?"

"You know how I am when I get a new problem to work on." She didn't say anything else, leery that he might inadvertently pass along the fact that she was doing research on something sent to her by her father. Doctor Rob Miller was persona non grata as far as the CDC was concerned.

He nodded at her. "But it's been three months and you're still working eighteen-hour days. You're always warning me about the effects of exhaustion."

The truth was, she was burning the candle at both ends hoping that what she'd discovered was somehow an error. "I know, but this time…I just feel like I need to work on this project around the clock."

"We're used to emergencies," he said.

She shrugged. How could she explain to him what she didn't really understand herself? She only knew that the virus her father had sent her needed her attention. She'd received the samples almost too long ago—in the world of infectious viruses, three months could be a lethal amount of time.

She remembered when she'd received the plainly wrapped brown package. It had seemed innocent enough, but she'd recognized the angular handwriting on the outside and opened it with trepidation. Anything from her father was suspect. The CDC and her dad went way back, but the relationship was no longer one that either side liked to acknowledge.

Why had he sent it to her?

Jane flashed her badge at the reader on the wall. Then she removed her glasses and leaned forward for the eye scan. She didn't like it, but had gotten used to it. Finally she could withstand the laser scan without blinking. The doors opened and she stepped through.

She slipped her glasses back on and noticed the biohazard warning sign that stood next to the door to the women's locker room. She entered the facility and changed from her street clothes into scrubs. In order to enter the lab, everything had to be removed from the skin out. Jane changed as quickly as possible.

She then made her way to a second set of scanners. Adrenaline and nerves warred for control of her body. Adrenaline won. It had been a long time since she'd had anything new in her hands. Once the doors opened, she stepped inside the ultraviolet-light chamber and waited a moment before exiting. She paused again, preparing to enter the level 3 labs.

She flashed her badge one more time. Security had always been tight at the CDC and with the ever-present threat of biological warfare looming on the horizon, it had grown even tighter in recent years. The guard at this station was new and he took her ID badge and read every bit of information on it. He also had her remove her glasses for him.

She knew what he saw. A rather average-looking woman with curly red hair. In her ID photo, it looked darker, almost auburn. Her eyes were wide-set and the exact same warm brown color as her mother's had been. Jane herself had no real memory of her mother's eyes, but her father had mentioned it often enough when she'd been a girl.

Finally, she entered a holding area that contained the space suits. She went to her stall and pulled on the one that had her name emblazoned on it.

She exited the room and walked a short distance to the decon—decontamination—showers, which brushed over her. Then she pressed her thumb to a keypad and the door opened. "Welcome, Dr. Miller."

The computer voice reminded her a little of the *Star Trek* computer. Maybe it was the space suits, but she always felt as if she'd left this world and was on a journey to another one when she stepped into the lab.

Small windowed doors lined the hall. Jane didn't bother reading name tags or signs of what the scientists inside were working on. She kept moving until she reached her lab. Her area of expertise was Ebola, and she'd recently finished working with a new strand of the virus that had shown up in the Sudan.

Ebola was reliable and she knew what to expect. But this thing her father had sent—it was a mystery. The puzzle was still a jumble in her mind and on her microscope slide. But she felt in her gut that she was getting closer to figuring everything out.

She swiped her badge through the scanner and the door unlocked. She walked inside, hitting the light switch with her elbow. Her lab looked like every other one on this level. Long countertops lined the walls and a small office area was in the back. She could just make out her Johnny Depp poster, which hung on her large bulletin board next to the *Dilbert* cartoons that her college roommate, Sophia, had sent to her.

There was a sophisticated replicating machine on the end of the counter and a freezer to keep samples at the proper temperature until she was ready to use them. The freezer currently held samples of her father's blood as well as the blood of a Yura tribesman.

The Yura were a tribe native to the Amazon. Some of them lived in Bolivia, but her father had spent the last few years with a group who lived near Manu in Peru's Amazon basin. Their lifestyle had changed little in generations save for the introduction of modern weapons such as rifles. They still lived off the bounty of the rain forest and whatever the Amazon River and its tributaries provided.

Jane had been working with the blood samples as well as medication her father had sent and monitoring the effects of the primitive treatment.

She took the clipboard from the wall and wrote *Blood samples from South America* and the day's date. She didn't mention the Yura tribe or Dr. Rob Miller. Three damned months and finally she was getting closer to finding an inoculation that worked. She'd decided to mutate the local remedy her father had sent, a powder made from bark and leaves, to see if that would work. Today she'd find out.

The powder from the bark wasn't a treatment. A treatment in the world of viruses was a way of stopping the virus. Kind of like a cure. But because of the nature of infectious diseases, virologists didn't use the word *cure*. As soon as it was uttered, a new mutation would show up.

She'd noticed that the bark wasn't a treatment after she'd administered a dose of the powder to the infected blood sample. It slowed the activity of the virus, but the virus returned to full strength one week later.

Jane had used her blood samples to start a colony of the mystery virus in the petri dishes. An application of the bark powder had initially slowed the spread of the virus through the petri dish, but within a week, the virus was flourishing.

The leaf used to make the remedy was related to the coca plant, which was used in the making of cocaine. Jane suspected that the side effects were more than just relief from pain.

There were no real healing properties in the plant. This meant that anyone using this remedy wouldn't live. They'd alleviate the symptoms for a time, and wouldn't be in pain while the disease spread throughout their body, but the virus would win in the end.

"Hey, Jane," a man said, from her doorway.

Jane glanced up to see Tom Macmillan, another scientist who worked on her floor. What the hell was he doing here? She didn't want anyone in her lab on the off chance it would get out that her father was involved in her current project.

Tom was an expert who worked with E. coli. He'd spent four years working in a monkey house in Africa, studying the multigenerational effect of the disease.

"What's up, Tom?" she asked. Everyone was really too busy to ever just hang out and chat in the labs.

"This came for you. Since I was coming back to start work, I told Angie I'd bring it."

Jane reached for the package and saw the same angular handwriting that had been on the last package from her dad. Her heart stopped for a second. The situation with the Yura must be escalating if he'd sent something else.

"Do you know what that is?" he asked.

Jane debated for a second, but being evasive would only raise his suspicion. "Some samples I was asked to consult on by a virologist currently living in Peru."

"Infectious?" Tom asked. He was a little geeky, but sexy in his own way. Tall and lanky, he wore horn-rimmed glasses that looked good on him. His eyes were hazel and changed color sometimes with his moods.

Right now his eyes were the swirling gray-green of the Atlantic when a hurricane stirs through—excitement, she realized. He stared at the clipboard in her hands.

He loved it when they got a new disease. And he wasn't the only one. There was a reason why they all worked back here, away from the public. Why they spent so much time in the lab. They all were obsessed with watching life change in their petri dishes. There was nothing quite like taking a potentially big biological threat and reducing it to nothing.

"Oh, yeah. I've been trying to find a treatment. This must be some new blood samples."

"Want some help?" he asked. He rubbed his gloved hands together as he stepped into her lab.

"Don't you have your own work to do?" She was reluctant to involve anyone else in this project until she had a firmer grasp on what her dad had sent.

"Yes, but I needed a break. I'm missing something and staring at the strand I'm working with isn't helping. Maybe solving your problem will help me," Tom said.

"Solving my problem? Tom, you do have a God complex."

"Ha. Stop teasing me. I know you've been working around the clock in here. You need some fresh eyes."

He was right. She went to her office and returned a minute later with the note from her dad.

"This is all I've got to work with," she said, handing the note to him. "So far I've analyzed the viral strain and it is definitely lethal. I tried all common treatments but they didn't work. Yesterday I mutated a strain of the local remedy—a powder from this tree—and let it incubate. I'm ready to test it."

Tom read the note. Jane already knew it by heart. She tried to keep her expression impassive.

Jane—not sure what this is, but the Yura are infected by it and so far two have died. I tried to contact the disease control office in Lima but they weren't interested. Local practices forbid examining the deceased and the bodies were burned. I was able to get this blood sample from an infected male. I've also sent mine to compare it with. The symptoms include fevers, hemorrhaging, swelling, shock and convulsions. I'm enclosing the local treatment. The bark and leaf are ground together to make a paste and then ingested. The treatment relieves symptoms for a 48-hour period before it has to be ingested again.—Dad

He'd included the coordinates of the tribe's location in the jungles of Peru. She'd already tracked the location on her own GPS unit.

"Rob Miller sent this letter. Is that from him, too?"

"Yes." She didn't elaborate. If he was like half the other scientists at the CDC, he'd leave now. Instead he just watched her.

"What'd he send this time?"

She went to a low workbench and opened the desktop freezer. Blood samples were submitted to the lab in a frozen form, something that had bugged her about her dad's original package. Where had her dad found a facility to do this kind of work? Especially since he mentioned that the CDC office in Lima hadn't been cooperative.

And if he'd had a lab do the freezing, why hadn't he stuck around to analyze the samples?

His first package had contained the Yura blood sample and a second, her father's, as an uninfected sample from the same environment. He'd included a piece of tree bark with a small bud and leaf still attached—the local remedy—and an insect. *Possible carrier,* the label in her father's handwriting said. Jane had spent the last few months analyzing the organic medicine and hoped to find some answers soon.

She'd called a peer at the World Health Organization in South America to check on the strain, but he'd assured her that there was nothing to worry about. He'd heard the rumors. They'd taken samples and conducted interviews in a village along the Amazon.

If the government officials were saying not to worry, she could be opening a can of worms. The World Health Organization and the CDC would both have consulted with the Peruvian government.

She was cautious by nature. She opened the new package. It was packaged the same way the original one was. Only this time the note on the packaging was labeled, *Male Caucasian, 55 years old, Rob Miller.*

Another sample of her father's blood. Her heart beat just a little faster. Did he suspect he'd been infected? Oh, man. He'd better not be infected.

She still had a lot of things to say to the man. And...she pushed the thoughts aside. Now she was going to have to test his blood sample. She wished Tom wasn't here.

There wasn't anything she could do about it now. Find a treatment, then worry about her father.

"Tell me what you need me to do," Tom said, taking the sample and going to a microscope in the corner.

"Each day, I've been checking the blood sample. I've administered the powder from this tree bark, which works as a temporary relief of this virus. But so far the change in the growth pattern in the petri dish doesn't resemble a treatment."

"I wonder if the insect is the carrier? It could have been a primate. Did the letter indicate?" Tom asked.

She glanced at him. "No. He wasn't sure what carried the disease, just sent this little wasp as a possibility. I've been concentrating on trying to isolate the virus and figure out what it is. If it's something we've already identified and can treat. I've been varying the sample treatment with known treatments for differing fevers found in the region."

"What'd he send this time?"

"His own blood sample. He included his with the first package to show a healthy test had been conducted. But this new sample means..."

"He thinks he might be infected. Want me to check it? He is your father."

Did she really want Tom to do this for her? Hell, no. She'd do it. "No. Why don't you take a look at these two slides, see what the treated and untreated blood looks like." She pointed to the slides containing the Yura tribesmen's samples.

Tom reached around her for the two samples before moving across the room to the other long lab table. "Let's crack this case wide open."

She smiled at him, trying to make sure he'd think this was a normal reaction. Trying not to let him see that she was afraid for once of the knowledge she'd always taken such pride in.

"God, you are too corny for words. Good thing you chose to go into science."

"Why's that?" he asked, arching one eyebrow at her.

"Any other profession wouldn't tolerate your eccentricities."

"Sure it would. I'm brilliant, and that kind of raises the tolerance bar," Tom said.

"Not far enough."

He threw his head back and laughed. "I like you, Jane."

"Thanks, Tom. Let's get to work."

Tom took his sample to a corner of the lab and Jane went to work. The space-suit gloves were for her protection, but she didn't like to use them. If she'd been alone in the lab she would have shed them. But she couldn't with Tom here, so she worked with them on.

She took her time preparing the electron microscope, a fully computerized technological wonder that took up as much room in her lab as her large desk did. Finally, her father's blood was being shot by the microscope's "gun," the lens focusing on objects too small for the most powerful light microscope to magnify. The computer screen finally showed her a photo of the tiniest of objects: a virus. Blood rushed in her ears and spots danced in front of her eyes. She reached behind her for support against the countertop.

"Jane? You okay?"

She shook her head and forced down the bile rising in the back of her throat. "Yeah. I'm fine. Let me compare this with the one you're looking at."

She concealed the panic and pain and infinite sadness that rose through her like a wave.

Tom didn't say anything, just stepped back out of the way. She ordered the computer to remove the sample. She studied the slide, adjusting the light. With this level of magnification it was easier to see the infection.

Saying nothing to Tom, she inserted a new sample.

She adjusted her glasses and glanced down. The cells began to take shape on the computer screen as she searched. Slowly it came into focus.

Jane's dad was infected with the same virus that was killing the Yura. And it was fatal.

"Where's the modified bark treatment you made?" Tom asked.

Jane stared at him. In her mind she saw every encounter she'd had with her father.

"Jane?"

"I'm sorry. I'm a little upset."

"I can see that. What can I do to help?"

She looked back at the slide again, this time as a scientist and not as a daughter. She looked at the cells and how they'd replicated. It seemed similar to Lassa fever, which was diagnosed by analyzing the platelets.

"Yes. Fine. Let's try the treatment." Jane left Tom and went to the refrigerator where she'd stored the batch from yesterday. This was the third mutation of a possible treatment she'd made.

She returned to Tom and administered a drop of it, praying it would work. She did the same thing with the other infected sample. Then, using a healthy blood sample of her own, she tried the treatment she'd culled from the same mutated strain.

"Well, well, well. You didn't need me after all, Jane."

She looked at the computer screen with Tom and saw that the new mutated treatment was indeed isolating and destroying the virus.

"I need to talk to Meredith and then call the director of the lab in Lima."

Tom said nothing else. "I'll run a test to see how long the treatment will stop the virus."

"Thanks, Tom."

Jane left the lab slowly, not wanting Tom to see her inward panic, but she walked as fast as she could. She barely tolerated the decon shower. She pressed her thumb to the keypad to activate the door. "Good day, Dr. Miller."

Jane sprinted to her locker, stripping the space suit from her body as she moved. She dumped the space suit in the environmental cleaning bin and tugged on her jeans. Dammit, why the hell had she worn a button-down shirt today? She struggled to get her arms into the shirt and started buttoning it before she realized the damned thing was twisted.

She closed her eyes. Her hands were trembling and she knew she had to focus. This wasn't helping anyone. She pulled the shirt off and calmly put it on correctly.

She flashed her badge at the new security guard and he keyed the door. She dashed down the corridor to the retinal scanner. Pulled off her glasses and bent to be scanned.

The door popped open and she forced herself to walk slowly through it. Stan waved at her as she emerged. She waved back. The urgency riding her was intense but her steps slowed as she neared her boss's office. How was she going to explain that her father had once again stumbled onto a fatal virus?

Meredith Redding had been with the CDC for more than twenty years. Jane remembered meeting her for the first time when she did a project for her sixth-grade science fair. Meredith hadn't looked like Jane had expected her father's peer to look. With her straight blond hair and model-perfect features, Meredith was the type of woman people often assumed had more looks than smarts. But Meredith quickly disabused them of that notion.

She'd been very helpful and encouraging to Jane. The relationship had maintained that mentor-type balance until Jane had received her degree and taken a job at the CDC.

"What can I do for you, Jane?"

Honestly, she had no idea where to start. She took a deep breath. "I just had a breakthrough with the treatment I've been searching for on the virus my father sent. Did you get anywhere with the office in South America?"

Meredith pursed her lips. Then she swiveled her chair and stood.

"I've found a treatment that works in our initial testing. Tom is running a test on the treatment to see how long it is potent. The virus looks similar to Lassa fever, but it's more dangerous and this new treatment is the only one that has worked on it."

"Damn. Are you sure?"

Jane realized she was staking her reputation to her father's, an action that had proven disastrous in the past for other virologists. "As positive as I can be in the lab."

"If any other virologist sent it…"

"I know. But the fact that he did send it makes me want to take it seriously."

"What aren't you telling me?" Meredith asked.

If anyone else had asked, Jane would have kept her mouth shut. She would have never even mentioned Rob Miller's name. But Meredith was the one person in the CDC, heck maybe in the world who'd understand the complications that surrounded her and her father. "One of the samples was Dad's."

Meredith flushed. "Is he infected?"

Jane clenched her hands in tight fists. Swallowing against her dry mouth, she said, "Yes."

Meredith sank back down in her chair. She and Rob had been friends and maybe more ten years ago. Then when she'd been promoted, he'd left Atlanta and gone to Belgium to work on the AIDS-HIV project. Jane didn't know what had happened between them, but watching Meredith now, she suspected there was still some connection.

"What do you want to do?" Meredith asked after a few minutes had passed.

"Call the office in South America and get them to move on this. I can send them my research and then they can…" Jane broke off. Meredith was shaking her head.

"What's going on?"

"I've contacted them. They are sure that there is no danger of a hot-zone outbreak. In fact, they insisted we stop trying to tell them they had one."

"Just ask them to visit the Yura."

"A three-man team visited a village near the Yura— Puerto Maldonado—and conducted interviews and obtained samples. No one is infected."

"The samples are definitely infected."

"I know that you think they are."

Jane looked at her boss with new eyes. "What are you saying?"

"That I can't authorize you going down there."

"Well, I'm going. Lives are at stake—my dad's life is at stake. I know you have bosses and they aren't going to like it, but I'm not sitting on this."

Meredith closed her eyes and leaned back in her chair. "I can give you a week. But you'll need to be on a leave of absence."

Jane had never felt so angry before, but she understood where Meredith was coming from. Discoveries like the one she'd made were worth a lot of money. Both the State Department and the Peruvian government worked very closely with each other. "I need at least ten days. It's going to take me a few days to get everything in place."

"Okay."

"I'll need equipment to take with me, and some backup." Jane couldn't do it on her own. It was stupid to go into the rain forest without someone at her side.

"I can't give you anyone from the CDC. But I have some contacts in the private sector that might be able to help you."

Meredith didn't look happy, and Jane prayed she made it to her dad before her boss pulled the plug. There were times when working for the CDC really chafed.

Jane stood and walked to the door. Already her mind was busy with everything she needed to do. And knowing she'd have to do it alone gave her a new appreciation for her father and the work he'd done. How many times had her old man come up against this kind of corporate maneuvering and come out on the other side the winner?

"Jane?"

She glanced over her shoulder at Meredith. There was something different in her boss and old friend's eyes. Something Jane wasn't sure she wanted to recognize.

"Be careful."

Jane walked out the door. She planned to be more than careful. She planned to come back to Atlanta with a major success behind her.

"I will."

Chapter 2

Jane sank deeper into her office chair and tried to organize her thoughts. If she was going to survive and save lives she needed a plan.

The images from the slides still flickered through her mind. Along with some nasty images from a death she'd viewed earlier in the year of a man who'd been infected with a similar virus. The man had been on an extreme vacation with his college buddies and had sustained a jagged cut on his hand while mountain climbing. He'd fallen while they'd been trekking down the mountain and wiped his hand on a leaf that had contained the microscopic bug. The bug had entered his bloodstream and seventy-two hours later he'd died.

In her mind's eye, though, instead of the hiker, she saw her dad's face. She shivered and forced the image from her head, focusing instead on what she knew. Her dad was infected with a lethal virus. This was her chance to save him. Her chance to do the one thing she'd always vowed she wouldn't do—go after him.

He'd been leaving her most of her life. He'd left her with her mother when Mary Miller had still been alive. Then he'd left her with her grandparents—his parents—after her mom had died. Mary had died of non-Hodgkin's lymphoma. As a ten year old, Jane had blamed the Amazon for her mother's death. She'd only cried once. When Rob Miller had warned her that crying solved nothing and was the weakest of the female traits, she'd worked hard never to cry again. And she'd vowed that, if he ever needed her, she wouldn't be there.

Hell, she'd been a kid and a petty one at that. Her heart wouldn't let her stick to that vow. Her dad needed her, and she was going.

She didn't want to think about him being sick. He'd always been a big bear of a man. A huge guy who was unstoppable. Even the scandal with the CDC couldn't keep him down. He'd dropped out of sight for a year, but then he'd shown up in South America, where he'd been living with the Yura tribe.

She rubbed the back of her neck. Peru. Damn. She really hated South America. She didn't like the heat and it would be damned hot in April, and wet. The humidity would feel like a living blanket. She didn't like the men, who were macho in the extreme and seemed to think that every woman who walked the street was in need of one of them to watch over her...to protect her.

She knew how to survive in the jungle. Had spent the first ten years of her life living with hunter-gatherer tribes. Her mother had been an anthropologist. And the truth of the matter was she was used to hot, humid weather. She lived in the South.

The real reason she didn't like South America was it held too many memories of things that weren't anymore. Things and people who'd left her life. She wasn't ready to add her father's name to the list.

For backup this trip, she'd contacted a group of independent virologists—Rebel Virology. Jane had worked with the group before. They were all well-respected but independent virologists who couldn't stand bureaucracy and now worked for themselves. She opened an e-mail from them and scanned it quickly. Upon arriving in Peru, she should look for either Maria Cortez or Mac Coleman.

She hoped her partner would be Maria, whom she'd worked with years ago at the CDC. Maria was smart and funny and Jane got along well with her.

She hadn't met Mac Coleman, but he had a reputation for being a maverick. In fact, he'd founded Rebel Virology. He'd worked with the World Health Organization and had been on his way to the top of his career, but had left for bureaucratic reasons. And scientists who were tired of working within the government structure had applauded him. But a few years later, in Southeast Asia, he'd had a fiasco that had led to the deaths of twenty-five people. She'd heard that he'd rushed to treatment and lost lives.

Jane rubbed the back of her neck. There were no details on the incident. She knew mistakes were made by both virologists and governments and she wasn't judging him.

She checked the laminated maps she'd stopped at Kinkos to make on her way home. The jungle wasn't kind to paper. She had a compass, a Blackberry phone with GPS unit that would work even in the depths of the jungle and two backups. She had a lethal hunting blade that her grandfather had given her. He'd been a Marine and had reinforced to Jane every summer when she saw him to always be prepared.

She packed rice, rice cakes and her favorite cereal bars. She brought the tea she loved so much in a metal canister that she knew might rust if she stayed too long in the jungle. She had medicine, as well, in a separate pack, treatments for a long list of diseases.

The phone rang. She glanced at the clock. She was waiting for a call from Angie, her assistant, who was making all of the arrangements for the trip. "Dr. Miller."

"Jane, it's Raul Veracruz."

Jane held the phone away from her ear. Had she conjured him up by thinking about her father? "What can I do for you?" she asked. It had been a long time since she'd heard from him. Three years, in fact. The day her father had left the CDC.

"Meredith contacted me about some research you were doing," he said.

Maybe Raul would be interested in helping her. "I found the information I needed here in the lab while working with the samples."

"Who sent the samples to you?" he asked.

"A virologist living with the Yura."

"Your dad?" he asked.

She hesitated. Raul had once been Rob's assistant

and the two men had been friends. For a brief time Jane had been involved with him. But that hadn't lasted. Like most of her personal relationships, theirs had ended because she hadn't found him as interesting as the specimens in her lab. "Yes."

"Jane, I talked to him already. I personally analyzed the samples he had. They were clean. No sign of any virus."

"The ones I received were infected, Raul."

"Who are you going to trust?" he asked.

Jane doodled on her blotter and changed the topic. "What are you doing now? You're not with the CDC anymore."

"That's right. I'm working for Thompson-Marks Pharmaceutical."

"Research and development?"

"Yes. I like it. It's challenging and it pays well. Why don't you come and join me in their labs?"

"No, thanks. I like where I am."

"There's a lot more freedom to work on the projects that are important."

"And the CDC doesn't?"

"You know what I mean," he said.

"I'll keep that in mind." Someone knocked on the door of her lab.

"Please think twice about revealing anything your father may have sent you to others, Jane. You know he's done some…creative tampering before."

"I will. Goodbye, Raul." Jane hung up the phone and went to the door. It was Angie Tanner, her secretary, lab assistant and research guru.

The short, dark-haired woman wouldn't enter the actual lab even dressed as she was in a full-body space suit. Jane thought it was kind of funny. Angie had spent the last twenty-five years working for the CDC and had in fact been her father's assistant in the early days. Her smile was friendly and she loved her job. And she was completely paranoid about germs.

"I've finalized all the arrangements for you. The area you want to go into is only accessible by air."

Angie was ultraefficient and a real wizard when it came to bringing together the details of an operation. She was a top-notch researcher and interviewer and Jane trusted her implicitly. "I know. That's why I asked you to hire a small plane. Why don't you come in my office and join me for a cup of tea?"

"Because I happen to like being healthy. I tried to get you a flight to La Paz, but they didn't have anything leaving tomorrow, and Meredith wouldn't approve using the CDC plane."

Angie's phobia about her health was something of a joke amongst those who worked with her. She kept a huge bottle of vitamin C tablets on her desk and popped them like candy throughout the day. "Meredith doesn't really want me to go," Jane said. Angie probably was risking her position by helping Jane out.

"She has to answer to her own conscience," Angie said, handing Jane a plastic wallet portfolio. "Here are the rest of your papers. You're going to be parachuting into the jungle. I called in a favor from a buddy of mine in the military."

"Okay," Jane said. She loved parachuting and had a lot of experience. The jungles of the Amazon basin would be perfect for skydiving. If it weren't for the fact that her father was in jeopardy she might actually enjoy this trip.

"I told him you know your stuff when it comes to parachuting."

"Thanks. I'm not so sure about the virologist who'll be joining me."

"I only made travel arrangements for you," Angie said in a surly voice.

"Can you add one to the parachute jump?" Jane asked, knowing that once Angie made her plans or finished her research she didn't like to have to go back and change it.

"I'll try."

"Thanks. Did you get the guide I requested?" Jane asked. Going into the jungle alone was asking for trouble.

"Yes. He'll meet you at the private airstrip on the morning of your sky dive."

"Thanks, Angie. Can I ask you to do one more thing for me?" Jane asked.

"What?"

"Will you check into the research the Peruvian government has done on this disease? According to everyone I talked to, it's not lethal."

"What do you want to know?" Angie asked.

"Who did the testing and interviews and when they were conducted."

"Is that it?"

"For now."

"Be careful, Jane, even virus hunters aren't immune to death."

It was almost two in the afternoon by the time Jane arrived in Lima two days later. Tired, hungry and anxious to get to work, she made her way toward her hotel. The air was hot, humid and blanketed the city in the kind of haze that often covered Los Angeles. She closed her eyes and tried to breath. But the air was hot. It burned her lungs.

In a way it was invigorating. The one thing that she liked, though she hated to admit it, about South America was that you still had the feeling of having to fight to survive. That life was brought in on its most simplistic terms. Here it really was survival of the fittest.

But she had no time to enjoy it. She was here on a mission and every second she delayed she risked losing another life.

Now she was here in Lima—the clock was officially starting to tick. Meredith was giving her one week. One measly week after eight years of always doing what she was told. Fear of failure weighed heavily on her. It was an odd feeling and not one she liked to admit she experienced.

The treatment and the vaccine were loaded into a galvanized-steel reinforced trunk with wheels and a handle. She towed it behind her through the hotel lobby. She had a meeting with Rebel Virology in a little over an hour in the lobby of her hotel.

She needed to switch the glass vials and their protective packaging into bags that would make it easier to carry them through the jungle. And she desperately wanted a cool shower.

The lobby was full of artifacts from Macchu Pichu. The site, north of the city, was accessible by a multi-day hike or a train or bus ride. Jane paused in front of a lighted alcove displaying an artist's rendering of the

Temple of the Sun. She felt small in relation to her place in time.

Working in virology and making case studies gave her a link to realizing how short time was. And how little things had changed. Modern developments in science made the epidemics of yesterday obsolete in some parts of the world, but viruses and germs always found a way to mutate in order to survive.

Not on my watch.

"*Hola,* Jane."

She tensed and glanced up from the artwork. Raul Veracruz stood behind her. She could see him reflected in the glass. He held a white hat in one hand and a cigar in the other. His dark hair was trimmed close to his head. He had a mustache now and when she turned toward him, he smiled at her.

"I didn't think to see you so soon," he said in his accented English. His voice was meant to seduce and despite that knowledge she had to admit she still liked the warm sound of it.

"I'm surprised you're here. How did you know where I was staying?" she asked. He hadn't exactly sounded as if he wanted to see her down here. She wasn't sure what kind of reception she'd get from him.

"It wasn't that hard to find you. I have friends in government."

"Why were you looking for me?" she asked, a little unnerved that the government knew where she was. She needed to stop being so freaking jumpy about everything. She gave Raul a bland smile.

"I'm hoping to convince you to change your mind

about going to the Amazon basin. Can you join me for a drink?"

She glanced at her watch. She didn't want to have this conversation but saw no graceful way out of it. "I can give you five minutes."

"Only five minutes for an old....friend?"

If he was only an old friend and not a former lover she wouldn't feel so awkward. And she might have given in. But she didn't know what Raul wanted, and for a man who hadn't talked to her in years, he was suddenly very interested in her.

"Come to Atlanta, Raul, and I'll give you all the time you want." In fact in a week's time she'd sit down for half the day with him. But not now. Now she wanted to keep moving, not be slowed down with chitchat.

"What's the hurry?" he asked, putting his hand at her elbow as they walked through the lobby toward the reception desk.

"I need to check the vaccine and treatment." Though the vials containing the vaccine and treatment were packed in dry ice and then Styrofoam, there was still a chance of breakage. She'd checked it at the airport but wanted to get it open and make sure everything was still in the frozen state.

"Tell me about your find," he said.

She couldn't. Meredith would kill her. She probably shouldn't have mentioned her results to him on the phone, either. She was a little tired from flying for so long. Lima was on Eastern Standard Time so there was no time change to blame.

She shook her head. "Why don't you tell me what you're working on."

"A new product to treat a potential problem on the Brazilian border. Keeping that border open is vital to the economy of Peru and to the village I grew up in."

"What kind of problem?" she asked. Did the virus she'd looked at have a mutated strain already? Was it related to the one she'd found and isolated? And how was this virus passed?

"A virus that brings on a paralytic reaction," he said.

"Like polio?" she asked. Actually it could even be polio. Although it had been wiped out in the U.S., it hadn't been eradicated worldwide.

"Yes."

"Well, good luck. I'm going to be down that way. If you'd like, when I'm finished with the Yura, I can check out your site. Maybe do some interviews."

Interviews were vital to virologists. Jane would go into an infected area and talk to locals. She'd observe eating habits, water and sewage conditions—basic daily life. Then samples of blood and saliva would be analyzed. The final report gave her and other virologists an accurate picture of a virus and its environment.

Raul gave her an odd look, and then shook his head. "I've got it under control. But thanks for the offer."

"No problem. I better go check in. It was nice seeing you, Raul."

"Jane?"

"What?"

"I'm...not sure you should trust your dad."

The change in subject surprised her. "I've seen the blood, and it's definitely infected. Do you want to see the initial report?"

"No. I'm not saying that there isn't something out

there. Hell, we both know that hot zones pop up all over the place. It's just going to make everything harder because your dad's involved."

"What do you suggest?" she asked.

"That we quarantine your dad and the tribe and then let my team make the first discovery."

"What do you mean, *your* team? I thought you worked for a pharmaceutical company."

"I do. And we're interested in helping the people of Peru," Raul said. "I only made the suggestion because putting Dr. Miller on any finding is bound to raise some questions."

"My reputation is a solid one. And putting my name on any report isn't going to jeopardize it."

Raul stepped back into the shadows, and she couldn't see his face. She walked away from him with a cheerful wave, but deep inside she was worried. Two outbreaks in the same area didn't bode well.

Mentally she reviewed what she knew about the area. She hadn't been paying close attention to world news. Were they doing any construction there? Sometimes clearing the land stirred up diseases that had been lying dormant in the heart of the jungle. She'd grab the local paper and use her rusty Spanish to find out what was going on in the Amazon basin.

What had they uncovered, and was it seeking bodies as carriers to spread itself out of the jungle?

Twenty minutes later she was sitting in the hotel bar relaxing as much as she could. She'd hated leaving the vials in her room, but they should be safe for an hour behind a locked door.

"Jane Miller?"

She glanced up to see a dark man with thick hair and more than one day's worth of stubble on his face. He was tall and lean and looked as if he'd been living in a rough area of the world for a while. His eyes were hidden behind sunglasses, and he wore khaki clothes that were worn and looked comfortable. His voice was a low rumble.

"Yes."

"Mac Coleman, Rebel Virology."

She stood and shook his hand. It was warm and dry, calloused on the ridge of his palm. He tightened it briefly and then let her hand drop. Jane sat back down and waited for him to do the same. She hoped her disappointment that Maria hadn't made it instead didn't show. Her earlier doubts about him crept into her mind.

He removed his sunglasses. His eyes were a light blue color at odds with his dark coloring. His pupils dilated adjusting to the light. Jane wondered if he had problems with light sensitivity.

He quirked one eyebrow at her. Oops, caught staring. "Do you have any problems with sensitivity?"

"To a beautiful woman staring at me? No."

She shook her head. "Not that. I meant to the light. Your eyes are so pale…"

"Some, but not much. The glasses help, and unless I have prolonged exposure without some sort of shield, then I'm fine."

He signaled the cocktail waitress and ordered a local beer for himself. "You want anything?"

"I'll have the same," Jane said, adjusting the frame of her glasses.

Once the waitress left an awkward silence fell between them. Jane marshaled her thoughts. She was the lead scientist here. She needed to brief him and then get some space. Something about Mac Coleman disturbed her on a very basic level that had nothing to do with virology.

Maybe the heat was to blame for her reaction. Or just being in Peru. This place always brought out all those instincts she tried to hide away with a veneer of sophistication.

"Did you have a chance to read the material I sent via e-mail?"

"Not really. I just got finished working in Belize and caught a late flight. Brief me."

"I received some blood samples from a virologist—"

"Who?" he interrupted. He rubbed the back of his neck and leaned forward, resting his elbows on his knees.

Jane wasn't going to hide or apologize for her dad anymore. She didn't know what had happened years ago—what had motivated her dad to behave the way he had. And was a little ashamed that she'd never asked him about it. But the Yura virus he'd sent her was a real threat and she wasn't going to leave him out of it. If Mac had a problem with her dad, better to find out now before they left Lima. "My dad—Dr. Rob Miller."

Mac leaned back in his chair and then nodded. "I've never met the man, but some of his work was legendary. Until a few years ago."

Jane was relieved that was all Mac said. He was the first person not to ask if she'd double-checked all her

research. She didn't want to talk about her father's
"find" or the fact that he'd sent the U.S. into a tailspin
of frantic hand-washing to stop the spread of a germ
that had in the end turned out to be nothing more serious than the common cold.

"Anyway, the Yura are infected with a virus strain
that produces symptoms similar to Lassa fever. After
weeks in the lab I developed a treatment as well as a
vaccine to protect those not already infected."

"Did you already make it?" he asked.

She'd debated with Tom the benefits of carrying and
preserving the treatment versus replicating it once she
got to her father. But in the end the quickest way to save
lives was to bring it with them.

"Yes, I'm carrying enough of both to take care of
everyone in the tribe my father's living with."

"How is it packed?" he asked. There was an intensity in those pale eyes that let her know he was analyzing every fact she gave him. And though she knew little
of his reputation aside from the incident in Southeast
Asia, she was impressed with what she saw in him as
a scientist.

"Dry ice and Styrofoam. I have a couple of large
backpacks that we should be able to get everything
into. I also have some lab equipment, but that breaks
down pretty small."

"When do we leave?" he asked. The waitress
brought their drinks and Mac took a long draw on his,
draining half the bottle in one gulp. "Bring me another."

The waitress nodded and left. Jane took a sip of hers,
savoring the coolness as the beverage slid down her
throat. "I'd like to leave first thing in the morning. The

batch I brought with me is only good for seven days. So we have to move quickly."

"No problem. Where's the jumping-off point?"

"Puerto Maldonado. I scheduled a charter flight to leave here at 6:00 a.m.," she said.

"Amazon basin makes sense. Are we going in by river or trekking?" he asked.

Jane couldn't get a read on him. He watched her assessingly, which made her uncomfortable. The last thing she wanted to do was have another person she couldn't trust at her side. Yet he'd been living in South America and working there for the last few years. He had information on the geography that she didn't. Perhaps Meredith's attitude was affecting her perception of Mac.

"Are you familiar with the area? I'm not sure which way would be faster."

"If we could get a motorboat, that might be quicker. Do you know where the Yura are?"

"On the Cashpajali River. It's a tributary of the Madre de Dios. I have a general area, but nothing exact," Jane said. She had satellite maps and her GPS unit, but Jane didn't want to reveal the exact location of the Yura camp to anyone. She wasn't sure who to trust and didn't want to endanger her father and the Yura by trusting the wrong person.

"Why did you contact R.V.?" he asked.

Now for the fun part. But he had to have guessed that there was some trouble in her office if she'd contacted them. People from the CDC and WHO usually didn't have to ask independent contractors for help in their work. The CDC had teams in place worldwide and they mobilized quickly when there was a problem. Jane resented that Meredith hadn't trusted her enough to outweigh any doubts about her father. "We're short-staffed. There has been some backlash from the local government. They're refusing to believe there is any outbreak in the Amazon."

"Why?"

"I have no idea, but my boss doesn't want to ruffle feathers and since the initial samples and work came from my father, she can't really go public. She agreed to let me come here, but I only have a week."

"That pisses me off. I remember when saving lives mattered more than reputations. That's why I formed Rebel Virology."

"I thought it was because..." Damn, she hadn't meant to bring up the incident.

He arched one eyebrow at her. "I don't talk about that—ever, understood?"

She nodded.

"Good. I'll meet you in the lobby at five tomorrow morning."

He finished off his beer and took the second one from the arriving waitress, then stood and left.

Well, he wasn't exactly what she'd expected. That didn't matter, though, she needed another expert with her. She just hoped the man knew his stuff.

There was something about him that made her instincts itchy. She'd keep her eye on him.

Chapter 3

Jane got off the elevator on her floor. She wished they'd been able to leave tonight but it was a two-hour flight over the Andes to the Amazon basin and Bob Jones, the military pilot who Angie had arranged to fly them, had refused to do it this late in the day. Bob was actually a friend of Jane's father. Another face from the past. She looked forward to seeing him.

A man was in the hallway apparently having trouble figuring out the key-card system. Jane fixed a small smile on her face, prepared to do her good deed and help him out.

"*Hola.*"

The man looked up and Jane realized he was at her door. Which explained why his key wasn't working.

"Excuse me, that's my room," she said in Spanish.

"I know," he said, moving slightly away from the door.

She saw he had a gun. Panic raced through her and she screamed, which made the man wince. Her gut instinct said to run the hell away from him but inside that room was the only weapon she had to save her father's life and many others'. She couldn't leave it on the chance that he'd figure out how to get into her room.

Thank God for her formerly flabby thighs and the kickboxing class she'd been taking off and on for the last two years. If only she'd attended more frequently! Dropping back into what she hoped was a strong fighting stance, she waited.

The man gave her a look as if she was crazy and raised the gun. She lashed out with a crescent kick aimed at his weapon arm and hit him, hard.

His arm jerked out of position and a bullet ricocheted off the wall six inches from her. Dust got in her eyes and nose.

She sneezed and her eyes watered, but she didn't stop. Pivoting around, she lashed out with a spinning hook kick to the head. He brought his hands up to block her, grabbing her ankle, then brought his elbow down hard on the back of her leg. Pain shot through her. She jerked her foot free and fell back.

Breathing hard, she pushed to her feet and put her weight on her injured leg. It was tender but would hold her. He rushed her and this time she used a side kick, putting all her power behind it. She hit him hard in the gut and heard him grunt on the impact. He doubled over. Jane brought both of her hands together and hit him as hard as she could on the back of his neck with her fists.

He fell to the floor. Jane kicked him one more time in the side. She hurried past him and fumbled to open her hotel door. Finally she jerked it open and rushed in, then slammed the door shut behind her. She locked it and threw the night-security chain.

She went immediately to the phone and called the front desk. Taking a deep breath she tried to lessen the panic which had been sweeping over her. She was safe now. Or as safe as she could be for the moment.

"There's a man with a gun in the hallway trying to break into my room. He shot at me," she said when they answered.

"We'll send someone up immediately."

Panic swelled in her throat. Pawing through her suitcase, she pulled out the hunting knife her grandfather had given her and stood ready.

Her blood pounded so loudly she couldn't hear anything else. She stayed to the side of the door in the small bathroom, knowing a bullet could easily penetrate the hotel door.

She scanned the interior of the room and realized that everything was safe and untouched. Someone knocked on the door. "Hotel security, ma'am."

She moved cautiously toward the door and looked through the peephole. The man standing there was dressed in the hotel's colors and had its emblem on his left breast pocket. And a name tag on the right that said Pedro. She saw no sign of the man who'd threatened her with the gun.

She opened the door.

"Thanks for coming."

"No problem. We take the security of our guests

very seriously. Tell me what happened. By the time I got here he was gone."

"He was at my door when I got off the elevator. I thought he'd mistaken my room for his, but when I spoke to him he turned, and I saw he had a gun."

She wasn't sure, but she thought she saw some doubt in the security officer's eyes. She thought the story sounded strange, as well.

"Then what happened?"

I screamed, she thought. But there was no way she was saying that out loud. "He shot at me."

"Are you hurt?" he asked.

"No. But the bullet hit over here," Jane said. God, she couldn't believe someone had shot at her. A trembling started deep inside her. The scientist in her recognized her body's natural reaction to the incident now that the danger had passed. But she wasn't ready to let that show yet.

Her leg throbbed and she wanted to sit down and put some ice on it. But she'd do that later when she was alone. She showed him where it had grazed the wall. He examined the area before radioing someone else. Her Spanish wasn't up to his rapid-fire delivery so she had no idea who he'd called.

"We'll keep an eye on this floor. I'll continue to investigate this area."

The elevator pinged five minutes later and another man stepped off. "*Hola,* Señorita Miller. I am Jorge, the duty manager, and I am here to make sure you feel comfortable staying at our hotel. We've called the police."

Jorge swept her out of the hallway and into her room. He stayed there while Jane took the opportunity to wash her face and get the dust from the ricochet from her eyes. She tied her thick red hair back in a ponytail. A glance in the mirror showed she looked every one of her thirty-three years, plus a few more.

She closed her eyes but still saw that gun pointed at her. She opened them and straightened up her toiletries. She took comfort as she always did in the familiar. She started organizing her stuff. But her hands were trembling, and her makeup spilled from its bag all over the countertop.

She started gathering the items and stopped when she touched the brightly colored compact that Sophia, her college roommate, had given her for her thirtieth birthday. A picture from *Pinky and The Brain* covered the lid. It was silly and frivolous. Sophia had said it was to remind Jane that life wasn't as serious as she liked to make it.

Thirty minutes later after talking to police and assuring the manager she wouldn't hold the hotel responsible, she was ensconced in a suite on the concierge level with a guard out front.

Propping her legs in front of her on the long, low coffee table, she adjusted the ice pack and closed her eyes. She had a tension headache building, and she wasn't sure she'd made the right choice in coming here.

She'd feel a lot safer once she was out of the city and in the jungle, where she knew what dangers to expect.

The new room was nice but Jane couldn't sleep. Every time she closed her eyes she saw her father's face. The one from childhood that had always been lined with disappointment. She sat bolt upright in bed fighting the fear that she was too late to help anyone.

She climbed out of bed and turned on the lamp. Working had always been her solace. She took comfort in it now. Powering up her laptop, she checked for messages from Angie, who was doing some comprehensive research on where the virus may have started. Jane had warned Angie that she wasn't working in her official capacity. Angie, who'd worked with Jane for six years, had said she didn't care.

She'd asked Angie to run a check in South America on cases involving the symptoms that her father had described. Diseases didn't have boundaries, and from her own investigation she'd discovered that the Yura didn't stay just in Peru. They also roamed into Brazil. That made the potential areas for the disease to spread even larger.

She had an e-mail from Angie that read:

There has been no sort of epidemic outbreak in any South American country that mirrors the symptoms you are talking about. I did find a missionary from Bolivia who contracted something similar, bleeding and hemorrhaging. He died in a skirmish with prococa planters. His body was burned. I'm following up and waiting for the interviews that were conducted in that region on this case.

Damn. This didn't sound good.

Jane sent back a reply thanking Angie for her work and asking her to check into the land clearing that was going on to make way for the first Peruvian National Highway. That was virgin territory and a virus could have been incubating there for years. The highway would run from Cuzco to the Amazon basin. Right now the only way to get there was by air or badly rutted roads.

She shut down her computer and repacked it in her backpack, then stood and stretched. A glance at her watch showed her it was almost five and time to meet Mac in the lobby. She changed quickly into clothes that would wear well in the jungle. Khaki pants and a T-shirt covered with a long-sleeved button-down shirt. She also had a hat her father had left behind when she was a kid, and all her of her supplies.

Her phone rang. "Dr. Miller."

"It's Mac. The front desk won't give me your room number," he said, his voice husky and low as if he wasn't awake yet.

"I had some problems yesterday and had to move."

She gave him her room number. "I'm on my way up. I'll bring all my gear, and we'll get organized."

"Great. I arranged for a taxi to be downstairs in fifteen minutes."

He hung up. She'd finished packing her personal items and was in the process of organizing the Styrofoam packs when he knocked on the door. She hesitated before letting him in. He entered the room as if he was in charge, dominating the space. She didn't like the way he loomed there. A night's sleep hadn't lessened his outlaw look. He hadn't shaved, but he had trimmed up his beard. His clothing was similar to what he'd worn yesterday.

"What happened?" he asked. He went to the coffeepot on the desk in the room and poured himself a cup.

Jane focused on her luggage and not on Mac. "Some guy attacked me in the hall outside my room."

He put his cup down and crossed the room to her. He put one hand on her shoulder. "Are you okay?"

"Yes. I got away with just a bruise." She stepped

away from him and went to the two large camping backpacks she'd brought with her.

Mac moved next to her, taking one of the packs. "Do you know why he attacked you? Did he follow you upstairs?"

She shrugged, not wanting to remember any of what had happened yesterday. But she couldn't forget the menace in the man's eyes as he'd aimed that gun at her.

"No, he was in the hallway when I got off the elevator," she said at last. "I think we should load our clothes in the bottom and use them for extra cushioning for the vials."

"Okay. Was he targeting you?" Mac asked.

"The hotel security manager mentioned they've had a few small problems with thieves targeting lone female tourists over the last few weeks. So, no, I don't think it had anything to do with me personally."

He nodded. "Okay. What kind of vials do you have in here? Dry-ice packed, or did you dehydrate?"

"Dry ice. The Yura virus has already infected a portion of the tribe—I'm not sure how many—so I brought a treatment that worked in the lab."

"Have you tested it on any subjects?"

"No. There wasn't time. As I may have mentioned, my boss wanted the research stopped and me moved to something else."

"What are you planning to do?"

"The treatment is only good for seven days. We've got six left. According to my research it shouldn't take more than four to reach the Yura. I think my dad will volunteer to be a test subject. In the lab we started seeing results within two hours."

"What about those not already infected?"

"Luckily the Yura virus is very close to Lassa fever. So I was able to manipulate a strand of the vaccine we have for that. As I said, it should be effective at preventing the rest of the tribe from contracting the virus."

"Sounds like you've covered all the bases."

The cab ride to the airport had been short but once they arrived they had nothing but hiccups. The guide she'd hired had left a message that he would be waiting in Puerto Maldonado. The pilot, Bob Jones, ran thirty minutes late and a government official almost refused to let them leave the private airport.

He'd double-checked all of her papers. Finally Mac had stepped in and called a contact he had in the government, and they'd been cleared to leave.

"Thanks," she said when they were finally standing on the tarmac next to the plane for their flight to Puerto Maldonado.

"No problem. I was beginning to think I wouldn't have much to do." He took one of the backpacks and hefted it into the cargo area.

"Why?" she asked, watching his muscles bunch and flex as he moved. He was very different from Tom, who spent more time in the lab than he did either eating or working out. She was pretty sure she could bench-press more than Tom, but that Mac could probably bench-press her. She didn't like it. She was used to being the strong one. It didn't matter—this wasn't a competition, she told herself. But when Mac reached for her pack, she pulled it out of his way and lifted it into the back without his help.

"Asks the ultraefficient, no-room-for-mistakes woman," he said, with a wry grin.

"Are you teasing me?" she asked. Few people did, apart from Sophia. She seemed too serious for anyone joking with her. But Mac, whom she couldn't get a handle on, seemed to see past her serious-scientist outer layer to the woman beneath.

"What do you think?" he countered.

She thought he was too cocky and too perceptive for his own good. But instead she said, "That we should get on the plane before something else goes wrong."

"I agree. Who did you book the boat through in Puerto Maldonado?"

"A local tour company. They wanted us to stay overnight in one of the river camps but we don't have time. I want to get on the *La Torre* as soon as possible. That's why we're parachuting in. We'll take that upriver to the Madre."

"Janey! I haven't seen you in years," Bob said as he approached them. He gave her a hug.

"Hi, Bob. Thanks for squeezing us in," Jane said.

"No prob. Why has it taken you so long to come and visit your dad?"

"Work. You know how that is. You work all the time, too."

"Yeah, but I'm a crusty old dude, you're not."

"Kind of you to notice," she said.

"I'm glad you're here," he said, then climbed on board.

"Me, too," Jane said quietly. She picked up her duffel bag and climbed in the seat right behind Bob. Mac sat behind her. A few minutes later they were in the air. The flight would take a couple of hours.

Jane liked the view from the air. The lush greenery of the Andes rose out of the low desert landscape that had surrounded them in Lima. Mac sat quietly behind her in the plane.

When the jungle finally appeared underneath them, Jane took out her GPS unit to see where they were. She determined they were less than forty-five miles from Puerto Maldonado. Almost there. She glanced over her shoulder at Mac. He was reading a copy of the *New England Journal of Medicine*.

She wondered what had brought this man to start Rebel Virology. He hadn't been fired after that incident in Southeast Asia. All her life she'd studied behavior patterns, usually inside the small biosphere that was her lab. But she was enough of her anthropologist mother's daughter to want to know why people behaved the way they did.

Especially when she was in a situation that she wasn't certain she could control. As she was this time.

It was a big task, probably the biggest she'd ever taken on, but she felt ready for it.

The plane lurched. Damn. Jane gripped the armrests as Bob battled with the air to get them evened out again.

"Just an air pocket," Bob said between his teeth, his concentration on flying the plane.

The plane dipped sharply. Mac sat up in the seat behind her. He put his hand on her shoulder. The plane was tossed about a bit more. Jane braced herself against the seat fuselage. Bob started cussing.

"Are we in trouble?" she yelled to Bob. He was struggling with the stick and watching the gauges. Jane waited, knowing he'd respond when he could.

"Something's wrong with the engine," he said at last. "Why don't you two get ready to jump. I'm not sure if I can take you all the way to the target."

"What should we do?" she asked.

"Don't panic," Mac said from behind her. He'd tucked his magazine away and was leaning forward, as well.

"I'm not. I've been skydiving since I was eighteen. And I did two parachute dives with the military when I worked in remote locations with a military team," she said.

The plane jerked and a stream of smoke billowed past the window. "Are we going to crash?"

Bob turned around and looked at the two of them. There was something in his eyes that didn't reassure Jane. "Not if I can help it."

Mac finished fastening his chute to his back and then climbed over his seat to the packs that held the medicine. He passed them up to her. Jane worked quickly to tie the packs to another parachute, which would auto-release at a certain level.

"This is as close as I can get you."

"I think you should come with us, Bob," Jane said. The plane lurched again and sputtered.

"I'll be fine, I'll bail out if I lose control. Go while you still can," Bob yelled.

Mac stood up and opened the door. The air rushed in and Jane closed her eyes feeling the familiar pump of adrenaline through her veins. Thank God they were already on the other side of the Andes. She didn't relish the thought of having to trek down the mountain to get to the river area.

"I'll go last," she said, needing to make sure the medicine got out and to watch where it went.

Mac shrugged and stepped out of the plane. Jane pushed their packs toward the edge of the plane and then out. She turned around and waved to Bob before she jumped out of the plane.

She torpedoed her body and caught up to the packs, flying close to them. She'd lost sight of Mac. The chutes opened and slowed her descent.

Her feet hit the tops of the trees. She pulled them up but it was too late. She was knocked off balance and continued falling through the thick green canopy of the tall rain forest trees.

Her chute got tangled in the branches and she was held suspended over the floor of the jungle. The momentum of her fall caused her to rock back and forth. Her cheek stung where a branch had cut her face on the way down. She was about four feet from the ground.

She heard a loud boom and guessed that the plane had crashed. A few minutes later she saw smoke billowing up from the sky. *Oh, my God.* She prayed Bob had made it out okay. She should have insisted he jump when they did. She looked up for another drifting parachute, but only saw the smoke and sky through the high canopy.

She had her Blackberry in her pocket, but had left her change of clothes and food behind. There just hadn't been time to get everything out of the plane. And the medicine had been the most important thing.

Her heart raced and her hands shook. She finally unbuckled her harness and let herself fall to the ground. Her injured leg gave as she landed and she rolled a few feet before stopping. When she got her bearings she looked up into the painted face of a warrior who held a spear with a sharp tip aimed straight at her.

Chapter 4

Jane gingerly got to her feet. Her leg ached. She had no idea how to defend herself against a spear-wielding native. The man's eyes were calm, cool. She made eye contact with him but didn't sustain it, not wanting him to think she was aggressive. After a minute he lowered his weapon but continued watching her.

His face was painted in broad stripes of red and blue. His eyes were a dark chocolate and his body was covered in modern clothing. Civilization had come to the Amazon basin and yet the old traditions remained. Jane was struck by the dichotomy.

She was still trying to deal with everything that had happened. She couldn't believe their plane had crashed. Her hands shook and her mind was racing. The jump hadn't been as bad as she'd expected considering they'd had to drop out before they'd planned.

Where was Mac?

Jane held her hands at shoulder level. The warrior continued watching her, spear in hand. She noticed he had an old AK-47 rifle slung over his shoulder.

"I'm a doctor," she said in Spanish. "I'm here to help the Yura."

He took a step closer and raised his spear. Jane didn't flinch or back up. She figured her rudimentary knowledge of martial arts would buy her some time if she needed it.

"The Yura aren't around here, they are closer to the Madre de Dios River," he replied in Spanish, gesturing to the south.

"My plane had engine trouble," she said.

The man just looked at her. There was nothing threatening in his gaze. Jane had the feeling that he'd come out to make sure there was no threat.

"Can you point me in the right direction?" Jane asked. She wanted to find Mac. But getting her gear and heading toward the Yura was her first priority.

"Why are you going to them?" he asked.

Not wanting to alarm the warrior, she sidestepped the question. "Have you had any dealings with them recently?"

"No. More trouble than it is worth to trade with the Yura lately."

"What do you mean?" she asked.

Three more men emerged from the forest. All were armed like the man holding her at spear-point. And all wore identical face paint. She wondered if any of them were infected from contact with the Yura.

"Where is your guide?" he asked. "Too dangerous for a woman alone in the jungle."

"I have a guide waiting in Puerto Maldonado. And another doctor parachuted out with me. Have you seen him?"

"My men are looking. Are you crazy?" he asked.

She couldn't help but smile. She'd been asked that question before. Mostly it stemmed from the fact that she always had to do things by herself. "No. Just in a hurry."

"You can travel with us as far as our village. From there it is a day's journey to the Yura."

"I'm Jane," she said.

"Reynaldo," he said. "Saturnino and his son, Daniel. That's my son, Aldo."

Jane nodded to the men. What had Reynaldo meant by trouble with the Yura?

He conversed with his men. Jane wished she understood the native dialogue. And she had more questions for them. Finally, Reynaldo came over to her.

"We'll travel in a line. Aldo will lead then you follow. We'll be behind you."

"I must find my friend and my gear," Jane said.

Aldo said something to his father in a language she didn't understand. She heard a few Spanish words mixed in, but couldn't follow their conversation. She pulled her Blackberry phone from her belt and checked her location via the GPS function. She wasn't that far from the Yura. She should be able to reach them in a day, maybe two if the terrain was rough, just as Reynaldo said.

Deadly Desire

But she had to find Mac first. She couldn't leave him alone in the jungle.

"Aldo saw your gear and a man, as well. We will take you to them now."

"Thanks, Reynaldo."

Aldo moved off at a fast trot and Jane followed behind him. She wasn't used to running like this and after a few minutes she was breathing heavily. The scent of fresh flowers mixed with wet soil filled the air. Monkeys chattered overhead.

Jane slipped on a patch of wet earth. Throwing her arm out to brace herself against a peach palm and stop the fall, she felt Reynaldo grab her arm and jerk her off balance before she could make contact with the tree trunk. She gasped when she noticed the needlelike spines on the trunk. She had forgotten such dangers.

"The spiny plants are dangerous. Just fall next time."

She nodded. Aldo hadn't stopped and the other men just looked at her. She felt incompetent and didn't like the feeling. She shook her head to clear it, pushed her glasses up farther on her nose and moved to catch up to Aldo.

Jane kept moving at a steady pace following the men through the jungle. It was hot and humid on the jungle floor. Rotting leaves and other vegetation provided a cushioning layer. She let the lush greenery soothe her mind as she moved. She flashed back to her childhood, remembering one time when the village they'd been living in had moved. Jane had been a child then and she'd traveled with the other children, singing a song whose words escaped her now. But the rhythm beat through her mind and body as she jogged along behind Aldo.

* * *

After fifteen minutes they stopped under a large canopy. Aldo pointed up and Jane saw her gear suspended from the trees. Jane looked at the base of the tree, which was the size of a compact car, and wondered how the hell she was going to get up there to retrieve her stuff.

But Daniel was up the tree before Jane could say anything. He pulled a knife from his waistband and cut the cords. The packs dropped and Jane hurried forward, afraid the fall might have damaged the vials.

Jane moved toward the packs, but Reynaldo stopped her with a hand on her arm. "Someone's coming."

"It might be—"

Reynaldo covered her mouth and the men all drew their weapons. Jane found herself in the middle of a protective circle. She thought about trying to explain that she could take care of herself, but it was such an odd feeling, having someone try to protect her, that she was bemused.

Mac burst through the underbrush. Mac had survived, but then she'd figured he would. He had the look of someone who had survived a lot of things. But she was still relieved to see his familiar face.

Mac put his hands up, showing that he was clearly not armed.

"Jane, tell them I'm with you." The command in his voice rubbed her the wrong way. Given the tension in the air she understood his impatience but she didn't like it.

"He's with me," she said to Reynaldo. But the men didn't lower their weapons.

Reynaldo said something to Mac in the same language Aldo had used earlier. Jane listened in shock as Mac responded. What was going on? Was Mac known to them? Why weren't they lowering their weapons?

The conversation continued for a few minutes and then Reynaldo and his men lowered their weapons. "You can check on your stuff now."

Jane moved forward. Mac joined her at the packs. She opened hers first and saw that the Styrofoam was cracked around one of the vial containers. Digging deeper in her bag she removed some medical adhesive tape to repair it.

"What was that about?" Jane asked in English.

"I've spent a lot of time in this area. They wanted to make sure I wasn't from one of their rival tribes."

"Why are you in South America, Mac?" she asked, suddenly wishing she'd asked a few more questions before leaving Lima with this man. He wasn't Peruvian, but here in the jungle he looked as if he was in his natural environment.

"You invited me," he said, his voice low and quiet.

She was well aware that he hadn't answered her question. She couldn't help but think there was more to this man than he'd revealed. There was so much ambiguity around this virus and the people who were denying its existence. Had Mac been sent to keep her from reaching the Yura?

Actually, she knew why she wanted to find out his secrets. Then maybe she could answer some of her own questions. She wasn't burned out by her job, but she did fear misdiagnosing something, or getting a treatment wrong as she'd heard Mac had. Going to an outbreak hot zone and killing everyone instead of curing them. That fear always lingered at the back of her mind. And with this trip it was in the forefront. What if something she did in the lab translated not to a treatment, but instead to death?

"And you always go where you're invited?"

"Always," he said, in a way that made her realize he wasn't as cocksure as he seemed. The man was a mystery to her. By rights he should have left the world of virology and locked himself up in a lab. But instead he was here still fighting to save people despite the devastating setbacks he'd encountered. How had he gone on?

She shook her head. "Reynaldo mentioned that the Yura were in trouble. I want to find out what he meant. Would you ask him?"

"I doubt your friend will tell me anything. He doesn't trust me."

"Why not?"

"Let's just say I'm friends with some of his enemies."

The way he said it sent shivers down the back of her spine. She realized she should have conducted a more in-depth interview of this man, looked closer at his past. "I need more answers."

"That's all you're getting right now. You'll have to trust me."

"Trust has to be earned."

He leaned in close, speaking in a very low tone. "Do you want me to leave you here alone with these men? Or do you want to get to your father?"

She sensed he was manipulating her. Deliberately using her father's peril to keep her from asking any more questions.

"I'm focused on what needs to be done."

She jerked away only to trip on the buttressed roots of a strangler fig. The trees were called killer trees by the natives because they completely covered the other trees in the forest and eventually strangled them. But they also provided much-needed fruit for year-round consumption by the animals.

Mac reached down and pulled her to her feet. She noticed again how strong he was. She just hoped she had someone at her side who she could count on personally as well as physically.

Jane wasn't used to counting on anyone, let alone a guy with a tough reputation. And Mac was hiding something from her.

Did Reynaldo know something that Mac didn't want her to know?

Jane didn't know who to trust. There were more dangers in the jungle than the disease infecting the Yura. Diseases she could handle. Liars just pissed her off.

The rains had held off for a while, but now they fell in a steady pattern. The water was unexpectedly cold, making her shiver with each drop that hit her skin. When she felt a chill moving up her spine she knew she needed to put on something else. She'd packed a vinyl rain jacket for just this kind of situation. She stopped. Aldo continued moving and Saturnino and Daniel jogged past her as did Mac. But Reynaldo stopped.

"What's wrong?"

"I need my jacket."

He nodded. Jane pulled out the vinyl shell and pulled it on over her clothing.

"How much farther to your village?" she asked.

"Not long now. You and your companion should consider staying the night with us."

Nothing sounded better to Jane. Especially when they arrived at the village fifteen minutes later. The cluster of huts was nestled in a small clearing, surrounded by tall trees. A well stood in the center, along with a fire where women were cooking. The dry huts were tempting. But her mission was urgent, and they had no time for rest.

Mac disappeared as soon as they got into the village. Jane was shown to a dry, clean hut. She didn't bother changing her clothing because she knew being wet was part of being in the Amazon.

She got out her Blackberry and called the airport. They hadn't heard from Bob.

She used her Blackberry to check her e-mail and was stunned to read a message from Meredith to the staff saying that she, Jane, was on a sabbatical and that her current projects were being reassigned. So she was really on her own.

Meredith hadn't mentioned moving Jane's workload around. Jane started to respond to the e-mail but decided it wasn't worth the effort.

She did send an e-mail to Tom and Angie, telling them that things weren't going too smoothly and that they'd been forced to jump early. She gave them her co-ordinates and asked Angie to check to see if Bob had survived the crash.

She found a table in the corner and removed everything from her bag. She found her grandfather's knife and attached the holster to her ankle. She also took out her insect repellent and doused herself and her bag with it. Then she repacked everything and knew it was time to get on the road.

She searched out Reynaldo and found him speaking to some men. He looked up at her, his gaze concerned.

"Would you send some men to the crash site?" she asked.

He paused before he answered. Her heart sank.

"These men have checked it out."

"Did they find the pilot?"

He shook his head. "There were no survivors."

Jane swallowed hard and wrapped her arms around her stomach, struggling not to cry. She closed her eyes, remembering how Bob had always seemed so wild and funny to her. He'd amazed her with his wild tales.

She felt a hand on her shoulder and spun around. Mac.

Reynaldo and his men drifted away, probably to give them privacy.

"Where have you been?" she asked.

"Getting some information from the villagers about who's warring with who. We don't want to get caught in the cross fire of a tribal war."

"That was a good idea."

"I heard Bob didn't make it. You okay?"

"Yes," she said. But she wasn't. She wished she was still safe in her lab, where she was in control. She turned away from him.

His voice made her pause and collect herself. "Do

you know where the Yura are? Reynaldo thinks we've got a good day's hike or more in front of us."

"I know. I programmed the coordinates into my GPS before we left Lima," she said. Focusing on business helped her shock at Bob's death. In his note, her father had left some coordinates for the tribe.

She thought about her dad and how much had changed since he'd left civilization. Not just in the way of available products, such as satellite phones in the private sector, but also in her. She was older now. More experienced with the CDC.

She wondered what had gone so wrong with her father.

Mac put his hand on her shoulder. She glanced back at him. "My watch has a GPS. I'll program the coordinates in there so we have a backup."

Jane gave him the coordinates. His watch looked as though it had been invented for NASA. He programmed it and then glanced up.

"I have some light sticks we can use once darkness falls. But I'm planning to keep moving if we can," she blurted out.

"That makes sense," Mac said.

"I've been thinking about hiring Aldo to come with us," she said.

"I've got enough jungle experience to get us to the Yura."

That was all well and good, but there was something about Mac that made her uneasy. He was hiding something and she didn't really want to find out on her own in the jungle that her faith in him was misplaced. "I'm going to check in with Reynaldo, but I want to leave in five minutes."

"Sure thing, boss lady."

Jane walked away, ignoring his smart comment. He liked to needle her, and she didn't know why. She spotted Reynaldo and he waved her over to him.

"Do you need anything for your journey?" he asked.

"We do need food. And some information."

"I gave food to your man. What do you want to know?"

"Could you tell me more about the trouble with the Yura?"

Reynaldo glanced across the clearing at Mac and then drew her farther away from him. "Six months ago something weird started happening with them."

"Weird how?"

"They stopped trading with us and refused anyone who journeyed to their village."

"What do you mean by refused?"

"They wouldn't allow anyone to come into the village. No food stores could be replenished. A white man…gave them orders."

"Did you see him?" Jane asked. Was it her father? Or someone else? Maybe Mac?

"No. But Aldo did."

"Was the man Mac?" she asked.

He shook his head. Jane started to ask another question but saw that Mac was moving toward them. "Thank you. Would Aldo be available to act as a guide?"

Reynaldo shook his head. "No. We are getting ready to start the Spring rite and Aldo is needed here. If you wait two weeks I can give you a group of men and a guide."

She didn't even have two days and well she knew it. "Thanks, but I can't wait."

Reynaldo nodded. He closed his eyes and put his hand over her forehead and muttered some words. Jane didn't know what he was saying, but sensed he had blessed her.

From his neck he took a necklace made of shells and bamboo and handed it to her. "Be careful. The way is not always straight or clear but don't doubt the path."

Jane nodded. "Thank you."

Mac joined them with his gear on, clearly ready to go. They said their goodbyes to Reynaldo and went back to get Jane's pack.

"So what's the plan?" he asked. "Just us, or did you find someone else to come along?"

"Just us. I'm not sure how far we can get tonight but I think I might go crazy if we stay here."

"Yeah, I kind of had that feeling. Why is this so important to you?" he asked.

"Saving lives is always—"

"Don't give me that. This feels personal."

"It is. My dad's involved." She hoped he'd leave it at that because she wasn't sure she even understood the deeper reasons why she was doing this. But she knew they involved being the one to right the past.

He moved closer to her, something she realized he did when he wanted to needle her.

"I think there's more to it than that."

"Well, save your brainpower. I just like to do my job well." He was more perceptive than she wanted him to be.

"Whatever you say. You want to take the lead?"

She nodded and lifted her backpack up, sliding the straps onto her shoulders. She groaned under the weight of it. Damn, it was heavy. She wished she'd done a little more than just weight training at the gym. She was going to have the mother of all backaches before this was done. But it would be worth it if she could save her father and prevent more people from dying.

The scent of fruit and rotting vegetation hung heavy in the air. They were far removed from the real world. She closed her eyes and saw her father's face. The pressure and the time clock beat loudly in her head once again.

"Tell me about this disease," Mac said as they moved out.

"The symptoms are similar to Lassa fever as far as I can tell. As I said in Lima, I didn't have time to do any tests on people."

"Do you think it'll spread to the brain?" he asked. Now he was acting like the other virologists she knew. She could almost hear his mind working as he processed what she'd told him and what he knew of viruses from the past.

"From what research I did…yes."

"Is your father infected?"

She swallowed. "Yes."

"How advanced is he?" he asked. There was no concern in his voice. He was just gathering information.

"I don't know." And somehow that made it worse. If she knew he was in the advanced stages, she could be better prepared. "He sent me two different packages. The second one contained his infected blood sample."

"Did he include notes?"

"Yes."

"Was his handwriting shaky?" Mac asked.

"No. It was the same bold strokes he always used."
She was tired of talking about this. It wasn't helping.
Somehow being here in the jungle made the threat all
the more real. Right now she felt out of control. Only
the glances she kept taking at the monitor on her GPS
unit made her feel more in charge.

Less a victim of this Yura disease that might spread
throughout the entire Amazon basin region. A disease
that the government and Raul Veracruz both denied existed. She didn't understand that. Raul had always been
a top-notch virologist. She couldn't believe he'd have
missed something this lethal.

"When we stop tonight I'm going to have my assistant send me some further information on Lassa. Did
you definitely rule that out?" Mac asked after several
minutes.

"Yes. Why are you questioning me?" she asked. Did
he doubt her research?

"I don't want to give an untried treatment to people,"
he said at last.

"Why not? The disease is fatal. A treatment gives
them a good chance to stay healthy." She'd bet that his
doubt had something to do with his Southeast Asia experience. She wanted to know more about it. Had he put
glory in front of human lives?

"Experience."

There was an expression in his eyes that she'd seen
once or twice on a virologist fresh from a hot zone.
There was nothing like fighting a disease in its environment and coming home barely the winner. "Does this
have something to do with—"

"I said *experience*. Leave it at that."

She stepped away from him. He was surly now, as if it was okay for him to probe into her life but not vice versa. He wiped his brow with the sleeve of his shirt. "I don't understand you," she said.

He closed the gap between the two of them. There was something challenging in the way he crowded her. Man-woman challenging, and it made Jane take a step back. She wasn't used to dealing with men who got in her face. She was kind of an ice queen at work and in the field she was all business. Damn. This trip was making her crazy already.

"That makes two of us," he said.

When he pulled his arm away she realized the sleeve had blood on it. She searched his face in the waning light, finding a cut at his hairline. "Are you injured?"

"It's nothing. Just a flesh wound," he said, moving out of her reach when she tried to check it out.

"We're in the jungle. A flesh wound—"

"I know it could mean death. I put some antiseptic on it."

"Let me see it," she said. He stood still. She had to step very close so that each breath he exhaled brushed her face. He smelled of sweat and mint. She hadn't been this close to a man in a long time. In fact, Raul had been the last man.

It had taken her a long time to get over him. Not because she'd been mooning or anything like that. But because she'd felt, of all the men she'd dated, Raul was the one she could have gone the distance with. They'd both shared so much. Work and career, similar outlooks on life and of course white-hot passion.

Mac stared at her and she realized she was just looking at him. Carefully she probed around the cut with her fingers. He didn't flinch, and she saw that the wound had started to close.

She went up on tiptoe for a better look.

"Going to kiss it and make it better?" he asked. His lips brushed the side of her cheek when he spoke.

Shivers spread down her body from the warmth of his breath against her skin. Maybe it was the fact that she didn't trust him or maybe it was just some sort of animal magnetism that he possessed. But whatever it was, he made her very aware of needs she'd ignored for too long now.

He was trying to rattle her. She knew it and he knew it. But Jane had been holding her own against hard-ass men her entire life. And it took a lot more than intimidation to scare her.

Jane put her shoulders back and stood a little taller. It helped that she'd spent a lifetime getting to know herself so well, because she had utter confidence in her ability to do what she'd come to the Amazon basin to do. Her nature wouldn't let her accept failure.

"Maybe it's worse than you think and I'll have to put you out of your misery."

Chapter 5

"How's your head?" Jane asked. Her mind was full of conspiracy theories that involved tampering. Their plane had been booked ahead of time and probably hadn't had high security around it. Add to that the man who'd attacked her, and it seemed smart to be paranoid. She couldn't shake the feeling that Raul had something to do with it. His interest seemed too convenient. Paranoia was something that scientists who worked for organizations like the CDC entertained all the time. The fact was, manipulating viruses and spreading them to create an epidemic and then stepping in with a treatment was something that could easily be done.

"Fine. I'd be better if I knew what had happened to that plane."

"Me, too. I have some thoughts," she said.

She wished she had a guide with her. Someone whose loyalty she knew she had.

Mac walked in step with her on this part of the trail. Was it just that he was a good trail mate, letting her set the pace? Because she knew his long legs could outpace her.

"What have you got, Jane?" he asked.

She glanced at him in the twilight. He kept asking her so many questions. She didn't trust him. Was that the fatigue of the day catching up with her? She was more tired than she'd realized.

"Just some thoughts," she said. Who in the Peruvian government would have anything to gain by denying a hot zone was in the offing?

"About what?" he persisted.

"The plane and the incident at my hotel. Plus, when I arrived a virologist working in the private sector warned me to leave."

"Do you think this virologist had something to do with the attack and the plane crash?" Mac asked.

"It's not like I have anything concrete, but I've know Raul a long time and he was acting weird."

"How well do you know him?" Mac asked. More than casual interest was in his eyes. It couldn't be jealousy.

"Very well at one time," she said.

The jungle exploded to life around them. Chattering monkeys in the trees shook raindrops down on their heads and birds took flight with excited calls. Jane froze, wondering what had scared the animals.

Mac pulled his gun and stepped in front of her. Touched by the protective gesture, she pulled her knife from its sheath.

"Something's out there and the way the animals are acting I'd say it's not just a friendly person. Stay here. I'll go check it out."

"Check what out? That's a stupid idea. I'll go with you. What if it's an entire hunting party?" He was a virologist, not Indiana Jones. And though she wasn't sure of his motives, she didn't want to see him injured.

"Then only one of us will be captured."

Jane heard the sound of rapid-fire Spanish moving toward them. She grabbed Mac's arm and tugged him behind the roots and waxy leaves of a *Bromeliad*. He'd been living in the Amazon basin for five years. He knew this place and its people way better than she did. "I need you alive."

"Great faith you have in my abilities."

"I do have faith, which is why I don't want you killed in a shoot-out."

Two soldiers moved into the clearing they'd vacated only seconds before. They wore jungle fatigues and face paint. They held AK-47 assault riffles loosely in their arms. They both had radio mikes clipped to their collars.

"No sign of them here," one of them said in Spanish.

The other one surveyed the area. He paused as he skimmed over the tree they were hiding behind. Jane held her breath, noticing that Mac did the same. They waited, hidden in the large root system of a tree that looked as though it solely supported the entire ant population of the jungle.

For the second time in as many days she was facing an armed man. She didn't like it. They were scientists, not guerilla soldiers.

"Search the trees and then report back to base," the second soldier said.

"For what? They don't know we're looking for them."

"The boss wants a thorough search."

They did a sloppy search of the area and then moved on. Jane let her breath out slowly.

"Okay, so your paranoid theory seems to have some substance," Mac said.

"Were those government soldiers?"

"I don't know. I just came from Bolivia. I haven't had time to meet the local law enforcement yet."

"Stop trying to convince me you're such a badass and help me figure this out."

"Near as I can tell, either your friend Raul sold you out to someone or the Peruvian government doesn't want you messing with the Yura."

"But why?"

"That does seem to be the million-dollar question," Mac said.

"The Yura travel in the triborder area."

"So anything that threatens the Yura threatens the border."

"I can have Angie look into seeing if there's a possible trade route that would be in jeopardy if this health threat was made public."

"Who's Angie?"

"My assistant back in Atlanta."

"I think you should stop communicating with your office."

"Why?"

"Because someone is sharing your itinerary."

* * *

Jane couldn't sleep. She was in a hammock above the ground and the mosquito netting that Reynaldo had given her kept most of the insects away. But her leg ached and she heard every sound that Mac made despite the distance between them.

What really disturbed her were the facts that Mac had laid out in a calm and concise way. She factored in that he was a little distrusting of organizations like the one she worked for, but even in the worst situations she couldn't imagine Meredith setting her up to die.

The more she thought about it the more she believed that someone *was* sharing her itinerary—and he might be in that hammock right across from hers. But then why would he hide with her?

There was no way that anyone would expect Jane to survive against a gun-wielding opponent. So far she'd gotten lucky. But now she was getting mad. The clock was ticking. Her dry ice was holding for now but it was damned hot in the jungle and she'd forgotten about that when she'd purchased the chemical coolant.

Everything she owned felt damp and was starting to smell musty. She searched deep inside herself to make sure continuing on this trip was what she wanted. Maybe Raul was right. What if she endured all of this and her dad was wrong?

But what if he was right? She'd seen the proof with her own eyes. That sample he'd sent was infected. She doubted he'd given himself a disease just to give them both a shot at treating something lethal. It made no sense.

She rolled over again and stared at the night sky through the canopy of branches. The hammock swung with her movements.

"Can't sleep?" Mac's voice was low and husky. He disturbed her on so many levels and tonight she was too tired to worry about keeping a barrier between them.

She glanced over at Mac's netting-enclosed sleep area. Her restlessness must have woken him. "No."

He sighed, propping himself up on his side. "We have a lot of walking to do tomorrow."

She knew it. She'd checked her laminated map before they'd gone to bed. They only had two days to get there. And she wasn't sure what Mac was up to. "I won't slow us down."

"I didn't think you would. Why are you so defensive?"

She didn't respond to that. Self-analysis wasn't something she was interested in playing tonight. "I'm just focused on getting to the Yura."

"Have you given any thought to where the virus may have started?" he asked.

She closed her eyes and let everything she'd read before she came here roll around in her mind. "Maybe the new highway they are building between here and Cuzco. They're doing a lot of jungle clearing and that always stirs things up. This virus could have been carried by a worker coming home to the Amazon basin, or by an animal."

"That makes sense. Some cultures might also believe that ancient spirits have been awoken," he said. "That belief makes sense to some part of me."

"Not the scientist," she said, carefully.

"Something deeper than science. It's there when I don't expect it. When you look at life in its smallest detail, the truth is revealed to you. And that truth…"

"That truth?"

"That truth is that there is something beyond what we can explain with our medicines and our microscopes. If a virus is spreading through the Yura and killing them, then…"

"Maybe it's bad spirits?" she said. The way he spoke reminded her of the artist Francisco Grippa, whose work was known for its Amazon themes, but occasionally included a piece that had underlying mysticism in it. There was something about the Amazon that brought out otherworldly thoughts.

"Yeah, but don't quote me on it," he said gruffly.

There was more to Mac than first met the eye. She'd heard in his voice his love of the Amazon basin and the peoples who lived there. She thought about what he'd said. About the spirits. Her mom had studied all kinds of peoples, and the Yura were the last tribe she'd lived with. Jane guessed that was why her dad had chosen to live with them when he'd left the United States.

"My mom was an anthropologist here," she said into the quiet. Mary Miller had lived for her work. Jane didn't have any pictures of her mom except the one in her mind in which Mary was standing on the banks of the Amazon helping a mother bathe her children while Jane splashed in the shallows.

"What do they believe here?" he asked, his voice jarring her from her own thoughts.

She thought about that for a minute. The people she'd met and lived with as a young girl had a deep mysticism that had nothing to do with modern religions. It came from the earth and the sky and that timeless quality that came from living in the rain forest. "Reality. Ancient cultures that practiced ritual beheading."

"Nice. A little virus that brings on brain hemorrhaging and fever shouldn't frighten them at all."

"Yeah, you have a point," she said at last.

She heard his hammock swing as he shifted. "What about you, Jane?"

"What frightens me?" she asked to buy time.

He waited for her response.

"The usual stuff. Spiders, snakes and men with guns. What about you?"

"You scare me," he said at last.

Shaman, she thought. There was a shaman's soul deep inside Mac. And she didn't know if she trusted him.

"Good." But she doubted she scared him. She wasn't big, even for a woman. The only thing she had going for herself was determination.

"One day that smart mouth is going to get you into trouble."

"I can handle it," she said, sitting up to adjust her mosquito netting. She didn't want to welcome in any of the jungle creatures to her bed. Even Mac.

"I have no doubt you think you can."

"I know it, Mac. Seriously, there's nothing out there I can't face on my own."

"I already figured that out. But what are you going to do when you have to face something with someone by your side?"

She didn't respond. Just rolled over and closed her eyes. She knew what he meant. It was the same comment that had dogged her entire life. *Doesn't play well with others. Too competitive. Not a team player.* Fuck that. Being a team player usually meant letting someone else screw up so that she had to fix their mistake and then solve the problem.

"I'm not your enemy," he said in that silky voice of his. She wondered if he was counting on it to seduce her.

"I know that. I just don't like to rely on others."

"I think the jungle isn't going to allow you to go it alone."

He wasn't helping. She knew what she needed to do. She had the packs with the dry ice and the vials under her hammock and she was planning to guard them with her life if need be.

"Good night, Jane."

"'Night, Mac."

She heard him slide around in his blankets and then finally he was quiet. She couldn't sleep. The night sounds of the jungle brought back flashes of her childhood. Including the jungle's creepy crawlies. She wished they were closer to one of the Amazon Center for Environmental Education and Research stations so that they could have slept in the treehouses there. She hadn't been kidding when she said she was afraid of spiders and snakes.

But they weren't going near the biosphere, unfortunately. And their camp was dry for now and provided a good shelter.

Jane had forgotten so many things about life in the jungle that were coming back to her. The memories she'd buried in her quest to leave the pain of the past behind. Closing her eyes didn't help. With each breath she took, she was flooded with the scents of her early childhood. She remembered her fear of scorpions and how she'd made her mother double-check her shoes before Jane would put them on.

She'd come a long way from that girl. Never look back, she reminded herself. Mac might think she was a little scary, but she knew he wouldn't like her the other way. Scared of everything.

She reached for the can of insect repellent that she'd brought with her and resprayed the inside of the net. They should have been sleeping in a shelter tonight instead of roughing it and would have if they'd been able to deplane at their target. They should have been traveling up the damned river and be halfway to her dad by now.

Something flew into her netting. Jane slid her knife from her sheath, which she'd stored at her hip. Red eyes glowed at her. She shook, wondering what the hell it was and how to get rid of it.

Shifting up as slowly as she could, she realized it was a small bat. Relatively harmless except as a carrier for rabies. She hoped Mac had closed his netting well.

She swatted at the bat and it flew away.

She was never going to be able to sleep. Sleeping humans were usually unaware of a feeding bat. She buttoned her shirt all the way to the neck and pulled the collar up.

"Mac?" she called.

"What?"

"I just saw a bat. Is your netting closed properly?" she asked.

"Dammit," he grumbled under his breath. Then she heard him adjusting the netting.

"Thanks, Jane."

"No problem. I didn't bring a rabies treatment with me."

"Good thing my shots are current."

"Why am I not surprised?"

"Are yours?"

"Of course. But I haven't needed a rabies treatment since I was a kid."

"Obviously I run with a lower-class crowd," he muttered. She saw him roll over to go back to sleep.

Jane tried to do the same but something wouldn't let her sleep. Starting with the animals in the trees, she began identifying all the sounds around her. Something wasn't right. She moved on to the insects and then kept cataloging until she realized that she was hearing humans moving through the jungle, and machetes ripping through heavy vines.

She jerked upright in the hammock and grabbed her boots. Shaking them upside down, she made sure they were safe before she jammed her feet inside. She left her blankets, but took her knife and her insect repellent. She shoved them into her pockets and grabbed the medicine that she'd brought from Atlanta.

Moving as quietly as she could, she made her way to Mac's hammock. Startled, she realized he was upright and ready to move.

"I knew you were going to disturb my sleep."

"Stop being a grouch and help me find a safe place to hide."

Mac pulled his gun. "I'm through with hiding."

"We have no idea how many men there are or how they are armed. Let's have surprise on our side."

He nodded and led the way beyond his hammock to an area heavy with vines that draped to the floor. Jane remembered the bats of just a few minutes earlier and paused before entering the dark area. She didn't know if she could do it. She hugged her backpack to her chest and stood there for a minute until something exploded behind her and Mac grabbed her hand, yanking her into the covering.

Glancing back at their camp she realized her hammock was now on fire. She gasped as Raul Veracruz moved into the clearing and shone a bright light at the empty hammocks.

She couldn't believe it. Raul was hunting her like some kind of prey. She gripped the backpack harder and tried to process this. What was he doing here?

Had he come to join her? Why had he fired on their camp? That made no sense. She started to stand, ready to ask questions and find out what was going on.

But Raul turned then and she saw nothing of the man she knew. He was dressed in full warrior battle gear, handgun held loosely in his left hand, assault rifle over his shoulder. Webbing around his waist held a knife, grenades and spare ammo.

Who was this person? She'd never seen this side of him before and Jane wondered how she could have been so blind. How she could have missed this side of Raul.

"Spread out and find them."

Chapter 6

Jane took Mac's arm, pulling him farther into the brush. She wasn't sure moving was such a great idea, but staying put was definitely out of the question. It ticked her off that she'd never suspected Raul had a dark side. Was she really so uninvolved in her relationships that she wouldn't sense this side of him?

Of course, one thing about Raul *had* made her uneasy. He hadn't really noticed her as a woman until she'd started to gain a reputation as an up-and-comer at the CDC. In hindsight, that could have been a warning sign.

The men searched through the hammocks and the netting Jane and Mac had left behind. They left nothing untouched. Water seeped into her cotton-weave shirt as she eased farther into the vines and brush.

A storm would provide them the cover they needed to put some distance between Raul and his men. But the sky was nice and clear. The setting moon and brightest stars still twinkled above them. Jane wondered if this was some sort of cosmic payback for not believing in her dad when she'd had the chance years ago.

Was she facing all these trials and things that were her worst nightmares as some kind of karmic penance? Cursing her own imagination, she watched Raul and hoped he earned at least a tenth of the bad luck that seemed to be dogging her lately.

She sensed his anger and the urgency he felt. This wasn't the Raul she knew. This man had a desperate look in his eyes that scared her. What was going on?

Mac slipped his hand in hers and pulled her back under the cover of a passionflower vine, which fell from the canopy down to the forest floor. "Got any ideas?" he whispered.

"Give me your gun," she said. "I'm going to injure Raul."

Mac didn't hand over his weapon. He took the kind of care of his gun that she reserved for the small glass vials that held the lifesaving serum she'd toted from Atlanta. He'd taken the weapon apart and cleaned it with ease before they'd turned in. Where had he learned such vigilance?

"It's not easy to shoot a man," Mac said.

"Have you done it?" she asked.

His eyes said yes, but he didn't answer her. The silence between them was uncomfortable, and Jane knew that she definitely should have asked a few more questions of Mac when they'd still been in civilization. As

soon as they were clear of Raul and his men, she in-
tended to.

"We've got to get out of here," she said. Using her
shirt to block the light, she turned on her GPS unit and
waited for a signal. According to the unit, if they continued in a southwest direction they'd be on track. "We
need to go that way." She pointed.

"How confident are you of that?" he asked, his voice
a toneless rasp.

"Ninety percent," she said, trying to mirror his low
tone, but failing. It was hard to talk like that. The last
time she'd tried she'd been thirteen and Sister Mary Ed-
ward had caught her in the back of the church trying to
talk to her best friend.

"Then lead away," he said, again in that toneless
rasp.

Jane turned and headed off through the long hanging vines. Her eyes adjusted as well as they could to the
dark. It'd be nice if they had some sort of infrared gog-
gles so they could see, but she hadn't anticipated these
kinds of problems.

Slowly the light of dawn started seeping through the
canopy high above them to the forest floor. Jane pulled
up and Mac stopped behind her. She could hear another
person moving parallel to them. Mac pulled his gun and
moved ahead of her.

"Give me your shirt," he said.

"What?"

"I don't want everyone out there looking for us to
hear the shot. I need something to silence it." Mac wore
only a dark T-shirt over his khaki expedition pants

Jane unbuttoned her blouse. The morning air was

chill and cold. She still had on the thermal T-shirt she'd gotten on sale last Christmas. God, why was she thinking about her clothing? Because clothing was safe, she realized. Quickly she removed her backpack and her shirt. "How do you want it?"

"Fold it up so I can use it as a silencer."

She nodded and did as he directed, handing it over to him. Mac knew a lot about guns. What the hell had he been doing since leaving the WHO? Most of the scientists she knew didn't have an intimate knowledge of guns or how to keep them quiet. But he'd lived in dangerous areas for a long time.

There was something feral in his eyes as he said, "You keep moving. I'm going to come around behind him."

"Be careful," she said. Was it just the fact that they were being hunted like animals that had him acting this way?

He disappeared in the direction they'd come. Jane adjusted the straps of her backpack and made sure she could easily reach the hilt of her knife. She continued moving forward. All of her senses were on hyperalert, listening for the sound of Mac's gun or one of Raul's men firing on him.

She heard nothing but her own footsteps and her heart beating very loudly. Continuing forward, she checked the GPS unit and realized she needed to move a little more to the west.

As she adjusted her path, she realized she'd have to leave the cover of the blanketing branches. She saw two men walking toward her position. She stayed where she was, drawing her knife from the sheath at her waist. She shrugged out of the straps of her backpack and set it gently on the floor of the forest near some lianas vines.

The men scanned the trees, keeping their guns at the ready. They looked young and tired in the filtered morning light, and she thought about what Mac had said. It was hard to kill another human being. She could only hope these young men would find it difficult to kill her.

"There's no one out here. I can't believe we're out here for—"

"Shh. I heard something in the bushes over there."

"Probably another one of those damned bats."

"I'm not taking any chances. Cover me."

She closed her eyes, remembering the look in Reynaldo's eyes as he'd stared her down. Utter calm was what she wanted. She could do this. There was no one else. As usual, when it came time to take care of business, she was all alone.

Or she could stay in her hiding place and wait for Mac to take care of the problem. She debated for a minute, but the men were moving directly toward her. She hoped that Mac was as good as his action had said he was, because this was one time when being her own team might not be enough.

Taking a deep breath she peered through the hanging vines and let her knife fly straight toward the man closest to her.

She hit one man in his left shoulder. He shouted in pain, dropping his gun. It hit the ground and bounced once. Jane wondered if she could get the gun from him.

The other man turned toward her position. Jane moved swiftly, dropping to the ground and rolling just as a spate of bullets hit the spot where she'd just been.

Damn. It was safe to say that this one wasn't some local handling a gun for the first time. Getting shot at wasn't exciting. It was terrifying.

Her heart beat so fast she thought she might have a heart attack. She realized that she was now weaponless and had only her wits to get herself out of this situation. *Please let me live through this,* she prayed. *Whatever happens I'll stop being so bossy.*

The first man bled steadily. Her knife stuck out grotesquely from his shoulder. He reached up and tugged it free, then tucked it into the back of his pants.

Her hands shook as she fought the need to take care of the injury she'd just created. She knew it was silly. She'd been protecting herself and she wasn't out of the woods yet. But her gut said that she was a healer.

Where the hell was Mac? If he'd been doing his part in their partnership she wouldn't be in this mess. Thunder rumbled in the distance. Come on, rain, she thought.

She heard a small pop and then saw blood spurt from a bullet wound on the second man's shoulder. He turned toward the jungle cover and began firing, but Mac hit him again in his thigh. Blood gushed from the leg wound, and the man fell to the forest floor, holding his leg and cursing in Spanish.

"Freeze," Jane said in a loud authoritative voice. She'd read one time that when you issued orders most people obeyed.

Jane emerged from the brush behind the man she'd gotten with her knife. He lifted his hands in surrender but he'd retrieved his gun. As she walked toward him, he tried to bring his gun up, but Jane lashed out and kicked the weapon aside. Thank God for kickboxing.

Mac came up beside her and held his gun on the men. Both men were groaning in pain from their wounds. Mac grabbed both guns and slung them over his back.

"Give me my shirt," Jane said.

Mac handed it to her and she went first to the man Mac had shot. She was afraid that Mac had nicked his artery. Jane applied pressure to the wound. "Keep pressure on this. What are your names?"

"I'm Juan. He's Carl." Juan pressed his hand to his thigh.

If only she'd brought a triage kit, but she hadn't anticipated this kind of emergency. She checked on his arm. "This is just a flesh wound. Clean it and cover it. There are parasites out here that would love to get into your bloodstream."

"Shake a leg, Jane. We need to move."

"Go get my backpack. It's just over there."

Mac did as she bid him. Jane squatted down next to Carl, who cursed at her in Spanish. She ignored it. "You need to apply pressure, too. When Raul gets here, he can treat both of your wounds. Don't leave them open."

In the distance, Jane could hear other men running through the jungle toward their location. She took her knife from Carl and returned it to the sheath at her waist after cleaning it on the back of Carl's shirt.

"Why are you hunting us?" Jane asked Carl.

"Screw you, lady."

"Let's go, Jane." Mac said.

He helped her get her backpack on and then grabbed her arm, dragging her away from the wounded men at an all-out run. At first Jane didn't think, she just moved.

Mac kept the pace steady and Jane trotted along beside him. She concentrated on not losing her footing as they traversed the uneven ground. The thick canopy overhead let only a little bit of sunlight through.

Her breath began to saw in and out. Slowly she stopped thinking about the weight of the pack and the difficulty she had keeping up. They couldn't stop. The men back there would kill them. Mac was her only ally in this hostile environment.

Her dad's favorite Hank Jr. song popped into her head as they were running. "Family Tradition" provided a nice internal sound track to the run. The song was perfectly syncopated by her footfalls. And she felt closer to her dad.

Maybe it was the jungle or the night or having come close to dying so many times, but she felt way more spiritual now than she ever had in the city.

The rough trail they were on sloped downward unexpectedly. Neither of them saw it in time to slow their momentum.

Mac swore.

The ground rolled away and Jane started to reach for a branch or something to break her fall but remembered that spine-bearing plants were dangerous. And unless she was mistaken, that was another peach palm. Its thorny spikes would bring about infection and inflammation.

"Don't try to grab any plants to break your fall," she called to Mac.

Jane struggled to just let herself roll with the fall. The ground was hard and she slid a good twenty feet before she stopped moving. Her left arm was scraped from shoulder to elbow and her right knee still ached from her hotel encounter.

Mac's head was bleeding again. "What happened to your head?"

"I hit it when I was getting your bag," he said.

Jane pushed herself to her feet and walked over to him. Her knee hurt, but she could tell it was only bruised. "I think we have enough time to bandage it."

"You'd make a good triage doctor."

Jane searched in the top of her pack for the first-aid kit. She didn't want to listen to him rib her about her treatment of the gunmen who'd been trying to kill them both. "Nah, I don't do well when I have to deal with people."

He took her chin in his hand. The intensity in his eyes made her feel warm all over. "I think what you did was…"

She took out an antiseptic wipe. "I hate the way you trail off like that. Just say it."

"I think it was courageous."

She rubbed his cut gently then applied a bandage to cover it. "It wasn't. I'm a healer. I had to."

"I know. It's hard to willingly injure someone."

Jane turned around, busying herself with putting the first-aid kit away and stowing the trash in her pocket. "You don't seem to have any problems with that."

"I'm not a heartless monster, no matter what you've heard."

She glanced back over at him. She may have had some doubts about his reputation before she'd met him. But now she knew he wasn't the bad guy that she'd perceived him to be. "I hadn't heard that."

"But you've heard some things?"

"I think we better get a move on."

Mac let her change the subject. She checked the GPS unit and led the way down the rough trail toward her father.

Mac took the lead when the jungle around them became denser. He pulled a machete from his pack and used it to hack a rough passageway through the thick growth. The thunder had delivered on the promise of rain. Walking through the steadily falling rain Jane wondered if she'd ever be dry again.

Though they'd put some distance between themselves and their followers, Jane knew that the Raul she'd seen tonight wouldn't give up. She listened for any sound of human pursuit.

"I'm surprised we haven't run into any tribes," Jane said. She'd noticed signs of people in the rain forest but they had yet to encounter anyone.

"Me, too. Frankly, we should have run into at least someone by now."

"So why haven't we?" she asked. The Amazon basin was filled with many different tribes, and they were often warring. There were also gold miners who ventured into this area. They didn't like anyone to come near them.

Mac shrugged and kept on walking. "I'm guessing your friend is responsible."

"How?" she asked. Raul could follow them because he knew roughly where they were going, but how could he get the word out to different tribes? One thing about the rain forest was that traveling on foot was the only way to move. Raul would be slowed down by the two injured men, which would give them the time they needed to get to the Yura and warn them.

"Hell, I'm not the one who's friends with the man trying to kill us."

Or was he? What had taken him so long to get to Carl and Juan? Why did he have the gun? And why couldn't she stop thinking about him?

She shook her head. He had a surly side that came out a little too often for her comfort.

Jane knew herself well enough to know that, though Mac seemed fascinating and different here in the Amazon basin, once they returned to civilization he'd be like all the other men she'd known.

Well, maybe not, but she'd be back to her old self. The woman who had little time for dating and romance.

Her awareness of Mac must be due to the weird adrenaline aftereffects from the encounter with Juan and Carl and then that fall down the slope. This was turning into the adventure of a lifetime. Where did Mac fit in?

"Tell me what happened in Southeast Asia. Why do you only work in the Amazon now?"

He shook his head.

"Sorry, you'll have to try something else," he said, closing the gap between them. In his eyes, she saw something she recognized. The signs of having witnessed the kind of death that no one wanted to remember. They all had stories like that. You couldn't work with level 4 viruses and not see death. Not feel its breath on your shoulder and its eyes fixed on your body.

"Like?" she asked. The rain was still a steady trickle, but she'd gotten used to it and hardly noticed it anymore.

"Are we really having this conversation?" he asked. Then rubbed the heels of his hands over his eyes.

She knew what he meant. Stop pushing, she thought. But her nature wasn't to leave things alone. Her nature was to shove and prod until she uncovered what made a virus—or a person—tick. And with Mac, who she sensed was hiding something from her, that instinct was even sharper.

Maybe she was going a little crazy from everything that happened. She knew poking at him was insane but it was the only thing that kept her from the fatigue that dogged her every step. That, and the fear that rode shotgun with it. She couldn't close her eyes without being assailed with some image that was so foreign to her everyday life that it made her feel as though she was someone else.

"I'm tired," Jane said suddenly. Bone-deep tired. She thought of Bob, hoped that by some miracle he had escaped the crash. If he were here with them, taking this trek through the jungle, he would lighten the mood. And she could talk to him about her father. It had been years since she'd heard the stories of her dad in his youth, with his life on the line. Not knowing if he was going to be alive when she found him, she wanted to revel in his life.

Maybe that was part of the problem. For the first time she was in a situation that she couldn't handle on her own. A situation she didn't want to handle on her own. God, she'd only known Mac a little over a day. He didn't mean anything to her. Yet at the same time, he did.

"I think the rain is stopping. I want to check the packs and make sure the dry ice is holding," she said.

He let her go but she felt his gaze on her the entire time as she opened her pack and checked on the vials. God, she was wagering so much on her own research. Wagering so much on a risk that she still couldn't believe she'd taken.

She'd kept her composure through some of the most trying times of her life. And this time was no different. Not just the situation with her dad, but other tense circumstances at the CDC. She was known for her poise and cool.

And it would take more than the rain forest or Mac Coleman had to rattle her. She closed her eyes for a minute and pictured herself back in Atlanta surrounded by Meredith, Angie and Tom. All of them congratulating her on following this possible outbreak from start to finish.

Mac stood there, watching her. She felt a million things at once, but mostly she focused on the sense of urgency in the back of her mind and the feeling that time was running out.

Chapter 7

Jane's Blackberry beeped with a new message as soon as they reached an opening in the canopy. She stopped. Mac was several yards behind her, moving at a pace that was just about as fast as her Granny Pearl. He was writing in his notebook, something she noticed he did a lot.

Jane dialed into her voice mail. "Jane, this is Tom. I have some concerns about the treatment you took with you. I ran an additional test that I'd like to discuss with you. I'm worried that you might be rushing into something you're not prepared for. Call me."

Tom wasn't on her team, but he'd always been a good friend. She started to dial him back then remembered what Mac had said the other day. Someone knew her itinerary and was sharing it with Raul.

Was it Tom? Her gut said no way. But Jane had been

badly shaken when she'd seen Veracruz rifling through their campsite. She sighed, closing her eyes for a moment. She needed to get her bearings. They only had two days left to reach her dad. All of the delays were taking a toll on her spirit.

She struggled not to let Mac see it. She didn't want him to have a clue that she wasn't as indestructible as she'd thought she was.

She wished she had her spare shirt, but she hadn't had time to gather everything when Raul had attacked the camp. She'd give anything for a bath and something to drink that wasn't ionized water.

Jane composed an e-mail to Tom.

Thanks for the concern. Plan to do clinical trials when I arrive with the tribe.

There was an e-mail from Angie about Mac. Jane skimmed the contents and then struggled not to let anything show on her face.

She read the message again.

Be careful, girl. I've gotten repeated requests for information about you from Rebel Virology. I've dug as deep as I can on Mac Coleman, but can't find anything except that he has spent the last five years living in the Amazon basin...according to one article I read in *Science Times* weekly...he is searching for the kind of fame that eluded him in Asia.

Unsure if Angie was warning her that Mac was working against her or not, she didn't know what to do.

Make a plan, she heard her father's voice say. *Pull out your pad of paper and jot down what you know,* that's what he'd always said. Every time she'd gone to him for an answer, he'd come back with that.

Jane shrugged the straps of her pack off her shoulders and opened the bag up. She dug around until she found a leather-bound journal at the bottom. She'd bought it when she first started traveling at age sixteen. She'd always had a vision of writing her travel escapades and then someday publishing a book of them. But only three pages of the book were used and they said things like *Germany was nice* and *Greece not as pretty as the pictures.*

Mac had caught up to her and stopped several feet away. He was still engrossed in whatever he was doing. At least he was hampered by not having a way to communicate with anyone outside of the jungle. Jane turned her back on him, pulled her knife from her waist sheath and sat down. The knife was uncomfortable when she sat. She dropped it on her lap and started making notes. Just things she knew.

Raul was definitely up to something and she wished she knew what. The man she'd known would want them to reach the Yura and stop the spread of the disease. So why was he hunting them down? She could only guess that he had been working on the disease at the same time she was, and had reason to keep it quiet. Had he contacted her father? She knew from what Meredith had found out that clinical trials had been conducted in the Amazon basin by a virologist. But now Jane wondered—was it Mac or Raul?

Hell, enough guessing.

Mac wandered over to her.

"Anything urgent?" he asked, not looking up from his notebook.

"Nothing too important. What were you doing in Bolivia before you joined me?"

"Tracking down a virus. Making sure that it hadn't spread down La Paz way. Why?"

"I know you've been checking up on me," she said.

He scratched his jaw and tipped his head to the side, studying her. "So?"

"Why?"

"Because something about this whole setup doesn't feel right to me."

"Me, either. Like someone is deliberately slowing me down," she said.

He didn't respond. She didn't care.

"Either keep up from now on or I'm leaving you behind."

"Yes, ma'am."

"Don't be a smart-ass," she said, pushing to her feet. She sheathed the knife and put the journal away. It hadn't helped. She'd known it wouldn't. She was a woman of action, not words, and even writing the reports she was required to do at work was tedious. She didn't like it.

"I'm not. Just remember that you've got gunmen on your trail and no weapon."

He made her situation sound more daring than she'd been imagining it.

She wouldn't be in this boat if Meredith had more guts. More than anyone in the world, Meredith should have understood and given Jane full support instead of off-the-record support.

"Are we moving out?" Mac asked.

"Yes."

He shrugged and put his pen and journal back in his pack, then stretched his arms over his head. His dark hair hung almost to his shoulders. The white bandage at his hairline stood out in stark contrast to his tanned skin.

"I'm not just checking up on you, Jane. I don't trust the CDC."

"Why not?"

"From my experience, when the chips are down and it's time for action, the CDC and WHO wait. They have to. There are too many outside interests that have to be satisfied before they can act," he said at last. This wasn't an observation he was making. Mac really believed that those organizations were willing to sacrifice to please their moneymen.

"Why does that make you so mad? Those outside interests, as you call them, are the source of most of the funding those groups receive." She sensed there was more to Mac's anger than simply what had happened in the past. What was his agenda here?

"Money is a powerful tool for manipulating people. I'm mad because it shouldn't be about doing what will make the most profit, it should be about saving lives."

"I'm not going to let you make the CDC into the bad guys. They want to save lives, too," she said defensively.

"Yes, but at a price."

"We all pay a price for doing what we believe is right. I learned that the hard way early in my career. I'm sure you've had some experiences with regret, as well."

"You know I have."

"Yes," she said quietly. "I do."

Jane started down the path. "We could probably get there quicker if we followed native tradition and jogged."

"You're the boss."

She glanced over her shoulder at him and caught him staring at her backside. She turned around before he looked up. "We only have two days left to get there. I don't want to push the clock any closer."

Jane started jogging at a steady trot. She checked the GPS several times to make sure they stayed on course.

Jogging left her mind free to wander, but it never went much farther than the man at her heels. He'd never answered her question, just changed the subject. She was stuck in the jungle with her ex-lover hot on her trail—and with a man who was hiding something from her.

The rains continued into the afternoon, getting progressively steadier. Jane trudged on but it was harder to keep the pace she'd set. She slowed from a jog to a fast walk. But then she slid into the mud, completely covering her entire left side in muck.

"You okay?" he asked, coming to her side and tugging her to her feet.

"Peachy." God, she hated this. She kept falling on the same leg. She hadn't had a chance to look at it yet, but she was sure her left leg was one continuous bruise from thigh to ankle. "I think we're going to have to find shelter."

Mac nodded. While he scouted around, Jane found two large, waxy rain forest leaves with drip-tips. She held one over her head. Mac returned a minute later.

"What is that?"

"Rain forest umbrella. I have one for you, too."

He took it from her. "Thanks."

"Let's string together some of these and use it as the roof of a shelter. We can use bamboo to make a rough sort of lean-to," Jane said.

Working together they made short work of gathering and cutting bamboo. Mac created a platform to sit on while Jane lashed together the large, waxy leaves in two large groups. Mac took them and finished putting the roof up, making a very crude lean-to. Jane shoved their packs inside first and then climbed in. Mac followed her.

The rain continued to fall and Jane watched ants and other insects moving about their business. Mac opened his pack and pulled out an energy bar, offering her one. That man had more stuff in his pack than she did. She was impressed with him and the way he'd packed. But then he'd been living here a lot longer than she had.

"What all do you have in there?" she asked at last. To make her pack lighter, she'd taken out a lot of the stuff she wanted to bring. Of course, she didn't have the chest and shoulder muscles that he did, so logically it made sense that he could carry more.

"Essentials for living," he said.

"Got something to make a shower from?" she asked. She'd brought some of those cleaning wipes to use for bathing, but they weren't going to cut through the mud.

"Do I smell?"

"No," she said around a laugh. "I can't take the mud anymore."

"I have soap. I'll be a gentleman and not look if you want to use nature."

She debated it for a minute then nodded. She held her hand out for the soap. "Okay."

He pulled the bar of soap out of reach. "It'll cost you."

Why wasn't she surprised? "What do you want?"

"Tell me something that no one else knows about you."

What? "Why?"

"No questions, just an answer. Being the nice guy that I am I'll even close my eyes and let you get started on washing."

"I can't talk to you while I'm doing that."

"Why not?"

"I don't know. I just can't."

He opened his eyes again. "Well…"

She had no idea what to tell him. There were literally hundreds of things that no one knew about her. She liked it that way. "I quit high school when I was fourteen and took the GED."

"Your boss knows that."

"Well, *I* never told her," Jane said, knowing she sounded peevish but not really caring. There was something about Mac that made her not want to confide any of her private thoughts.

"Why is this important to you?" she asked. She couldn't imagine why he wanted to know more about her unless he wanted something more than just this trek through the jungle with her.

"It just is," he said.

She thought it over. She knew Mac well enough by

now to know he'd give her the soap even if she didn't tell him anything. He was more than the tough hombre he looked like on the outside. And she did want to know about the incident in Southeast Asia. "Okay, but you'll owe me something."

"More than a bar of soap?" He arched one eyebrow at her. And leaned closer.

"Yes. Deal?"

"Depends on what you're going to share. If it's another high school story, forget it."

"What do you want to hear about?" she asked again. She hadn't been kidding when she said her life was boring.

"Tell me about Jane, the woman."

"She's not very exciting." Actually Jane was more comfortable in her Jane-the-virus-hunter skin than she was in her Jane-the-woman skin.

"I'll be the judge of that," he said with the kind of roguish charm she was coming to expect from him.

She closed her eyes and tried to think of something intimate that wouldn't leave her feeling vulnerable. "I like country music."

"Which artists?" he asked. "I'm partial to rock music. Stuff like Van Halen and Guns 'N Roses."

"Do you wear your leather pants and muscle T-shirts when you listen to them?"

"Ha ha. Who do you like?"

"George Strait and Garth Brooks."

"Why?"

Suddenly she was cautious, she knew he wasn't going to be satisfied with just any answer. "Because they sing about things I've always wanted."

He didn't say anything else, but she felt his silence as he waited for her to explain. She picked at the laces on her hiking boots, talking to them instead of to him. She removed her shoes and took off her socks, draping them on top of the boots. She stared at her plain, un-polished toenails and knew that there was nothing in-triguing about her. Was he perceptive enough to under-stand the true depth of her longing when she listened to songs by those men?

"Things like love, family and loyalty," she said at last.

Jane had said too much. She knew it, and she wasn't saying anything else. She put out her hand and he dropped the bar of soap into it. She dug in her pack until she found her spare pants and underwear.

Mac pushed his pack toward the back of the lean-to and laid back, eyes closed. She wasn't disappointed, she told herself. But on one level she was.

Jane crawled back into the lean-to twenty minutes later a much happier and cleaner person. The rain had been very cold but she didn't care. She needed to be clean.

Mac sat up immediately and she was a little un-nerved to realize he hadn't been sleeping. There was intensity in his eyes when he watched her that made her uncomfortable.

"I didn't realize you were awake," she said, her voice a little husky from fatigue. She handed his soap back to him and he put it away.

"I'm not tired," he said.

"I am," Jane said, rubbing the back of her neck.

Tired of the jungle, and yet at the same time she wasn't. The jungle was so alive and so different that there was a part of this environ that constantly challenged her mind. There were so many sights and sounds to catalog here.

She became aware that Mac watched her with his dark gaze. She wished she knew what he was thinking. "What?"

"If you'd let go of having to be in charge of everything…"

He was right but she didn't know how to let go. And to be honest the one time she'd let him make a decision, it hadn't worked the way she'd planned. Carl and Juan had almost found her and the medicine while he'd been tracking them.

She hoped that Raul made sure that those men got proper treatment. Mostly because it would slow them down. "Do you think the plane was sabotaged?"

He let her change the subject. "I wouldn't be surprised."

"I feel responsible for Bob."

"Why? Did you sabotage the plane?" He rubbed his jaw. The hair of his light beard and mustache was filling in. She remembered the texture of it, soft and tickly against her.

"Of course not, but I should have thought of the possibility that someone might have."

"Let it go, Jane. You're not Wonder Woman, though I think you'd look great in the costume."

It was a sexist comment and she had no doubt that he meant it as such. But she also realized that was just Mac's attitude. He knew she was capable and he liked the fact that she was. "You'd better be happy I'm not Wonder Woman. If I were, I'd have the lasso of truth, and then you'd have no secrets from me."

"You want to know my secrets?"

"You wanted to know mine."

He leaned back on his elbows in a pose of total relaxation. They could have been on a beach in Lima enjoying the afternoon.

She did. Find out what his weaknesses were so she'd have some defense against the way he watched her. But that was dangerous.

"Maybe someday. Right now I want to figure out why Raul and his men are trying to kill us."

He closed his eyes for a second and when he looked at her again the fire in them was banked. "Let's start with what we know."

The rain still beat down on the top of the lean-to and small drops made their way through the thatched roof, rolling slowly down the side before disappearing under the bamboo. Jane hoped she'd learn something new from him.

"The Peruvian government denies there's anything infectious out here," Jane said.

"Did they conduct interviews and run tests?"

"Yes. They sent an expert to the Yura to do the testing."

"Who?"

"I don't know. I wasn't given that information."

"Can you get it now?"

She pulled her phone out of its protective plastic-and-leather case and saw that she had a decent signal despite the rain. She quickly pulled up the e-mail function and sent a note to Angie asking her to find out who'd done the initial field research with the Yura. Despite what Mac has said about not communicating with her office, Jane had no choice. She couldn't do a lot of computer research on her phone.

"Something must have happened to make Dad send me those samples." She wondered if the Yura were even aware that they had an outbreak. Outbreaks always started small. One person dying from bleeding, hemorrhaging or some other foul way. Her father would have investigated and then possibly isolated the others from the deceased.

"That's what I was thinking. Your father doesn't want to be involved in our business anymore so he wouldn't have sent this to you unless he felt there was no other way."

"I wonder if Raul did the research."

"He's not with the CDC anymore. He's private, so he couldn't conduct the interviews alone."

He was right. But who would have been sent? Someone familiar with South America. Someone like Mac.

"What do you know about the Yura?" Jane asked.

"Next to nothing. I got some notes from our research wiz at R.V., but didn't have time to read them before we left Lima."

"Do you have it on you?" she asked.

"No, I was told to travel light."

She tossed her phone to him. "Why don't you see if they can e-mail you what they found?"

He started typing on the thumb keyboard. Jane leaned against her pack. The rain didn't really cool things off but it was a nice respite from the humidity.

Mac finished typing and tossed the phone back to her. She caught it and put it away.

"We should start moving again," Jane said. The rain was letting up a little and moving through the jungle in it wouldn't be that hard.

"I was thinking the same thing. If we use the light sticks we have left sparingly, we should be able to travel at night, as well."

Jane nodded. She checked her boots before she put on her socks and shoes. Mac pushed the top of the lean-to off of them and they both got to their feet. Jane adjusted the weight of her backpack, which felt heavier as the days went on. They started walking.

"Tell me about the group you lived with in Brazil," she said.

"There's not much to tell. A friend asked me to come and check out his people."

"Why you?"

"Yabidwa and I went to school together."

"When?"

"Second semester of college. I came down here to study at the American University in Lima and so did he. I've always been more comfortable in the jungle then in the city and Yabidwa was the same way."

"So he asked you to come and check out his people and you did?"

"Yes."

"What was wrong with them?" she asked.

Mac stopped abruptly. "Did you hear that?"

Jane tilted her head to the side. The forest around them was very quiet, which wasn't right. Where the insects and birds had been chattering noisily just a few minutes ago there was now silence. A predator was on the loose in the jungle. *Please don't let it be a snake,* she thought. Though she knew that snakes didn't attack people who left them alone, they creeped her out.

Something caught her attention in the hanging vines across the way. A movement that didn't seem like a rain forest animal. She moved closer to investigate, but Mac caught her arm, holding her in place. He pulled his gun from the holster and moved forward with his weapon drawn.

They both froze in their tracks as three guerilla soldiers stepped into the open. They all held assault rifles pointed directly at Jane and Mac.

Chapter 8

Mac moved in front of Jane, pulling his gun. Two of the men lifted their rifles. They were at point-blank range. Mac would be killed if they fired. Thinking quickly, Jane stepped to the side and the third man moved to keep her covered.

"What do you want?" Jane asked in English and then again in Spanish. She was sweating despite the rain. A part of her was oddly detached from the situation. Deep inside, she started to wonder if she was ever going to leave the jungles of Peru or if she was destined to die there.

"Are you a doctor?" the leader asked in Spanish. He was her height with a stocky build. His face was broad and his eyes held a serious intent.

"We both are," Jane said, carefully. Mac had some

field skill and they both had training in treating infectious diseases, but she wasn't trained in delivering babies or anything like that.

"We need your help. Our village is sick," he said haltingly.

There was something in his voice that she could respond to. "We would like to help you, but we have another village to get to first."

He glared at her. "We can't wait. People are dying."

Jane looked at Mac. *People are dying.* That was a call neither of them could ignore. What if the virus her father had sent was already spreading through the Amazon basin? They were still a day's journey from the Yura. In English she said to Mac, "It could be the Yura virus."

"It wouldn't hurt to check it out. Do you have the equipment needed to take blood samples and analyze them?" he asked.

Mac never took his eyes off the two men who held him at gunpoint and she had the gut feeling that if need be, he would have been able to fire on them and still converse with her.

"I have a small microscope and some needles and plates, so we should be okay. I have a small centrifuge machine, but that requires electricity." She'd wanted to bring more supplies, but in the end they'd had to bring only the necessities and the medicine took precedence over lab equipment.

She turned back to the leader. "We will help you if we can. We are both scientists, not regular doctors."

He nodded at Jane. The men lowered their weapons and Mac holstered his. Jane walked with the leader and

Mac followed behind with the other two soldiers. Jane's first thought was to conduct a preliminary interview as they moved through the jungle. But the men fell into a single-file line as Reynaldo's men had and moved at a trot through the jungle. Jane followed the leader with Mac right behind her.

In her head, Jane went through what she knew of the virus plaguing the Yura. From her dad's note she knew that fever and hemorrhaging were both symptoms.

"What kind of sickness is it?" Jane called as they were moving. "Fevers?"

The leader glanced over his shoulder at her, slowed his pace to jog side by side with her. "Some, but not everyone has it."

That was good but it didn't mean that they didn't have the same thing the Yura did. "What about bleeding?"

"No. Nothing like that. Our shaman has tried several sweats and his vision told him of you."

"Me?" she asked, surprised. How would a shaman know about her? The mystical part of the jungle made her uncomfortable. She'd seen enough to make her realize there were things that happened here that she didn't understand and never would.

"A doctor traveling through the basin," he said after a few moments. That was vague since Mac and Raul were both doctors, as well. So was her father.

Jane said nothing. The scientist in her didn't accept things like a shaman's vision. Her mind automatically cataloged the facts. Reynaldo had acted as if he were shaman of his village. Perhaps he had relayed their presence to someone else who had in turn passed it to this man's village.

"I'm Jane," she said at last.

"Tambo," the man said.

"Is your family sick?" she asked.

"Wife is, and son and daughter are starting to show signs," he said. In his eyes she saw the anguish she'd felt when she'd realized her father was sick. Having dealt with illness all of her adult life, Jane had never really worried about it until now. She'd sometimes thought about what might happen if she contracted whatever virus she'd been working with, but she'd also always believed she could master the virus and find a treatment. *Until it had became personal.*

"Stomachaches?" Jane asked.

"Yes. They can't keep any food down."

"Do you live near a waterway?" Disease could come from a polluted water source.

"No, but we travel to the Ucayali River to fill our water reserves when we start to run low."

With the everyday rains, lack of water wouldn't be a problem especially now that it was the rainy season. She wondered if the Ucayali was running high and maybe had spilled over its banks, contaminating the river.

"Has there been any…" Jane didn't know how to ask the man if his wife's stools had been soft and bloody. In some cultures speaking of such things was forbidden. Tambo looked at her but she could only shake her head. "I'll check with her when we get there."

Tambo and the other men moved quickly, at a pace that was a lot more vigorous than she and Mac had been traveling at. Soon she had a stitch in her side and couldn't speak without gasping for breath. The forest

floor beneath her feet was wet and she was aware of it
as she hadn't been earlier. She narrowly missed stepping on a slick spot that could have caused her to fall.

"What...do you...eat?" she gasped.

"Fruits and vegetables from our gardens. Capybara
and palm grubs."

Jane nodded and processed that a capybara was a rodent and palm grubs were larvae. She'd eaten both
when she'd lived in the jungle as a child. And though
they sounded a bit nasty, the grubs were tasty. Kind of
an acquired taste, like oysters.

Jane wouldn't rule them out as the source of whatever was bothering Tambo's people, but she didn't think
it was the food. If they weren't suffering from the same
virus the Yura had, then it might be dysentery. She'd
know more once they arrived in the camp and had time
to examine the villagers.

But time was in short supply. They'd have to work
quickly because Jane couldn't afford to give Tambo's
people more than a few hours.

The village was comprised of several thatched huts in
a circle around a cleared area. The homes were small and
the activity in the village was very limited. There were
no trees—the area had been totally cleared. There was
minimal standing water in the lower spots around the village.

Jane cataloged it all as she bent double at the waist
to regain her breath. Mac crossed over to her and put
his hand on her shoulder.

"You okay?"

"Yeah, just out of shape."

"Too much time in the lab, Dr. Miller," he said, but there was a grin in his voice.

"Thanks. That's just what I needed to hear now."

"Well, then how about some good news."

"I could use that."

"I doubt that this is the same virus the Yura have."

"Me, too. From everything Tambo said I'm leaning toward dysentery."

"I'll check out the food and water supply while you examine the patients."

"Why do I get all the fun jobs?" she asked. But she wasn't serious. She loved this part of her work. Being in the field and helping and educating people were why she'd chosen this profession.

She paused, realizing that she was more like her dad than she'd ever admitted before. He, too, spent the majority of his life tending to others. He'd explained it to her once when she'd been about twelve. She could still remember the words he'd spoken that eerie dawn before he left for South Africa. His voice had been quiet and almost soundless. He'd said… *"Saving lives, Jane, that's what I'm good at. I could stay here with you but then I'd be only helping one person when I could be saving many more."*

Those words echoed in her mind as she headed to Tambo's hut. This was her father's legacy to her. No matter how different she liked to pretend she was, she knew that she was cut from the same cloth Rob Miller was.

Tambo stood in the doorway, his gun slung over his back, his eyes pleading with her in a way that this strong warrior never would do with words.

She put a hand on his shoulder and entered the hut. There were windows cut out of each of the walls and the afternoon light spilled through them. The hut was hot and humid and flies buzzed around. On a bamboo bed in one corner lay a woman of indeterminate age. She moaned and clutched her stomach.

Jane moved closer and bent to examine her. "My name is Jane and I'm a doctor. Can you tell me what's wrong?"

Tambo's wife looked up at Jane with eyes like large pools of obsidian. Jane saw evidence of pain and dehydration.

After asking a few questions, Jane was certain that dysentery was affecting the village. Mac was waiting outside of Tambo's hut when she emerged.

"It's dysentery. I think we can mix up a salt-water-carbohydrate combination that should help with the dehydration," Jane said.

Mac tossed her a Ziploc baggie filled with salt tablets. "I had these in my pack. We can use fruit juice as the carbohydrate."

"Are we sure that the dysentery wasn't caused by the fruit?" Jane asked. The same water that had infected these villagers was probably used in irrigation.

"No. We can boil the juice and then add it to the mixture," he said. "We'll test a sample first before we give it to anyone."

She wondered at his caution. Aware of the clock ticking in getting the medicine to her dad, she would have made assumptions. But Mac clearly wouldn't. She decided right then that the next time they were alone she was going to get the details of whatever happened to him in Southeast Asia. It had clearly shaped the virologist he was today.

"How was the water?" she asked when she realized she was just staring at him.

"I'm not sure, yet. I couldn't find your microscope."

"It's in my pack," she said. "It should be right near the top. Did you check under the dry ice packets?"

He shook his head. "I have a thing about going through a woman's bag."

Jane didn't mind, she thought it was respectful that he hadn't just started going through her stuff. She went to her bag and took out the equipment she had.

"Can you heal her?" Tambo asked, coming up behind Jane. He still wore his gun and she wondered if he ever put it down. He probably didn't. This area wasn't just plagued with warring tribes but also with drug runners, miners and other badasses looking for trouble.

"Yes. We know what's wrong and can treat it. We're going to need to boil some fruit juice," Jane said. She didn't know whether Tambo totally trusted her, and she prayed that she and Mac had made the right diagnosis.

"We will take care of that," Tambo said. "Do you need anything else?"

"A table would be great," Mac said.

A few minutes later they had a table to use. Jane left Mac setting up the microscope and starting to check out the water samples he'd taken. Jane continued through the village, talking to those who were sick and reassuring them that they'd be better in a few days. Only two of the people she examined had extreme cases of amebic dysentery.

She had brought along a few pills that the CDC used

in those cases because Jane had gotten a mild case of dysentery one time in Sierra Leone. The diloxanide furoate would kill the bacteria. Jane used her Blackberry phone to contact the local CDC office for Peru. They promised to send a field team to follow up with Tambo's village when they could.

When she rejoined Mac, he'd mixed up the drink to be given to all those who were sick. "Ready for the Mac-Ade."

She shook her head at him, but noted that he was in his element here. She could understand why he'd left the WHO. This is what he was meant to do—and really, what she knew deep inside that she was meant to do—get out in the field and help people without having to deal with the government's red tape.

It took a little over three hours to treat everyone. While Jane explained what they needed to do for the sick for the next forty-eight hours, Mac took a few of the men aside and discussed the fact that the water supply and the sewer needed to be separated. He showed them some simple steps they could take to ensure their village stayed healthy.

When Mac found out the CDC had promised a team but not given an immediate response, he also used Jane's phone to call one of his field operatives, Maria Cortez, and asked her to come to the village as backup. She'd promised to come as soon as she was done in Brazil.

Forty minutes later, Mac and Jane were finished in the village. Jane was very aware that the afternoon they'd spent in Tambo's village was cutting into the precious hours they had to reach her father. The clock was ticking and she knew that each moment they spent getting to the Yura was another life in jeopardy.

"Thank you, Jane. I will follow your instructions so that this doesn't happen again," Tambo said.

"In a few days, Maria will be here," Mac said. "She'll stay until everyone is well. A team from Peru's CDC will also be by, although I'm not sure when."

Tambo nodded and then turned, gesturing to the thatched huts. "We'd like for you to stay the night in our village."

"Thanks, Tambo, but we can't. I have to get to my father," Jane said.

He shrugged his shoulder. "Then I can send two of my men with you. You will be traveling through dangerous territory."

"Are the dangers from the wild or from men?" Mac asked. He'd been quietly watching the interchange between her and Tambo. The men in the village were guarded around Mac, as if they sensed he was the dangerous one.

"Men—there are tribes we are warring with. As well as the dangers of traveling during the rainy season."

"Then your men should stay here. Jane and I will be fine with the other tribes," Mac said.

Warring men Jane understood. It didn't matter what environment they were in—that was the nature of the beast. They fought for supremacy and leadership because it was part of the basic DNA of all men. She'd seen examples of it in Atlanta at the lab where sometimes two virologists went head-to-head to be the first to find a treatment. She'd seen it in the jungle with Mac and herself.

Tambo offered them both a plate of palm grubs before leaving to check on his wife. Mac took one without even blinking. She watched him slit the back of the grub open and then bring it to his mouth and suck out the protein. Jane did the same.

He raised one eyebrow at her. "I see you've been here before."

"I lived in the Amazon basin as a child, remember?" she said. "Makes a nice change from protein bars."

She remembered the first time she'd realized what she was eating. She'd been a grossed-out eight-year-old, but it was too late to change her habits. She liked the taste of the grubs. After her mom had died and she'd returned to the United States, she'd tried oysters—the texture was much the same as the grubs—but she'd never cared for their taste.

"I'd forgotten how good the local delicacies could be. Although I've never been able to stomach eating a rodent. But then again, I'm not that hungry yet."

"I'm better when I don't know what it is I'm eating," Jane said.

Mac laughed and Jane joined him, finding release after the long, tension-filled day. Working had made her feel useful. As if she'd accomplished something worthwhile.

"What about Bolivia? Did you feast on local things there?" Jane asked.

"Only if I had to. I'm a meat-and-potatoes kind of guy but I can subsist on protein bars."

"I'm glad we were able to help them," Jane said. She was still worried about the two women with amebic dysentery. She hoped that they stayed on the strict regimen that she'd prescribed.

"This is the kind of thing that Rebel Virology is all about. You know the CDC isn't able to do this."

"Don't start," she said. But she meant it more for herself. Angry at Meredith for not allowing her a full team and at Raul, who must have manipulated someone inside the CDC, she wasn't in the best mind-set to discuss anything about her employer.

"I'm not. I just think you should consider that working for a big health organization is just like working for a big company. You can't do things that are important to you but aren't important to anyone else."

Jane handed him another grub. A part of her—the part that was afraid to trust those she'd left behind in Atlanta—wanted to hear more of what he was saying. But she also knew that, without the money that the CDC provided for research, it would be hard to do any kind of work in the jungle. "Stop talking and eat. I want to put some serious distance between us and them tonight."

"Do you think your buddy will follow us here?" Mac asked.

Jane hadn't thought of Raul. If he was still on their trail, it was possible he'd end up here. She didn't really fear for Tambo and his people. Tambo was one tough warrior who knew how to defend his own. But half the village was sick and it would be a few days before anyone would be up to their full strength. Also, Mac had sent for Maria. Jane didn't want Maria encountering Raul and possibly having trouble with him.

"Honestly, I don't know. We should warn Tambo to be on the lookout." Jane didn't really know how to explain the situation. But she needed to try, and she'd do it. It seemed as though she spent most of her life dealing with things that were uncomfortable.

"I agree. You about done?" Mac asked.

Something had changed in Mac since they'd been in the camp. She wouldn't say he was being completely open with her but there was a definite feeling that he was warming toward her.

"Yes," she said. She and Mac shared a bottle of water from his pack. "I ionized some water and refilled the bottles so we should be good for another day or so.

"When I was a kid we used to get water from leaves in the forest, so if we get desperate I can do that," she said. The memories of the rain forest came more frequently now. She'd worked so hard at forgetting that part of who she was, that part of her life, but being here—the scents, the sights and the people brought it all back. And it made her miss her mom in a way she hadn't allowed herself to since she'd been ten years old.

There was something in his eyes that looked almost like lust and Jane realized that Mac was looking at her as if she was some kind of sexy woman. But she wasn't.

She walked away before he could reply. But he stopped her with a hand on her shoulder.

"What is it you're running from?" he asked.

"I'm not running from anyone but Raul." Except Jane knew that wasn't true. She ran from everything except the diseases she had in her lab. She'd spent a lifetime keeping everyone at arm's length. Even Raul—was that why she'd never noticed his more deadly side? How could she have been blind to the man's real nature?

"Then why do you keep turning away from me?"

he asked. He stepped closer to her, invading her personal space.

Jane fought not to take a step backward. Instead she tipped her head back. "This isn't real, Mac. You look at me and see...I don't know what you see, but I know it's not real."

He leaned in, brushing against her, surrounding her with the heat of his larger masculine body. "I'm not a boy, Jane. This isn't jungle fever or a temporary aberration. There's something about you that makes my soul take notice."

She knew he was no boy. No mere boy could make her recognize primal instincts that she'd never acknowledged before resided deep inside her. No mere boy would invade her thoughts so often. But no man had yet affected her the way that Mac Coleman did—and she didn't like it.

"I don't know what to say to that. We're here to do a job. Don't let it be more than that."

"It's too late. I suspect you know it, too," he said. He let go of her shoulder and strode past her. She watched him retreat and realized he was right about many things. It was growing too late in more ways than one.

Chapter 9

The rain started again. The flooding was almost to her ankles in some areas. The thing with this area of the Amazon basin was that some years, it got hardly any rain. So she was feeling particularly cursed.

Mac had said nothing as they moved along the path that they'd decided on. He spoke to her if she asked him a question, but otherwise there was none of the open and friendly banter that had marked their earlier time on the trail.

She knew she was to blame and part of her regretted the wall that was between them now. But Jane knew that, to survive, she needed to concentrate on the importance of this mission. Not on Mac, with his sexy eyes and deep voice. No matter how much she might wish otherwise.

The lush greenery all around them was getting to her.

She felt as if she was at the dentist, staring at the tiled panels on the ceiling. The patterns of the leaves and vines were blurring in her mind, creating nothing but a wall of green.

She worried about Raul, hunting them with armed men. Hunting them. But for what? From what she'd gathered, he'd done some research in this area and she knew that the Peruvian government was keen to keep the border with Brazil open. Would that play a part in their denying any disease was present in the Yura?

"Mac?"

"Yeah?" He didn't turn to look at her but kept on moving. Dusk was starting to fall, though it was still possible to see where they were going.

"Did you ever encounter the closing of a border because of a disease?" she asked.

"Where did that come from?" he asked, glancing over his shoulder at her.

"I'm trying to figure out why the government would deny the existence of the Yura virus," she said. Mac had a razor-sharp mind and the longer she spent in his company the more she realized that he had a grasp on the global worldview that she didn't. Frankly, if it didn't affect her work, she didn't pay attention to it. "Everyone seems to know that something is wrong. Reynaldo and Tambo both were not surprised that that was where we were heading."

"Personally I only encountered it once when I was with the WHO. But from a financial standpoint, depending on how much Peru relies on the monies generated from trading across the border, that would be an excellent reason to keep it open."

"That's where I was going. But Raul works for a private pharmaceutical company, not the government. So how's he involved?" Thompson-Marks was an international drug company, but Jane didn't know how big a presence they had in South America. She pulled out her phone and accessed the Internet.

Mac continued walking but he had slowed his pace so that they were walking side by side. "Maybe his company has some deal with the government to take care of the virus before it becomes public."

"Can they do that?" she asked. The Internet search on the drug company had netted a few links. She stopped walking.

"They can pretty much do whatever they want," he said, stopping as well.

Jane clicked on the first link. It was a Web site with consumer info. Mac leaned close behind her, reading over her shoulder.

"This isn't the kind of information we need. Let's try another link."

Jane shook her head to clear it and clicked on the other link. She scooted a half inch away from Mac because she couldn't think when he was that close. She doubted he noticed. She read the page and found that Thompson-Marks was huge in South America, dealing with Venezuela, Peru and Brazil. Most of their work was done in the Amazon basin.

"What do you think of this?"

"That closing the border wouldn't be good for Thompson-Marks unless they were going to rush in looking like white knights with a treatment. How good is your friend at his job?"

"I've never worked with him. But he was on my dad's team when they found that alleged epidemic that turned out to be the flu. To be honest, he always seemed to be a day late. Does that make sense?"

"We'll have to ask your father for more information about him. Do you think he could find a treatment on his own?"

"I'm not sure. But he did ask me a lot of questions about my work on this virus when I saw him in Lima."

"Enough to make you suspicious?"

"Not at the time. But now that he's the one chasing me through the jungle, yeah."

Jane added that new fact to what she already knew. Could money be at the root of all her troubles in getting to the Yura and her father? But for Raul it would have to be more, too. He wouldn't do it for the money. What else was motivating him? "Do you really think someone from my office is working with Raul?"

"I already mentioned that I did. It's the only thing that makes sense. Someone sabotaged our plane."

"Hmm. I'm not totally convinced." Though a part of her agreed with Mac, she wanted to make sure she wasn't jumping to any conclusions. She'd seen Raul at their campsite so she knew he was on their trail, but everything else was just supposition at this point.

"What else have you got?" Mac asked.

"What makes you think I have anything?" He couldn't be that perceptive where she was concerned. Other people never got the way her mind worked and how it jumped from topic to topic.

"I can almost hear the wheels moving in your head," he said.

"Well, if it is someone in my office, I want to set a trap and see if we can flush them out."

"What kind of trap?" he asked.

She wasn't sure. She needed to figure out exactly what Raul wanted and then they could plan accordingly. "That's where I'm running into a block. I have no idea what Raul's objective is. To stop us or to steal the treatment and vaccine."

"From what I've observed, I'd say both."

Jane clipped her phone back on her belt and started moving through the jungle. Mac kept pace with her and she wondered what he was thinking about. Probably the problems they'd been encountering and Raul.

She slipped on a patch of mud and started to go down, but Mac grabbed her upper arm, holding her upright. Her heart was pounding from her near miss and when she looked into his eyes, she saw something there that she'd been trying to ignore.

It was full dark by the time Mac spoke again. She'd pulled away from him earlier and taken the lead. She knew it was only a matter of time before one of them said something, but Jane had kept quiet, not wanting to discuss the intimate things that Mac always wanted to talk about.

"Hold up. Something just bit me."

Jane hurried to his side. "Didn't you use the bug repellent when we stopped?"

"Yes, but with the damned rain it's probably washed off." She held the light stick out to him and he took it, holding it over his arm. The wound was already starting to swell and was the size of a dime.

"Damn. It looks like a spider bite," she said. She was trying to remember what to do to treat one.

"It hurts like a mother."

"I'll bet," she said, brushing her hands down his arms and over his back to make sure the spider was gone.

"If you're done patting me down, I could use some antiseptic on it."

"Stop being a wiseass. I didn't think you wanted another bite."

"I already brushed it away."

"Do you know what kind it was?" she asked, grabbing his wrist and searching for his pulse. It was accelerated and his wrist was sweaty under her fingers. Hell, she couldn't remember what the other symptoms of a poisonous spider bite were.

"Are you feeling dizzy?" she asked, when he swayed on his feet.

"No," he said, jerking his arm away. "I'm not dizzy or nauseous. I just need some salve and then—"

She glanced down at his arm as he stopped speaking. It was swelling as they spoke. This was not good. "Oh, my God. I bet it was a banana spider."

"Yeah, that's what I was thinking. Got any lidocaine in that bag of yours?" he asked, his voice low and husky. The pain from the bite would be hideous.

"I do," she said. She shrugged out of her backpack and quickly found her first-aid kit. She pulled out the tube she needed and replaced and closed everything quickly.

She applied a liberal amount on the wound, which continued swelling. "Do you want to make camp for the night?"

He rubbed his arm lightly around the affected area, then scrubbed the other hand over his face. "I'm fine. I've had worse bites."

"Are you sure?" she asked. He didn't look fine. For the first time since they'd entered the jungle he looked tired and worn-out.

He gave her a look that spoke volumes and picked up the light stick instead of answering. He led the way deeper into the dark night and Jane followed.

"There's nothing wrong with saying you need to stop," she said, knowing she should let it go but unable to. This man was so hardheaded it made her want to scream. Didn't he realize that, if he collapsed, she couldn't carry him anywhere? He was a big, muscly guy. And she wasn't that strong.

"Leave it alone. We don't have the time. The dry ice isn't as effective as it was yesterday."

"I know." She'd noticed it, too. Though she'd double-checked on the potency of the dry ice before they left, she hadn't considered the constant rain or the humidity.

"Well, as soon as that stuff leaves a frozen state, we're going to have a hell of a time using it."

"I was just trying to be nice," she said. He made her feel stupid for suggesting he rest. She knew they had to get to the Yura, but he was hurt.

"Don't be nice to me, Jane. I don't want that," he said, pivoting around. He stalked over to her, holding the light stick at eye level with his uninjured arm.

"What do you want?" she asked. In this light, he looked tough. The beard on his face and his eyes glowing out from under the dark rim of his hat. She knew he was angry and she suspected some of that was from earlier. But she didn't know what to say to make this right. And at this moment she needed to know that she wasn't harming one person in order to save more.

"Lots of things. Right now, for the pain in my arm to go away," he said on a sigh.

"I wish I had something else to give you. I might have a topical numbing agent. Want me to check?" she asked.

"How will it react with the lidocaine?" His eyes were calmer now and he leaned toward her.

"I have no idea." He was using the last of his strength to stay on his feet. She looked around, trying to find a place where they could assemble a camp for the night.

"Then let's skip it. I don't want to worsen it," he said.

"Yeah, but you're in pain."

"I'll live. Let's keep moving."

"No. We need to stop and make camp. You're wavering on your feet and we're not going to get far enough down the road to make a difference."

"Jane."

"Don't argue. Help me find something we can use to keep ourselves off the ground."

"Dammit, woman. You are the bossiest person," he said. His breathing was heavier than it had been earlier.

"We can argue about bullheadedness later. Right now, let's get a camp together."

He said little else and went to work. In no time they'd assembled another rough lean-to. As soon as possible Jane had Mac under the shelter and helped him remove his shoes. She placed her rain jacket over him and made a pillow from his pack.

"I'm all tucked in," he said, his voice a soft rasp. "Want to kiss me and make me better?"

"Will that really work?"

"It can't hurt. I'm in pain, Jane."

She leaned over him, cradling his face in her hands. In the darkness, with just the moon and stars providing a scant light through the trees and their thatched roof, she could see his dark eyes.

Bending down she brushed her lips over his, whisper soft. He sighed and opened his mouth. She leaned closer and kissed him more gently. His eyes closed, but she kept hers open and pulled back. She had positioned herself on his right side since the bite was on his left arm.

She lay down next to him, keeping her hand on his wrist to monitor his pulse. It was still too fast for her peace of mind. She didn't want anything to happen to him. She needed him strong and edgy. She needed him making smart-ass remarks and bugging her about how bad the CDC was. She needed...him.

Jane woke with a start. It was still full dark but her gut was screaming at her. She jerked upright and looked at her watch. It had been about four hours since she'd forced them to make camp.

Mac was breathing fitfully and talking in his sleep. His words were disjointed and made little sense to her. She touched his brow. Damn, he was hot.

The rains had stopped but there was water trickling everywhere. Jane wondered if that was what had woken her, or if it was Mac. She used some of their water stores to bathe his face.

He started and grabbed her wrist in an unbreakable grip. His eyes were wide and she felt the adrenaline rushing through his body. He gazed at her for a few moments then said, "Jane."

"You have a fever. I have some painkillers in my first-aid kit, do you have any allergies to them?" she asked, dropping the wet cloth and reaching for her pack. Now that he was awake, she was reluctant to touch him.

"No allergies. But my arm is throbbing," he said.

She got the painkiller and handed him the tablets. He swallowed them with only a small sip of the water from the bottle. She checked his arm. The swelling was starting to go down.

"I'm glad it stopped raining. Whose idea was it to come to Peru in the rainy season?" he asked with a shadow of his usual grin.

"You know how it goes—viruses don't care what the season is." That was the truth. In fact, they seemed to thrive in seasons when people didn't want to be moving about.

"I'm really thirsty," he said. It was the first time he'd admitted to any weakness and it bothered her. Maybe it was worse than she'd thought. What if he couldn't move for days? But according to all the research she'd done on spider bites, the effects should be gone by morning.

She handed him the water bottle and he drained it in two long gulps.

"Sorry about this."

"Don't be. It could have happened to me."

"Nah, things like spiders know better than to bite you," he said.

"Yeah, right. I've been stung by scorpions and wasps. The ones at my house in Dunwoody don't seem to know that they aren't supposed to bite me." She wondered exactly how she'd given him the image that she was indestructible. While it was true that she'd never let anything stop her from reaching her dad, she was still struggling the same way he was.

"Maybe I'll have to follow you home and inform them," he said.

She knew Mac wasn't going to follow her any farther than the Yura. Then he'd be on his way back to wherever he made his home. She wasn't the kind of woman who inspired men to follow her.

"Where's home for you?" she asked.

"I grew up in Texas, but I have an apartment in Brussels. That's where Rebel Virology is based, but I spend most of my time in South America, traveling with various tribes."

"Do you like Brussels?" she asked. When she'd been a teenager she'd dreamed of living in Europe. Okay, not just Europe, but Paris. She'd always had a secret burning in her heart to be an artist. But reality had reared its ugly head in high school and she'd had to admit that the only path for her career-wise was science.

"I guess. It's really just a place to crash in between assignments. A lot of the funding that R.V. gets comes from the European Union, so it makes sense for me to be there."

"Any wasps there?" she quipped.

"I haven't been stung by any."

He sat up and brushed his hands over his face. "Is there something crawling on me?"

She leaned closer to him. "No. Nothing."

"Must be a side effect of the bite," he said. He kept running his fingers through his beard. "My arm feels moist, too."

She leaned over to wipe his arm, but it was dry. "I have no idea how long the effects of this will last. Why don't you try to get some more sleep?"

"No. We need to get moving."

"Why? You're injured and I don't really want to risk any further damage," she said.

"Because it's not raining and the moon is bright. We should be able to see well enough."

Seeing the path through the jungle wasn't her biggest concern. Seeing him collapse in front of her was. "Are you sure you're okay?"

He gave her a look that was purely masculine. "As okay as I'm going to get."

She doubted that, but sensed this was important to him. She knew she'd be champing at the bit to get going if she'd been the one injured and slowing them down. "Then let's go."

She shook out her boots and pulled them on. Mac had some difficulty in tying his laces, so she tied them for him. Jane dismantled the lean-to, throwing the branches and sticks into the dense jungle growth so that they wouldn't give Raul a clear idea that they'd been here.

"I'll take the lead."

"That's fine, I like the view from back here."

"Stop with the sexual stuff. We both know you're not going to act on it."

"I just want to remind you of what you're missing."

"I'm not missing anything. I'm just focused on work. Why can't you be?"

"I don't know, Jane. There's just something about you that puts me in this state of mind."

"Lust isn't a state of mind."

He laughed and that made her feel good because she knew he was still in pain.

"It's more than lust," he said after a few minutes had passed. His voice was low and husky and she liked the sound of it too much.

"I don't want to know."

"I've figured that out. The one thing I can't control is getting rid of it."

"I'm really disgusting. It's been days since I've had a real shower."

"As a woman you worry too much about that. I like your scent."

Jane tried to ignore his words, but they echoed in her head.

She came to an abrupt halt as they reached the edge of a river. She wasn't sure, but she suspected this was the Ucayali River.

"Let me guess," Mac said. "We're going to make a raft?"

Chapter 10

Jane would be happy to never see bamboo again when she got home. But the abundant shoots had been life-savers so far. Working with her knife, she cut down vines to use to lash the bamboo together. Mac wielded the machete with less than his usual skill and she had to admit she was still worried about him.

The predawn light filled the air. Jane watched Mac working in the forest of bamboo trees. The swelling in his arm had almost gone completely. But his skin had a greenish cast to it and she suspected he wasn't feeling as well as he wanted her to believe.

She'd make him rest once they got on the river. She'd practically grown up on the water and she knew enough about water safety to take them safely through anything they might encounter, even rapids.

For the past two summers, she, Angie, Tom and a few others from the CDC had been going up to Nantahala National Park in North Carolina and running the rapids there.

Mac glanced up and caught her watching him. He quirked one eyebrow at her. She was used to polished men who were well-groomed and clean shaven. Maybe that was why Mac affected her. He was different. He pushed his way past boundaries that no man had tried to get behind in a long time.

"Don't get excited. I'm just making sure you don't fall over."

"I've got staying power," he said. His voice was ripe with double entendre.

"I guess it is true that men think about sex every three minutes."

He tilted his head to the side. "I've never timed it, but that sounds accurate to me."

"You about done with the bamboo? Where'd you learn to handle the machete like that?"

He tossed the last of the eight-foot bamboo logs he'd cut toward her. Jane cleared a spot on the forest floor and sat down to begin notching out holes in the ends of the logs to pass poles through.

"I learned to use the machete from the guides I've had over the years. Most of my career has taken me to places that aren't...civilized."

"Much like the man?" she asked, continuing to work on the logs. His career was fascinating to her. On one hand, he'd been asked to leave the WHO and he'd done some things in the name of science that she didn't approve of. But seeing him in action made her realize the true mark of the man. And she had to admit she admired what she saw.

"There is a part of me that I like to think is untamed. But I have my moments when I prefer the creature comforts."

"Feather bed?" she said, knowing that was what she missed the most. That and her hot tub.

"I'd settle for a nicely cooked salmon steak and a bottle of good wine. Now who's thinking of sex?" he asked in that silky tone of voice of his.

"I was thinking of sleeping." But there was a part of her that couldn't let go of the suggestive images he'd planted in her head.

Mac brought her the last of the bamboo logs. He'd cut twelve logs. "We're going to need some sturdy poles to run through the notches you're cutting."

"You're the man with the big knife," she said. Her knife wasn't made for this kind of work. And cutting poles from the bamboo was dulling the edge. She worried that the only weapon she had was no longer going to be effective.

Mac searched until he found four poles that would run the width of their raft. Jane had notched out half of the logs by that time and he began assembling the raft. Jane finished the others and then brought over the vines she'd found to bind them together.

"We work well as a team. Say the word and I'll give you a job at R.V.," he said as they assembled the raft.

"I'll think about it."

He glanced over his shoulder at her, his light blue eyes penetrating. She had a feeling that he was seeing past her facade straight to the heart of who she was. She didn't like it. She wanted to have secrets from him. The same ones she kept from others. She needed that distance to preserve the heart of who she was—a loner.

"But not really, right?"

"No, not really," she said. She was upset with Meredith for not standing up against her bosses and supporting Jane in this matter. But it wasn't enough to make her want to quit. Jane knew that anger and resentment were futile and quitting because her boss made her mad wasn't a good enough reason. She wasn't ruling out ever leaving the CDC but right now, she wasn't ready to do that.

"You like being with the CDC," he said.

"Yes, I do. And the people in R.V., well, they've all had some kind of incident that no one talks about in their pasts."

"Like me."

"Yes. I have a solid reputation. I don't need to go looking for—"

"Forget I mentioned it."

His movements were choppy—angry—as he finished constructing the raft. She was very aware that she'd offended him, and that hadn't been her intent. "I'm sorry. I didn't mean it that way. I'm just tired and not thinking straight."

"I know the kind of establishment bull crap that is said about us. But I thought you were different, Jane. I thought that maybe you'd had a chance to look at the world in a different way."

"I have, Mac. Believe me. Which is why I'm apologizing. It doesn't help matters that you're all so secretive."

"Maria didn't leave in the swell of a controversy."

"I wasn't thinking of Maria."

"You were thinking of me, weren't you?"

"Yes. I can't help it. I want to know more of what shaped you."

"As a man?"

"And a virologist. I think they are closely intertwined. I can tell by the way you talk about your politics."

"You're right, they are. And as soon as you trust me, I'll trust you."

"I wouldn't be here with you if I didn't trust you."

"There's trusting and then there's trusting. You know what I want."

"Why don't you make the first move?"

"Touché. Ready to see if this thing can float?"

She nodded. They moved to the edge of the river and he set it down, holding firmly to the raft. It stayed afloat and Jane waded into the water, placing their packs on the raft. They lashed them with a few more vines. Mac tied the raft to a tree on the bank and then working together they made a rain shelter on one end of the raft using more poles and notches and the large waxy leaves. Then they made a rudder so the raft could be steered.

Neither spoke much. Jane was glad for the silence. She wasn't going to probe into Mac's past anymore. He clearly wasn't ready to talk about it.

The currents on the river had them going, by Jane's estimation, about five miles per hour. Not a lot, but faster than they'd been moving before. The river was wide here and each side was lined with virgin forest and thick vines.

Mac was leaning back against his pack, eyes closed. She heard the calls of exotic birds and for once the sun was shining. It warmed her from the inside out. She turned up her face toward the top of the tree canopy. Monkeys raced through the branches and dappled light filtered through to the riverbanks.

She checked her Blackberry GPS unit again. They were heading in the right direction. In fact, she thought they'd be at the Yura village by the end of the day. It would do them both some good to interact with other people.

The Blackberry beeped. She had two new e-mails. Holding the rudder with one hand and operating her phone was nearly impossible.

"I've got it. Check your e-mail," Mac said. He brushed her hand aside.

The swelling in his arm had completely gone. Only an angry red mark remained where he'd been bitten. "You're not even facing the right direction."

He opened one eye and stared at her balefully. "I won't steer us too far off course."

"You really can't."

"My point exactly. Stop arguing."

Jane hit the button to open her e-mail function and saw that one of the waiting messages was from Angie. Jane opened the e-mail and scanned the contents. "This is odd."

"What is?"

"Angie said that the original interviews and research of the Yura were conducted by the CDC. She's trying to track down who, but so far hasn't found out."

"That rules out your buddy unless he just left the CDC." Mac sat up and rubbed his eyes with the heel of his hands, letting go of the rudder for a minute. Jane fought the urge to grab the stick. They were in calm waters and the river wasn't that wide.

She really hated not being in control of anything.

"Stop calling him my buddy. You know he isn't. Raul left the CDC more than eighteen months ago."

"He could still be working with someone there," Mac said. The possibility bothered her. It would have been nice and neat—hell, convenient—if Raul had been the one to do the study.

"It's possible. You know how small our community is. I recently finished work on an anti-Ebola grain that was done in conjunction with an ex-CDC person who now works for the agricultural lobby."

"So who would be working with Raul? Surely someone is. Are you sure you trust the source of this e-mail?"

"Angie wouldn't betray me." But Jane wasn't sure. Angie was a career employee and had only five years left until she reached retirement. Jane realized that Angie's loyalty might not be to her.

"You're betting both of our lives on it," he said in that gravelly tone of voice that made her keenly aware of him.

Yes, she was. And strangely that gave her pause. She didn't want to be responsible for putting Mac in further danger. She decided not to respond to Angie's e-mail. That way, if Angie was passing on information, she'd have no way of knowing if Jane received it or not.

"I have another message but I think it's for you," she said, instead of answering his question on Angie.

"Why, does it say *Hot young babes?*"

"No, it says *For Mac Coleman.*"

He held out his hand and she passed the phone to him. Jane took command of the raft, shielding her eyes from the sun to watch the river ahead. She'd been able to determine that they definitely were on the Ucayali. She knew it from the way the river was running, the color of the water and the vegetation on the banks. She figured they had about four hours more on the river and then they'd have to hike to where the Yura village was on a river that was an offshoot of the Madre de Dios. But by nightfall they should be there.

"My e-mail was from Maria. Rebel Virology has received some information that she thought I should have."

Jane got a sick feeling deep in her stomach that had nothing to do with the fact that she'd been eating protein bars for too many days. "Do I get to guess what it is?"

"Sure, guess." He leaned back against his pack again, crossing his arms over his chest.

"It has to do with me?"

He nodded.

"Am I officially in trouble?"

"It seems like it. Maria was told that you did not have official sanction to take the treatment and vaccine you developed in the CDC lab in Atlanta."

Jane felt betrayed in the worst way. "I was put on leave, but no one officially forbade the actions I'm taking."

"They threatened R.V. with legal action if we assist you in any way."

Jane swallowed hard. This wasn't Meredith not wanting to confront her bosses. This was someone effectively coming after her. Slowly the pain of betrayal was replaced with the fire of anger. Jane wasn't going to simply give up and stop trying to reach her father. She knew now that something bigger than this disease was going on.

"Should I find a nice place to pull over and let you off?" she asked Mac. He was chairman of the board of Rebel Virology. If he was found with her, it would mean the end of funding to the group of scientists.

"Hell, no. We don't give in to that kind of pressure. Maria told them to kiss our ass."

"That seems more like what you'd say."

"What I'd say isn't fit for a lady's ears."

He was angry on her behalf and that warmed her. She couldn't remember any time in her life when another person had cared enough to get upset because of her. Maybe he was defending her because they'd involved his company, but she sensed it was more that she'd been let down by the very company that she'd given nothing but loyalty to.

"Thank you."

The river ran smooth and wide. It was a boring ride with little to relieve the monotony. Jane checked the packs of dry ice, and the vials were still in a frozen state. Thank God.

Mac had been quiet and pensive since they'd checked the e-mail and he'd made that gallant gesture toward her. She wondered if he was as tired of staring at the green banks as she was. The words of Garth Brooks's "The

River" kept circling in her mind. She steered their vessel, very aware that she couldn't fail to reach her destination.

"Tell me about Rebel Virology," she said. Her future at the CDC wasn't as certain as she'd once believed it to be. And she had a new appreciation for her father. Though her situation was nothing like his.

Or was it?

Jane had maintained a distance toward her father while the clinical trials were being analyzed and found inconsistent. She'd stayed away when the CDC had released a report saying that the work of Dr. Rob Miller was flawed and that the public health scare was not really a danger.

The entire time she'd stayed away, fearing deep inside that the flames of that controversy might singe her career. All her life, in the back of her mind, had been the thought that her father had never been there when she needed him. And a part of her had felt justified in not being there for him. But she knew what it was like to be alone. She should have gone to him.

"What about it?" Mac asked.

What had she asked him? She could scarcely remember. Swamped with guilt and worry over her father, she prayed that they'd reach him in time for her to make the past right. But Mac didn't know that.

She'd brought up his company. "How does the funding work? Is helping me going to put you under?"

"No. It could hurt us when we apply for visas the next time to go into a country. But for the immediate future we're okay. Most of our funding comes from the finds of our viral research and development team. We sell what we discover to the pharmaceutical industry and use the funds to do this kind of work."

"So you work with large pharmaceutical companies?" she asked. She hadn't realized that. But then, where else would the money come from? And money was the grease that fueled all science. It was too hard to come by the supplies needed for experiments without it.

She knew from personal experience that there was resentment on both sides of this issue. The money people resented having to wait for the virologists to come up with a new product. The virologists resented having to wait for the money to kick in so they could do their experiments.

"To some extent. We also work for different governments, as well. But we don't report to them. We do our research and go into hot zones. Then, when we're back at our offices in Brussels, we compile the data and take the product to market."

"How is that different from what I do?" she asked, because he wasn't making it sound more appealing.

"As a virologist at R.V., you'd have complete control. We'd never deny you a team or support in any way." There was pride in his voice. He'd accomplished something that all scientists—hell, all people—wanted. To have his cake and eat it, too.

"Even if it was something that came from my dad?" she asked, quietly.

"I told you in Lima. I liked your dad. We're more willing to forgive mistakes at R.V. But then, as you mentioned, many of us have something in our pasts that makes us questionable."

"Want to tell me about it?" she asked. It no longer mattered to her what had happened. She'd seen enough of him in action to know that Mac was very good at what he did. Even without knowing the details of what happened, she sensed that it wasn't something he'd done for a quick fix or for money.

"No. I still see those faces, Jane. I don't expect you to understand this but I still see every one of those damned faces and I don't want to discuss it."

She took his hand in hers. God, the pain in his voice echoed the pain in her heart when she saw faces of her own. There were always a few people that a treatment didn't work on. There was always a small group whom they were too late to save. Those faces stayed with her. "I know. I see them, too."

Jane checked the GPS map and realized they needed to get off the Ucayali and walk overland seven miles to get on the Madre de Dios. "I think this is where we stop."

Mac steered them to the shore. Working together, they pulled the boat out of the river. "Should we carry this or just make another one when we get to the Madre?"

"How heavy is it?" she asked. Though the last two days of carrying her backpack through the jungle had strengthened her muscles, she wasn't sure they'd bear the weight of the raft. Her new muscles ached and she'd be glad to sleep in a real bed and not have to carry everything she owned on her back.

"Not too bad. Even for a girl."

"Comments like that are going to get you pushed into the river." There was a streak of chauvinism in

Mac. It wasn't unappealing, because he was so up-front about it. And she knew he thought of her as some sort of exception to the rule. She liked the fact that he knew she was capable and in fact was counting on her to be capable. She held back a groan as they lifted the raft, and shot a glare at him.

"Hoping some piranha will get me?" he said, wriggling his eyebrows at her.

This was the man who tempted her. His teasing relieved her of the lingering fear she'd had when he'd first been bitten by the spider. "I don't think I have to do more than give you a shove and you'll find the stinging venomous things on your own."

"You know how to hit a man when he's down," he said, but there was a smile on his face.

Mac was almost completely recovered so she didn't feel the least bit bad about it. "Just calling it like I see it."

"It's one of your more endearing qualities," he said.

"What is?"

"You don't sugarcoat things like some women do. A man knows exactly where he stands with you."

"Is that a good thing?" she asked, not sure she really wanted to know. Mainly because she was too old to change her ways. And she liked herself, so changing wasn't really an option.

"Hell, yeah. For the right man, that's a very good thing."

She didn't know how to react to that so she focused instead on finding a path. Mac let the conversation lull as they walked toward the Madre de Dios, but he'd given her a lot to think about. Things she'd never considered before were dancing around in her head. Suddenly her career wasn't her sole focus, and she wasn't sure she liked that.

Chapter 11

The seven-mile trek along the portage between the Ucayali and the Madre de Dios was hard and long. The rain started again. Cold water dripped down inside the collar of her jacket. She was so sick of the rain. At first she'd enjoyed watching the way it cycled every day, bringing life to the plants and animals of the forest. But now she was tired of it.

Jane shivered and longed for a five-minute oasis where she was dry, had a hot cup of tea and a man to massage the tight muscles of her back.

"How you holding up?" he asked.

She'd be a lot better once they got back on the river. They were close to reaching her father and she was anxious. Anxious to insulate herself from Mac and from the questions she saw in his eyes. And the ones that went unanswered in her mind.

"Fine," she said. But honestly, she didn't know how much longer she could keep her arms over her head. They were starting to ache and go numb.

"Well, Wonder Woman, I need a break. I feel like my arms are going to fall off."

She envied him the fact that he had no problem admitting to his weaknesses. Maybe he didn't have as many as she did. "Okay."

They set the raft down. Jane tried to lower her arms, but it hurt. *A lot.* She groaned and forced them to her sides. She had no idea that there were that many muscles in her arms and that they could hurt this badly.

Mac came up behind her and started massaging her left shoulder. "I won't think less of you if you say you need a break."

"I didn't need one," she said, stubbornly. Mac was getting too close. He was making her want to do things that weren't in her nature. Things like relax back against his big, solid chest. Things like ask him to hold her for a few minutes. Things that she knew better than to believe were real.

"Take your shirt off," he said.

She shrugged out of her shirt and felt his hands return to her. He rubbed and applied pressure all over her shoulders and back until all of the tension left. Then he moved to her arms. They'd taken shelter under one of the waxy-leafed trees which kept most of the water off them. Just a fine mist continued to fall.

Mac started at her shoulder and rubbed his way down her arm. When he massaged from the wrist up, the back of his fingers brushed her breast. She sucked in her breath, waiting.

He moved his hands again on her upper arms and she twisted her body toward him until his fingers brushed the side of her breast with every movement. Mac's nostrils flared and he leaned closer to her. So close that she could see the gray flecks in his blue eyes.

"Thanks," she said, glancing over her shoulder at him.

"You owe me one back rub."

She nodded. She had been planning to offer. She had to keep things even and fair. Why was that? She was too tired to ponder it now.

"Hungry?" Jane asked.

"Yes," Mac said, tightening his arms and pulling her firmly against his chest. She was completely surrounded by him. His warmth, his strength, the goodness of his heart.

She tipped her head back and realized that it was too late to insulate herself against him. Completely trust him or no, there was something about this man that touched her deep inside.

He kissed her. She felt the restrained passion inside him, but he kept the embrace light. As if he were giving her part of his strength and taking some of hers.

She tunneled her fingers through his thick hair, holding him to her. His beard was a soft abrasion against her cheeks. His tongue thrust deep into her mouth with long languid strokes that she felt all the way down her body. She wanted to get closer to him. Wanted to do whatever she had to, to make this embrace never end. Wanted... more than she knew she could really handle right now.

Slowly she pulled back from him. Dragging her lips away from his. He let her go. She held his face in between her hands, looking up at him and realizing there was something in his eyes that mirrored the longing in her soul.

"We need to keep moving."

"I'm not apologizing for that."

"I didn't ask you to. Why do you insist on treating me like some kind of fragile woman?"

"Because you're not. And I think you're too used to leading men around."

She pulled away and went to her backpack and jerked open the straps, searching for something to eat.

"You run away every time I get too close to you."

"I'm not running. Stop saying that. I've never run from anything. I've always stood my ground even if I wanted to run."

She found the protein bars. There were only two left. She pulled them from the pack and tossed one to Mac. He caught it easily.

Jane pulled her cell phone from her belt hook and activated the GPS unit. They were on track. Finally getting much closer to the Yura. She accessed the Internet file she'd saved on the rivers of the Amazon basin. "Once we hit the Madre we'll make up some time but not a lot. It's not a deep river and we'll have to be on the lookout for the Cashpajali tributary, which feeds off of it. Do you have any experience with white water?"

"Some. I'm not an expert, though."

"I've got some experience, too, so we should be okay."

But it had been a long trek and they weren't through yet. She was amazed that they'd made it as far as they had. But she knew a lot of that was due to Mac and her working as a team. Being part of this team was the only thing she'd ever enjoyed as much as being alone in her lab.

"Why are you staring at me?"

"Just tired. I wasn't really staring at you."

"Your mouth says that, but your eyes…well, let's just say they were devouring me."

"I think you're having one of those out-of-body experiences—something mystical from being in the rain forest."

"You think so?"

"Either that or some sort of vivid fantasy."

He threw his head back and laughed. "Damn, woman, you make me glad to be here in this lush green nightmare."

She didn't respond, but her heart beat a little faster and she knew that she was glad to be with Mac. She only prayed that he never realized how much.

They reached the Madre de Dios in the middle of the afternoon. An uncomfortable silence had fallen between them. For Jane's part she was trying to decide how to regain the ground she'd lost by letting Mac glimpse her attraction to him.

Her father weighed heavily on her mind. It had been almost too long and there was a part of her that feared the worst when they finally arrived at the Yura village. Carrying the raft had drained much of her strength and Mac's, as well. And though he'd said nothing she noticed that the bite on his arm was an angry red color.

"You're staring again," he said.

"Is your arm okay?" she asked. She wished they'd taken more time to let him recover. Aside from the simple fact that there hadn't been time. Right now they were a day behind her original schedule.

"It hurts like a mother but otherwise, yeah. I'm fine."

"We should be to the Yura soon. Then we can take care of it properly."

"I'm looking forward to sleeping in a bed tonight."

"Me, too. We should do a sample swab of your arm area and make sure the infection isn't spreading."

"I'll let you do that if you promise—"

She broke off as she saw movement on the shore. "Duck!"

She hit the deck as a spate of bullets flew over their heads. Mac was lying awkwardly by her side.

"Are you hit?" she asked. She couldn't see any blood.

"Quit coddling me," he said.

Jane shrank back. He pulled his gun and fired judiciously. She knew from a yelp he hit at least one of the men firing on them. She kept her hand on the rudder and noticed it was shaking. The current was starting to pull them more quickly downriver. "I think we're getting close to rapids."

"Great. That's just what we need."

"I go rafting all the time in North Carolina and Tennessee," she said, but in the back of her mind was the knowledge that she'd never piloted any kind of log boat through the rapids. That was going to be far different from her kayak.

"Good. Then you're in charge," he said between

shots. She wondered how many bullets were in his clip. Was he going to run out?

"Funny man. I already knew that."

More bullets stirred the air overhead, one of them embedding in the bamboo by her cheek. "Are we out-armed?"

"Hell, yes. I have a spare pistol in my pack. Can you get it?"

Heart pounding, she belly-crawled the short distance to Mac's bag. Loosening the drawstrings, she reached inside and searched around for his spare pistol. It must be toward the bottom. Her arm wasn't long enough to reach without sitting up.

"Cover me," she said and took a deep breath. Sat up on her haunches and dug deeply into his bag. She found an extra box of ammunition and the second gun.

Bullets were flying around the raft with rapid speed and Jane froze as she felt one graze the top of her arm. She felt the burn. Blood oozed steadily from her arm. Quickly she flattened herself at the base of the raft. Mac grimly fired back and she heard the shattered cry as he hit his target.

Jane flattened herself out, trying to ignore the pain in her arm. She handed Mac a second clip for his semi-automatic handgun.

"Can you fire that?" he asked.

"I guess so. I've never fired a handgun before, just a rifle. Though I almost won a turkey at the turkey shoot one year." She'd only participated in the turkey shoot because one of the neighbor boys had said she'd never beat him at it. In fact, she had.

"Forget it. Hand the gun to me."

She did as he asked, well aware that she was going to have to expose herself to the gunmen again in just a few moments. Her arm was burning and she didn't want to think about the fact that there was a very real possibility they were going to die on this river. That the Mother of God was going to be their eternal resting place. *Like hell.*

"How come you're so good with weapons?" she asked to distract herself.

"I've spent a lot of time in this part of world. For some reason people are always firing at me."

"Must be your winning personality," she said grimly.

"Must be," he said, flashing her a grin.

The gunmen continued to fire on them but the bullets weren't coming close. Finally, Jane thought, we're outdistancing them.

"I need to see what's coming up," she said.

"I think you're safe to sit up."

She sat up just in time to maneuver them around a large tree trunk that was in their path. Mac took his small pocketknife and cut the sleeve away from her injured arm.

"Can't that wait?" she asked.

"No. Pull into that eddy over there and let me take care of this. Plus, it's a good idea to scout the rapid on foot first."

"There are men back there firing at us. Did you forget about that?"

"No. I can handle them. But we can't handle the unknown."

"You're right. I'm going to trust you to handle those guys."

Mac tied down everything to the raft, securing it as she steered the boat to the banks of the Madre. He got out first, hauling them up to the shore and anchoring the boat.

"Thanks for trusting me."

She looked into his blue eyes and almost stopped breathing. He looked like a bandito who'd been on the trail for too many days—but to her he looked like a hero. It didn't matter that she didn't need saving. That she'd spent her entire life rescuing herself. For once she had someone by her side. A man who she knew she'd already begun to count on.

"You should stay here with the raft while I go check out the rapid," she said.

"I don't like it. We should stay together."

"We don't have time for an argument. You're going to have to trust me, too."

His eyes narrowed. And he cursed as he walked over to her. She noticed he had a small white bandage in his hand. He grabbed her arm in a firm but careful grip and smeared antiseptic on the wound then slapped the bandage on. "Be careful."

"I always am," she said with a saucy grin and walked away.

Jane made her way down the river. The rough footpath was a little overgrown but not impassable. Moving as quickly as she could, she stumbled only once and had to force herself not to reach out to steady herself. When she got home she was going to the spa and not coming out until every ache, pain and bruise was gone.

She climbed back to her feet and followed the sound

of rushing water to the bank. The rapids were large and there were rocks and tree trunks on either side of them. In the middle of the rapids was a large boulder. Would the raft fit on the left side?

She knew it wouldn't make it past the right. She climbed down a little closer to get a better look at the area beyond the white water. There were two fallen trees she'd have to be careful of. In her kayak this would be a piece of cake.

Should they even risk it, or would it be better to just walk the raft down past the white water and get back in at the bottom? She glanced back up at the bank. The path she'd used to make it this far was not very wide or clear. In fact, calling it a path was being very generous.

"'It's hard to fight an enemy who has outposts in your head,'" Jane muttered to herself. It was a Sally Kempton quote that she always used when doubts started to crowd in.

She was a Pisces—part fish, as her grandmother used to say. And running these rapids wasn't going to stop her. She climbed back up the bank, took one last look at the water and then started back to Mac and their raft. They'd take the river. It would save time and Jane knew that even if it was rough, she could steer them through it.

Her phone beeped and she pulled it from her belt. She had a new voice mail message. The case had condensation underneath it. And the display screen had two new scratches but the unit was intact. She dialed in quickly.

"Jane, it's Meredith. I'm having a hard time keeping a lid on your presence in Peru. Call me. I think you are in over your head."

Jane debated for a minute. She knew that Mac would argue against calling her boss, but Jane felt that she needed to do it. With the signal clear she dialed Meredith's number.

Her boss answered on the second ring.

"It's Jane," she said.

"Thank God. I just got a report that you were killed. Where are you?"

"I'm not dead, yet. But they sure as hell are trying. Someone knows every move I'm making."

"Tell me where you are and I'll send in reinforcements."

Jane ignored that. "Did they make you give them my itinerary?"

"No. Angie is like a barracuda protecting her young, she won't share it. But two officials from the State Department visited me yesterday and demanded we turn over your research."

There was a long pause. Jane heard the chair creak and pictured Meredith in her office. Nice and safe in Atlanta. No cuts or bruises on her body. No one shooting at her. Anger began to build.

"Did you?" Jane asked. There was something in her boss's voice that made Jane realize she was really on her own. In the back of her mind she'd taken comfort from the fact that Meredith had always looked out for her. But not this time. And Jane remembered that, when her father had had his problems, Meredith had pulled away from him, as well.

"No. But it's only a matter of time before I have to.

I'm meeting with the head of the lab this afternoon. He's probably going to order me to turn it over."

"Meredith—"

"I'm doing my best here. I just wanted to warn you."

And her loyalty would always be first to the CDC, second to her staff. "Thanks, I think. We're almost to Dad. I was going to ask for more time."

"I wish I could give it."

"I won't call again."

"That's probably for the best," Meredith said, hanging up before Jane could.

Jane rubbed the back of her neck. She needed someone to get her notes from the lab before Meredith buckled and gave them everything. Part of the reason that Jane figured she was still alive was that Raul and whoever had sent him hadn't figured out the treatment for the Yura disease.

Angie wouldn't go into the lab so that left one of her colleagues. And she knew that someone had done that report. Quickly Jane dialed Angie's number.

Angie answered her phone on the first ring, as always the ultraefficient assistant. Her tone was very cool and very professional, which was Jane's first clue that something was wrong in the office.

"It's Jane. I need a favor," Jane said quickly.

"I can't really talk now, Lori," Angie said. Lori was Angie's daughter. Jane understood that someone was in her office. This wasn't good.

"I understand. Did you find out who did that research originally on the Yura?" she asked. She didn't want to risk contacting the person who was working for

Thompson-Marks and the Peruvian government. And in Jane's mind there was now a clear connection.

"No, I can't come over to your house on Saturday. I'm going to have to stay in the office and take care of business."

She was running out of time. "Damn. I need to get my notes out of the lab."

"I'm sorry, hon, but I can't do that for you," Angie said. For once Jane wasn't amused by Angie's phobias about the lab. But she understood, and she wasn't going to ask her friend to risk herself that way.

Jane sighed. "I know. I'm not sure who to trust."

"I'm in the same boat," Angie said. Jane realized that Meredith might have already sold her out. Angie had never said anything in the past that would make Jane question the loyalty of her boss.

"Is it Meredith?" she asked. Please don't let it be Meredith, Jane thought. She couldn't handle being betrayed by her mentor. Finding out her ex-lover was after her and would probably kill her if he had the chance was enough to deal with.

"I'm not positive, but I think so. Your father wants to go to the races," Angie said.

"Okay. Thanks, Ang."

Jane hung up the phone. Maybe Mac would have some ideas. Hurrying down the path she pushed aside her worries about Meredith and the lab. And the suspicion that maybe her father was set up all those years ago. But why? Jane knew she had to get her head together. Get it in the present to navigate them through the white water.

Mac was sitting on the raft when she returned, writing in his journal. He looked up as she approached.

"Can we get through?"

"Yes. And we can't afford to wait. Someone is putting pressure on my boss."

Chapter 12

Jane had maneuvered down class III rapids with no problem, but even with a plan in her head she wasn't as confident as she normally would be. Mac didn't look good and she wasn't entirely confident they'd lost the men following them. Things really couldn't get worse. And if they did, Jane thought, she just might have to contemplate putting herself out of her misery and surrendering to Raul.

She found two large sticks to use as oars. Rowing was key to successfully navigating the rapids. She wished the trail around the water was clearer and that Mac was in better shape. But she knew the best way to get both of the large packs and Mac downriver was to shoot the rapids.

For the first time since she entered the jungle Jane

felt more than ready for the challenge that lay ahead. She knew this was something she could do. Damn, she was getting used to meeting the challenges here. And she liked it.

But Mac didn't seem to be rising to the occasion. The jungle was wearing on him. The spider bite was definitely affecting him. Even as they worked to secure everything to the bamboo raft he was swaying on his feet. He sweated profusely and his face had a gray-green cast to it.

Had the Yura moved? Is that why Raul needed her to lead them? Or was his pursuit tied to the vials? She wondered if Raul was still acting as a virologist. If he'd asked her as a colleague to let him see her notes, she wouldn't have shared them. But she would have answered his questions.

Why was he so hot to get to her? Her head ached from trying to figure it out.

The water started moving more swiftly. They'd lashed the packs to the bamboo and Jane had taken down the lean-to. "I'm going to need you to shift your weight around to help move the raft through the rapids. Are you up for that?"

"Yes," he said, a gritty determination in his eyes.

"You're also going to have to row at times. I'm going to try to get us to the right of the rapid so that we come through it at a perpendicular angle so we don't flip. Do you know what to do if you fall off?"

"Dammit, Jane. Yes, I know what to do. I'll wager I've been down more class IV rapids than you have. So stop treating me like some kind of neophyte."

"Excuse me. But you are gray and you're swaying on your feet. You look like you won't make it until bedtime."

"I'll make it."

"Good. So you know how to swim a rapid?" she asked. He finally had some color. Should she keep him angry?

"Yes. Let's go. The more time we spend here the better chance your friends have of catching up to us."

She didn't say anything, just pushed the boat away from the shore and started rowing. She closed her eyes for a brief second and imagined herself downriver, safely through the rapid.

She steered into the current and let the river move her. The raft was heavy and awkward. Perfect for cruising down the smooth, slow-moving river, but she had no idea if it would make it through the tempestuous white water.

"I've only ever done this in a kayak," she said suddenly.

"Me, too."

For a minute she felt an odd sort of kinship with Mac, and that scared her more than the white water.

She heard the rapid before she saw it. She lined the raft up as best she could, praying she wouldn't have to try to spin it and enter the rapid backward, which was sometimes safer. The current picked up pace and Jane held her breath until she realized what she was doing.

She piloted the raft into the rapid. "All forward."

Mac paddled, the muscles on his arms bunching with each strong stroke of the rough oar. Jane did the same, watching for the obstacles that she knew were there.

"All back," she called when a tree trunk she hadn't seen from the bank appeared directly in their route.

Both of them were rowing backward, fighting the uwieldly raft and the water. But they made very little progress.

"Dammit, brace for impact."

Mac grabbed the side of the raft. Jane held on to her oar and the raft with one hand. She reached for the packs containing the vials of medicine with the other. She couldn't lose them to the river after bringing them this far.

She clung to the raft as it slammed into the tree trunk. They spun around but jerked to a halt. The water slammed into them, coming up over the sides.

Jane tried to crawl over to where they were lodged but Mac waved her back. "I'm closer."

He pushed his way toward where they were caught and got his oar under the water. She watched the muscles bulge in his arms and back as he pushed and cursed. The water rushed over the sides, cold and fierce. Jane hung on, realizing that the stakes were different this time. Being on the water wasn't just a thrill in her normal mundane life. This was the real thing and the risks were much higher.

Finally the raft broke free. The balance of the lashed bamboo wasn't sturdy. Mac wasn't braced and fell overboard.

"Mac!"

He popped up out of the water and then was pulled back under before she reached him.

Jane kept her eyes open for him as she steered the raft through the rest of the rapids. The current was still very fast here and she tried to slow the raft the best she could. She searched in front and behind her for Mac but couldn't find him.

Her throat closed and she couldn't breathe. What the hell had happened? She steered toward the riverbank, got off the raft and tied it to the buttressed roots of a tree. Oh, God, was he dead?

Her phone was water-resistant, but Jane didn't want to test it if she had to swim underwater to get to Mac. She took it off and tucked it into the pocket of her backpack.

Wading into the water she tried to find him. Had he gotten stuck underwater on a tree root? Was he caught in a hydraulic—spinning water that was almost impossible to swim out of?

The current was strong but Jane fought it. Was that his shirt? She reached out to snag the fabric. It was his shirt. He'd had it unbuttoned against the heat of the afternoon sun. Jane tossed it onto the shore and moved deeper into the water, moving downstream.

The far bank blurred as she took her glasses off and wiped them on her own shirt. Her hands were trembling. She knew it was just excess adrenaline coursing through her body. She'd always felt at home in the water and this was the first time she'd come close to losing someone.

She shoved her glasses back on, bringing the distance back into focus. She thought she saw him. Yes, there he was on the opposite bank, at the next curve in the river. Clinging to one of the many vines that hung down to the water's edge.

"Hang on, Mac. I'm coming to get you." She took her glasses off again, securing them in one of her zippered pants pockets, and dived into the water. Using a strong scissors kick and a breaststroke she made slow progress but finally reached his side. Mac was done for. He clung to the vine but his eyes were closed.

Jane reached up and put her arms around him. "Relax into me. We need to get over to the other bank."

She'd worked as a lifeguard for two summers in

high school when she'd wanted to work on her tan and meet guys at the pool. The advanced lifesaving she'd taken then came back to her. She put her arm around him as he released his grip on the vine.

Using an over-the-shoulder grip on him, she let the current push them back toward the center of the river, then sidestroked, gradually getting them to the other side. She pulled Mac up onto the bank. He was breathing, but his breaths were shallow. Jane took his pulse. It was steady and strong.

"Mac, can you hear me?" she asked. She put her glasses back on.

His eyes popped open and he regarded her carefully. The bandage had come off his head wound and he looked like the bandito she'd first mistaken him for.

"Yeah, I can hear you. Just barely. My ears are ringing."

"I thought you were…"

"Yeah, me, too." He paused. "I lost my shirt."

"I found it."

"You found me, too," he said. In his eyes was an emotion she didn't want to read.

She didn't know how to respond to that. She only knew that she couldn't have left without getting him back.

"Thanks, Jane. I…"

"What?"

"Nothing. You're not what I expected."

"What were you expecting?" she asked.

"Someone who was focused on their career and not on the people it affected."

"Well, I am focused on my career. But people are at the heart of what I do."

"I know that now," he said. He leaned up and touched her face with gentle fingers. "You cut yourself."

She couldn't breathe. His touch was warm and gentle and felt…dammit, the swim in the river must have addled her worse than she'd realized, because she felt cared for. And she'd never needed any man to care for her.

She pulled back from him. Shrugging, she got to her feet. Mac sat up, bracing his head on his knees. She watched him carefully.

"If you're okay, I should go get the raft. The river carried us downstream from it."

He pushed to his feet and swayed, reaching out blindly. Jane grabbed his arm and used her body to support him.

"Give me a minute and I'll go with you."

He wasn't ready to hike back the quarter mile or so to where she'd left the raft. She led him over to a fallen tree and helped him sit down on it.

"Will you be okay while I go get the packs?" she asked.

"Yeah. I think so," he said. He rubbed the back of his neck.

"Rest. I'll be back in a few minutes."

"Be careful, Jane."

She nodded and walked away. She'd seen no sign of Raul's men, so she figured they'd either continued on foot or stopped to make their own raft. She only hoped they were hampered by the rough handmade raft the way she and Mac were. If Raul had an inflatable raft, they were going to be in serious trouble.

Jane located Mac's shirt and the raft about forty-five minutes later. The rain had started again and she was cold and shivering by the time she got there. Everything looked undisturbed. She rubbed the back of her neck, warily realizing that they still had a few miles to travel by river and then a ten-mile hike to the last known location of the Yura.

Jane pulled out her Blackberry phone and checked the coordinates on it. She was on track. She checked the packs. The Styrofoam that had cracked in their initial fall was leaking dry-ice vapor. It was only a matter of time before the others started, too.

Jane dug out her vinyl rain jacket and pulled it on. It would be so nice to sleep inside. Or just sit inside where she'd be out of the rain and the mist.

The phone beeped, signaling messages waited for her. Jane used her jacket to shield the phone and read her messages.

The first one was from Tom, asking her if she needed him to do any follow-up and suggesting that she might want to send him her reports for safekeeping. He went on to say:

Meredith has been down here twice this week checking into your lab and searching for something. I had nothing to tell her. But she's not happy, Jane, and she's looking for someone to take her anger out on.

Where was the anger or the upset that her job was in danger? She waited for it, but it didn't come. In the Amazon basin, she'd found a new strength. Not just one that came from being a virologist, though she did have a new confidence in her abilities to heal. She also had a confidence in the woman she was—in her level head and calm reasoning. She'd never have thought that about herself before she'd come to the jungle. She smiled a little, unable to believe the difference a few days could make.

She checked the next message and realized it was from Angie.

Can't get any further information. Someone from our office did the original test but I was told it was worth my job to keep asking questions. I'm sorry, Jane. I feel like an ass writing this. If I can find what you need I'll send it. Watch your back.

"Screw you, Meredith," Jane said loudly. Her voice echoed back to her. Threatening Angie was really going too far. Jane knew that Meredith must be feeling desperate, but that was no excuse.

Jane clipped the phone back on her belt and pushed the raft into the current. She jumped on board, her muscles barely straining with the movement. She was getting in shape. She'd have to remember to tell her friend Sophia about the weeklong jungle-adventure fitness program. Jane paddled and steered her way to where she'd left Mac.

The way Mac talked about his company and the freedom he had to act without checking in with his boss was enviable. But she'd always been on the same page as Meredith before this and so it was odd to think of leaving the CDC. Was that what she was contemplating?

Mac was an interesting man. She still suspected that he was keeping something secret from her.

Mainly because he went from being this really easygoing guy to being very secretive. She thought part of it related back to his past. The incident in Asia that had driven him from the WHO. But she suspected it was something more. Perhaps something that involved her.

Did he suspect her of having gone along with her father in falsifying documents for the glory of making a find? It was so hard to remember those days. For the first time since she'd been sent to live with her grandmother, her dad and she had been living in the same city and working together. She'd been trying to rebuild bridges that she'd torn down in a fit of rebellion years before. Then Raul had asked her out and she'd found herself spending more time in their lab than she should have.

She'd always wondered if she'd been partly to blame for what happened. Her father had wanted to mend things between himself and Jane when they'd both worked at the CDC. She shook her head. Even now, five years later, she still felt guilty and ashamed of the way she acted. Of the way she'd demanded that he make time for her on his schedule.

She'd been a brat, she realized. Unreasonably demanding things from her father because he'd felt guilty for leaving her alone all those years and the mantle of age was weighing heavily on his shoulders.

She closed her eyes. Pictured the big bear of a man who'd always seemed so distanced from her. Acknowledging to herself that she was partially responsible for that gap didn't make her feel any better. But then Jane knew the truth to be uncomfortable. "Please, God, let me get to him in time."

The river was slow moving. Jane kept an eye out for water predators. She carefully kept her hands in the raft and away from the carnivorous piranha that were known to inhabit waters here. She'd had no fear when she'd dived in after Mac earlier because a big human body didn't look like a meal to the fish, but a few fingers was a different subject.

The rain slowed to a drizzle and the sun shone weakly on the river. Jane wished it would come out in earnest. She wouldn't complain about the humidity anymore, she just wanted to be somewhat dryer than she was right now.

Before she knew it she was back where she'd left Mac. He was still slumped on the log. She stepped into the clearing and he turned to face her. His eyes flashed a warning and she realized he had his gun drawn and leveled in the opposite direction. Jane pulled her knife from the ankle sheath.

She owed her grandfather more thanks than she'd ever given him for teaching her to use the knife. It was hard for her to believe a skill she'd used only in the wild swampland around her grandparents' house would prove so useful in saving her life in the jungle.

Before she could move or say anything she heard what had alerted Mac—a voice talking in a low murmur and the sound of people moving through the jungle. Jane got down on her belly and crawled over to Mac's log and lay hidden behind it. "Get down."

"Too late," he said out of the side of his mouth as a group of five men stepped into the clearing.

Chapter 13

The men entered the clearing and stopped right in front of Mac. Jane edged deeper into the undergrowth where she couldn't be seen. Something was crawling up her leg. Jane was afraid to swat at it, but feared it might be some poisonous insect.

The men who entered the clearing all had red-and-blue war paint on their faces. They wore camouflage pants and vests with pockets in them, but no shirts. Two of the men had ammunition belts draped over their chests. All of the men held assault rifles loosely in their arms.

The men kept Mac pinned down and moved closer, holding the gun on him at point-blank range. Jane had a moment's fear that Mac would do something really stupid, like shoot at one of them.

She remembered Reynaldo and Tambo. They'd both responded to calm rational thinking. The very things she was known for.

She stuck her knife in the back of her pants and got to her feet, hands held at shoulder height. She refused to keep hiding like some sort of cowering girl.

"*Hola!* I'm Dr. Jane Miller and I've come to the Amazon to find the Yura."

The men divided their attention between both her and Mac. But the leader lowered his gun and stared at Jane.

"You've found them, Dr. Miller. I'm Ernesto," he said in Spanish. His accent was a little different than Tambo's had been, but she had no problem understanding him.

"Wonderful. Is my father still with you?" she asked. She worried that her father might have contacted his old friend Raul. Which wouldn't be good for any of them.

"Yes."

"I'd like to be taken to him."

Ernesto shook his head. "That's not possible."

"Why not?" Jane asked. She had just spent days battling things that she didn't want to remember to get to these people and her father. There was no way she was turning around this close to the finish line. No way. She thought perhaps this man didn't realize that she was much more than her father's daughter and had more than her share of his stubbornness.

"Because we're not accepting visitors right now," he said.

"I'm not a visitor. I've come to help you. I know that your people are sick and dying," she said.

He raised his gun again, his eyes narrowed suspiciously on her. "How do you know?"

Jane didn't know what to say except that she'd come because they were dying. "My father sent for me."

"That's not much of a recommendation. The last men he sent took two of our sick with them and they never returned," he said.

Someone had taken the Yura? Had Raul gotten the people that Ernesto was talking about? And if so, why was Raul following her?

"I'm not going to take anyone with me. Listen, just take me to my dad and he can explain everything," Jane said. Her father had to be anticipating her arrival. Jane felt certain if Ernesto took her to his village everything could be straightened out.

"No, he can't. He's not speaking anymore," Ernesto said. There was no emotion on his face and Jane wasn't sure she'd heard him.

Then the words sank in and Jane's heart stopped for a minute. And the blood drained from her face, stars danced in front of her eyes and she swayed on her feet. Mac got to his feet and put an arm around her to steady her. "Is he dead?"

"No," the leader said. "Not yet."

"I'm not taking no for an answer, take us to him. This is why I came. To save him and hopefully to help you."

Ernesto watched her carefully.

"Someone is following us," she continued. "The treatment I brought with me to help the sick of your tribe is only going to be good for a few more days unless I get it into a freezer."

"Who is this man?" Ernesto asked, totally ignoring what she'd said.

"This is—"

Mac spoke over her in a native tongue. The men conversed for several minutes before Mac holstered his gun. Ernesto turned to speak to his men.

"What did you tell them?" she asked.

"That I'm considered a friend to the Yaminahua. They are relatives of the Yura and I'm here to protect my brothers."

"Is that the truth?" she asked, because several things were starting to clear up.

"Yes, it is."

"Why didn't you say anything to me earlier?" she asked. But she had an idea that he hadn't been sure what team she was playing for. And that angered her. She'd never had her motives questioned.

"Because I didn't know if I could trust you. I thought you could be working with the men that Ernesto spoke of."

"Is that why you were slowing us down?" she asked. Suddenly she understood his slow pace on the trail. And the way he'd seemed almost reluctant to keep moving.

"Yes. I couldn't find evidence either way, but I didn't want to chance you harming anyone else."

She understood his motives, but it really angered her. She'd done nothing to endanger anyone, something that Mac couldn't say.

"That's rich coming from you," she said, pulling away from Mac's loose embrace. "I've never killed half of my patients in an effort to hurriedly find a cure."

"That's a low blow. And I might deserve it, but now's not the time."

Jane agreed. "Well, it doesn't matter to me. I just want to get to my father and do what I can to save him."

* * *

Jane looked up as Ernesto approached them, very aware that she'd just been arguing in front of a man who wasn't sure he wanted anything to do with her. The only man who was really standing between her and her father. Without Ernesto on her side, she could kiss off any chance of seeing her dad.

She knew it, and as he stood and moved a few feet away from her, she realized that Mac knew it, too. Jane rethought her position and determined to do whatever it took to get to her dad. Even if it meant dealing with Mac's distrust.

"We are a small hunting party out to trade for goods up the Madre. We only stopped when we heard gunshots. We chased the shooters away and followed you down the river. You are a very brave woman."

"Not really, I just don't give up," Jane said. So that's why the pursuit had stopped.

Ernesto almost smiled at her. Jane took that as a good sign. "I think we got off on the wrong foot. I'm really here to help. And I have to see my dad."

Ernesto put his hand on her arm. "Calm down. We are heading back to our village. We will bring you to the border of our village and the shaman will decide if you can enter."

"Okay."

Ernesto studied her and Jane felt as if he was trying to read something in her eyes. She hoped he found what he was searching for, because she realized that she didn't know what it was. She had no idea how to fix this problem.

Ernesto turned and called something to his men and

they all laughed. Mac grunted but didn't bother to translate. Now that her temper had cooled, she knew she owed him an apology. But, dammit...

No buts, she heard her dad saying to her in her memory. How many times had she done that? Spoken without thinking of the consequences?

"Get your gear together and we'll move out," Ernesto said.

"Wait. Mac was injured in the river—"

"I don't need to be coddled by you," Mac said in English.

To Ernesto he said in Spanish, "I'm fine."

Jane waited while Mac got to his feet and then shrugged into his pack. Deliberately she turned her back on him. She didn't want to try to figure out if she could smooth the relationship between them with an apology or if she even owed him one.

"Ernesto?"

"Yes?"

"Will you tell me about my dad? Is he bleeding?"

"No bleeding now. But a lot of our people who are sick are bleeding through the nose."

That fit with the symptoms her father had described. "How long will it take us to reach them?"

"Only a couple of hours. But you'll have to wait until morning before you can enter the camp."

"I'm ready," Mac said, coming up behind her.

Ernesto nodded and they set off. Mac stayed right behind Jane and finally she couldn't stand it any longer. She glanced over her shoulder. "I'm sorry. I have a nasty habit of speaking before thinking. What I said was—"

"Totally true. I understand how you feel. My mother was diagnosed with ovarian cancer six months ago and I think I told off every doctor in the oncologist's office at least once."

"Still, I shouldn't have brought up your past. I know from experience that there's always more to the story than what the gossipmongers spread."

Mac moved abreast of her. His stride was longer now and she realized how much of his strength and knowledge he'd hidden from her on the first leg of their journey. It was only now seeing him with the Yura that she realized how well he fit with them.

"Why didn't you trust me?"

"Like you trusted me?" he asked.

"Well, I didn't lie to you."

"Sorry. I wasn't sure who was on what team and I wasn't taking any chances. Like Ernesto said, someone took away some of the tribal members to 'treat' them and they were never returned."

"Was it Raul?"

"I have no idea. I wasn't with the tribe then. I'd just returned from visiting my mother in the States. My Yaminahua friend Yabidwa left a message asking me to look into it. One of the missing men was his cousin. Before I could find out more, I learned that Yabidwa had died of an unnamed virus. I suspect it's the same one the Yura have."

He watched her carefully, as if looking for a reaction.

"I'm so sorry, Mac. I have no idea what's going on," Jane said. And any chance she had of getting information from the CDC was gone. She couldn't ask either Angie or Tom to risk their careers any further.

"I think that Veracruz did take the men to run tests on. I think he tried all kinds of treatments and they didn't work," Mac said, pushing a hanging vine out of the way as they walked. One man had gone ahead of the group, Jane assumed to scout the area.

Ernesto was behind them with two other men and there was a small man in front of them. Jane thought he was probably in his late teens. He still had the wiry frame of someone who wasn't finished growing yet.

"Why hasn't Raul gone to the authorities? The Peruvian government and Meredith were quite specific when they said no evidence existed supporting my find."

"I don't know. It could be greed. Peru is in the middle of some very delicate negotiations to keep the border open here to Brazil and Bolivia. The rubber trade down here is very profitable. So they wouldn't want a health scare to shut it down."

"But that still leaves Raul. He doesn't work for the government. I checked."

"I can't get any information about his company, either," Mac said.

"Well, Thompson-Marks hasn't had a major find in at least three years. They were scooped by Pryce Drugs last year. So they need something big."

Mac stopped walking, cocked his head to the side and just watched her.

She continued. "Do they need it bad enough to not care how many Yura die until they find the treatment first?"

After they'd been walking for about an hour, Jane noticed that Mac was sweating more profusely than anyone else. That spider bite was still getting the best of him. She knew he wouldn't say he needed to stop. So she did the girl thing and asked for a break. Ernesto looked as if he wanted to say no, but then she nodded discreetly toward Mac. Ernesto called out to his men and they all stopped.

Mac sank down on the jungle floor and put his head to his knees. Honestly, she didn't know how much farther he could travel.

"Can't we go by river?" Jane asked.

"It's being watched," Ernesto told her.

"Oh. Is that how they knew where we were?"

"They didn't set up posts until after they spotted your raft."

"Was it a mistake to take the river?" Jane asked.

"I would have."

She had a feeling that she'd just received a compliment from Ernesto. Mac was still resting and the others in their party were taking privacy breaks in the trees.

"Your dad has spoken of you often. I expected someone different."

In what way? But she didn't ask the question out loud. She couldn't. She didn't want to deal with whatever her father thought of her. She just wanted to get to him and…hopefully put the last of her guilt behind her. And whatever Ernesto had heard about her, she guessed it wouldn't be good. She'd been at her haughtiest the day her dad had tried to talk to her at the CDC while a television crew waited in the lobby for him.

"Did you get the supplies you needed?" she asked Ernesto.

"Yes, we did. And not speaking of it won't make it go away," he said.

"What are you, some kind of mystic?" she asked.

He gave her a half grin that made him seem somehow less fierce. "Yeah, I am."

"That's one of the things I love about Peru," she said softly.

"What?"

"The soul of your people."

He nodded. "You're not as different from your father as you'd like to think."

Before she could respond to that he stood and whistled sharply. Everyone reassembled and Mac climbed to his feet. He looked better than he had before the break. When she started toward him, he turned away.

Jane found her place in the group as they all moved out. She thought about Mac's reaction to her and she realized that whenever she tried to do something nice for him it backfired. To hell with him, she wasn't pretending anymore. This was who she was and she certainly wasn't compromising any more of herself for anyone.

Jane watched the trees and the animals as she moved through the forest. She felt small and very aware of the tenuous position of frail human bodies in this forest. The trees here had survived aeons and could crush her in seconds if they fell. She'd read a statistic that said that more people died from being hit by a tree than from snakebites in the Amazon basin.

It started to rain again and she stopped to pull her

rain jacket out of her pack. Mac stopped, as well, but Ernesto and his men merely slowed the pace.

"I'm not feeling well," Mac said in the silence.

"I can tell. I think you need to take a break," Jane said. He should be getting over the effects of the bite. She moved closer to examine his arm.

She pushed the sleeve up his arm and saw that the wound was still red and irritated. "It's not getting better. I think you might need a hospital."

"I gave my word to a blood brother, Jane. I have to see this through."

"Let me put some more salve on it."

"It's not helping," he said. He pushed his shirtsleeve down and fastened the Velcro clasp at the wrist.

"Did you show it to Ernesto?" she asked, wondering how to get him to go get the help he needed. She wasn't sure that staying in the jungle was the best idea for him no matter who he gave his promise to.

"No. I don't want them to know that I'm…" His voice trailed off.

"What, human? They can tell something's wrong." She couldn't keep the sarcasm from her voice. He arched one eyebrow at her, but didn't respond to that comment.

"I don't want to slow anyone down. But I think the spider venom may have entered my bloodstream."

"With the sweats I was thinking the same thing. Your body is trying to purge the poison."

"I'm dizzy, too. This isn't how it's supposed to work," he said weakly.

"What?" she asked. She'd never seen a man so strong even when he was obviously weakened. He had a strength of will that she really admired. She wished she had half his fortitude.

"Didn't Peter Parker turn into Spider-Man after one bite?" Mac asked her with a weak attempt at a smile.

"Yeah, lucky him," Jane said. Then she had the funniest image of Mac in a red-and-blue leotard, flying through the trees on webs he created. She chuckled.

"I'll say." Mac had his pack on again. They caught up to Ernesto and the others. As soon as they were back in line the pace increased. Jane kept checking on Mac and realized that he was dropping behind. And she knew that, this time, he wasn't trying to slow them down deliberately.

Jane was debating what to do when they heard gunfire from up ahead. Ernesto pushed Jane to the side and the other soldiers drew their guns. Mac took his gun out, but his hands were shaking. She knew it was from the spider bite. She reached over and removed the gun from his grip.

Mac gave it to her with no resistance. In fact, she thought she saw relief in his eyes. They were fevered and unfocused.

She took a position in the circle of men standing back-to-back and waited to see who or what would come out of the jungle. Jane worried that she wouldn't be able to shoot if it came down to it. But then she straightened her spine and thought that if these were Raul's men, then they were probably responsible for the deaths of at least two innocent men. Jane vowed there wouldn't be any more.

Chapter 14

"Those aren't men heading toward us, Jane, they're the enemy," Mac said quietly. He helped Jane remove her pack and set it next to him on the ground. "The gun pulls a little to the left when you fire it."

Jane glanced over at him. He was in the center of the circle. Clearly no one expected him to defend himself. But she appreciated his advice.

"I know," she said under her breath. Didn't he remember when she'd hit Carl with her knife? She did. She felt a queasy feeling in her stomach and she knew, just knew that this time it was only going to get worse.

"Shouldn't we hide in the jungle? I feel like bait standing here."

"Leave it to the Yura. They know this area better than we do."

"That's what I'm afraid of. I don't want to get caught in the middle of some tribal war. We've got enough of our own problems," Jane said.

"They know. Trust me on this."

Trust him? She wasn't sure she could. But she didn't dwell on that. Someone was moving closer to their location. Jane heard the footsteps, but even more telling was the lack of chatter from the birds and monkeys. The men around her started chanting. The rhythm of their voices seemed to swell in the air all around. She felt it creep up her body almost as if it were coming from the middle of the earth to fill her.

The words were foreign and their meaning not known to her, but in that instant she knew. She knew that whatever it took, she was part of this warrior circle. A solid part of it, she thought. Not the weak link. She closed her eyes and harkened back to her childhood, to that one experience with the rifle, and remembered her grandfather's advice. To keep her eye on her target and to watch out for the kick. The rifle had kicked in the shoulder and Jane suspected the semiautomatic handgun would kick, as well.

"Mac, put your back to mine," she said.

He did it without question and Jane lifted her arms, bracing her left hand under her right. If her foes or the enemies of the Yura came around the bend she was ready for them.

The man closest to Jane turned toward her and fired over her shoulder as three men entered the clearing. The first man was a dark, Spanish-looking man. His eyes were filled with deadly intent. Jane hesitated for one second before she fired. She aimed for his shoulder, but hit the fleshy part of his upper arm. He swung his gun around and up. Jane fired again before he could, this time aiming for his trigger hand and barely grazing his side. He cursed and dropped the gun for a minute.

Her arms were starting to shake from holding them up. The men around her were firing. Jane kept her eyes on the man she'd hit twice. Mac was at her back, steadying her with his strength. She could feel the energy coursing through him and she knew he wished he were the one firing instead of her. And damned if Jane didn't wish that, too. Later, she thought. She'd deal with regrets later. She fired on the man again as he shakily lifted his gun. Luckily her hits kept his aim way off. He covered the ground in front of her with a spray of bullets.

She fired again, hitting him in the upper thigh and he dropped to one knee. She ran forward and lashed out with a kick to the nose. The man grabbed her ankle and jerked.

She fell hard on her ass. Dazed, she watched as he reared back. She had an instant awareness of his fist swinging toward her and tried to duck, but his fist connected with her cheekbone, snapping her head back. *Damn.* That hurt. Stars danced in front of her eyes. She fumbled for her knife, still tucked into the waistband of her pants.

She pulled the weapon out and leaped at him, using her weight to push the man back on the ground. Jane put her knife to his throat. "Surrender or die."

He said something in a thick accent that Jane didn't understand. She pressed the knife blade harder against his skin.

Mac came up behind her and spoke to the man. "He surrenders."

Mac was at her side. He reached over her shoulder and pinched the artery in the man's neck. A few seconds later he was unconscious under her. Together they took his gun, ammo and bound his hands and feet. When Jane stood she realized the chanting had stopped and she glanced around the clearing. All of the Yura warriors were standing. And the men who'd attacked them were on the ground.

Jane wasn't the only one to have sustained an injury. Mac's eye was black and getting darker. Ernesto carried a wounded man—she thought his name was Paulo—back into the clearing and two other men had bleeding wounds.

Jane wanted to sink to the ground and scream. She wasn't sure she'd ever experienced anything as terrifying as the last few minutes had been, but she had to keep her head. Medical attention was needed. She went to her pack and pulled out her medical kit.

Focusing on bandaging wounds and making sure everyone else was okay worked an odd sort of magic on her. Jane found her own adrenaline from the fight slowly ebbing. Mac was still unsteady on his feet but he helped her bandage the wounds and luckily he had a pressure pack that they were able to use on Paulo, the scout, who was worse off than everyone.

Soon they were ready to move out and Ernesto came over to Jane. He looked into her eyes again. That deep stare of his that made her feel as if…as if she was being scanned by an alien mind probe.

This time he grunted at whatever he saw there. Then

he placed his hands on her head. Holding her in a vise grip, he said some words she didn't understand. She couldn't break her gaze away from his. When he dropped his hands and gave the order to move out, Jane adjusted the straps of her pack to follow, but Mac stopped her with a hand on her arm.

"Do you know what that was about?" he asked.

"I think Ernesto is having a bit of fun at my expense."

"No, he wasn't. He looked into your soul and asked a question to God. The fact that you didn't answer told him that you weren't ready."

"Is that going to affect my chances of seeing Dad?"

"Probably."

Jane didn't know what to say to that. She walked away from Mac, realizing she needed to learn how to speak Ernesto's language so that she wouldn't miss another opportunity like that one.

The pace was a little slower, but they arrived at the Cashpajali River earlier than Jane suspected she and Mac would have on their own. Ernesto and his men had stored three longboats in the trees and retrieved them. Mac got in a boat with Paulo and Leo. Ernesto and Ron were in her boat, and Maney and Jeff were in the last boat.

Ernesto seated her in the center and handed her an oar. Jane put her pack between her feet and was ready to row as soon as they pushed off from the shore. The Cashpajali was so different from the Madre. It was a slow-moving river with wide banks dotted with palm trees. Jane stared at the area around her. This place was totally unfamiliar to her and yet she felt at home here as she'd never felt in any other place.

Something was changing deep inside her and she didn't know what it was. She didn't know if she was ready for change because for so long she'd gotten by simply through existing. By following her routines and not challenging herself outside of the lab. But this entire journey was outside the lab.

"Why didn't you answer me before?" Ernesto said in Spanish when they'd been on the river for about fifteen minutes.

"I don't speak your language."

"I heard you chanting while we were fighting," he said.

"I…no, you must be wrong. I felt…I don't know. I wasn't chanting," she said at last. There were things she could believe in, but they were all backed up by scientific fact. By researching, careful attention to detail and the kind of single-minded focus that had enabled her to graduate cum laude. But speaking another language and not being aware of it. *No way.*

"What did you ask me?" she questioned after a few minutes had passed.

"You'll understand it when you understand me."

"Ernesto, that makes no sense."

"Even in your heart?"

"I'm a scientist. I make decisions based on fact."

"I know. Your father and I have spent much time talking of his brilliant daughter."

"You must have been talking to the wrong man," she said.

Ernesto said nothing and Jane was glad for the si-

lence. She didn't want to remember her relationship
with her father. She'd ignored most of what had gone
on between them for as long as she could. But she knew
that Ernesto had hit on something that was a secret
longing in her soul. Everything she'd done had been to
impress her dad.

She'd never realized that until now.

Her head ached. She'd taken two aspirin when she'd
finished bandaging everyone up. But it wasn't helping.
She had a feeling that the weight of the outcome of this
trip was keeping the pressure and tension high within
her.

"How many people are sick?" she asked, turning
her mind to what she'd come to Peru to do.

"Half the tribe. We've separated them and isolated
them for eating and bathing. Your father was very ad-
amant about these things as soon as he realized that
something was spreading through the camp."

"When did you notice the first signs?"

"A little over a year ago. We had a group of mission-
aries staying with us. So at first we thought it was something from them.

"But Maney's brother died and your father didn't
like some of the things he saw. He talked to our council and asked to perform an autopsy on the body."

Her father had done this many times before, Jane
knew. He liked to do all of his research and scarcely let
anyone else help him. "What did he find?"

"I didn't understand everything he said, but one
thing stood out. This wasn't a virus brought by white
men. It was more…how you say…killing?"

"Fatal?"

"Yes. He contacted his colleagues. I told you about them. But when they took my brothers and didn't bring them back, we refused to participate in any more research."

"How many people came to the village?"

"Three. All men. They spoke English and Spanish. One man was a native from a tribe we consider allies."

"Can you describe the others?"

"One of them was Peruvian. He has family in Puerto Maldonado. We spoke at length because at first the men and your father were convinced that we had been infected from our water supply."

Jane processed what he was saying. She didn't know if Raul had family in the town that Ernesto had mentioned but it made sense to her that he was the Peruvian. "Was the third man American?"

"Yes. Your father had worked with him and the Peruvian before."

"Was the Peruvian Raul Veracruz?"

Ernesto nodded. "He was the leader."

"What was the American's…"

Name. The word remained unspoken as Ernesto ended the conversation by turning and calling to his men to get on the move.

Jane's eyes narrowed. Someone had really done a number on Ernesto's and the Yura's trust. Raul and his teammates.

Ernesto might not trust her enough to reveal everything now, but she wasn't giving in. She'd wear him down and get into the Yura village to see her father and do what she could to help. Failure was not an option.

* * *

Jane's arms ached from rowing and she was happy when Ernesto steered them to the shore. There was a rough dock and the men tied the boats off to the posts. Jane climbed out of the boat and Ernesto handed her bag to her. She shrugged it onto her shoulders.

Scanning the shore she tried to see the village, but it wasn't in sight. "How much farther?"

"Not too much," Ernesto said. He went to talk to the other men. Mac was swaying a little on his feet but his skin didn't have the gray cast to it any longer.

Jane went over to him. "How are you holding up?"

"I'd kill for a bottle of tequila and a comfy chair."

She smiled and took his wrist in her hand, checking his pulse. He raised one eyebrow at her and she knew he was aware that she was checking his vitals, but didn't care. The man wasn't in good shape as he well knew.

"You two follow Paulo. He will take you to an area away from our village. You will be given food for dinner and then you should both bathe. We will have a decision for you by morning."

"Ask me again," she said. "Ask me in Spanish."

"You're not ready to answer yet. You know this, too."

He turned to leave, but Jane stopped him with her hand on his arm. "Promise me that if my father has worsened you'll come for me. I can't... I need to see him before it's too late."

Ernesto nodded and then turned and strode away from her. Jane watched the others move away rapidly and she felt impotent. She couldn't change this. She could do nothing but wait and hope that the right answer presented itself.

Mac's hand moved in her grip, turning to grab her hand. "I'm confident we'll get into the village."

"Me, too," she said. "I've never failed at anything once I set my mind to it."

"Why am I not surprised?"

She just shrugged.

Paulo returned and spoke to them in his native tongue. "Do you speak Spanish?" she asked.

"*Sì*. Sorry, señorita. Follow me."

Jane and Mac fell into step together following Paulo. She noticed the trail here was clear and wide, easily accessible. The Yura must use this path a lot.

"Where are you taking us?"

"To the missionary place."

Jane hoped it wasn't some sort of church. She didn't think she'd be comfortable sleeping and eating in a church. She realized that it probably wouldn't look like St. Joseph's, where she attended Sunday services, but still. She knew she'd never be comfortable in a place of worship. She was too grounded in science to believe in things that couldn't be proven.

"What do they use it for?"

"Sleeping. We don't like outsiders in our midst. I'm going to scout ahead. Keep following this path."

Mac said nothing as Paulo left them. They continued in silence until Jane realized that they were going to be alone together for the night. She tried not to dwell on it but the images were there in her head. Images of a sick man that she'd need to take care of.

"What did you learn from Ernesto?"

"That the virus doesn't travel through water, which I'd already found through my research."

"That makes sense. With all the clearing being done for the new highway I bet something stirred to life."

"That's my thought. The strand of this virus is a derivative of Lassa fever, so it could have been languishing there and not affecting anyone until the construction crews started clearing. I'd really like to know if any of them are sick."

"I can ask Maria to look into it," Mac said.

"No. I have a hunch that someone from my office came down here originally." Jane knew two people close to her had been out of the office during the period that Ernesto had indicated the men had first visited the Yura. One of them was a man named Josh Parson. He'd worked on her team before and was currently in Africa working with the AIDS/HIV team. The other was Tom.

"Who?"

Jane couldn't say it out loud because if she was right then she'd been set up by her friend. By someone she'd trusted. "Let me check a few facts first."

"What facts?" Mac asked.

"Ernesto said three men visited the Yura when my dad first discovered something was wrong. One of the men was Raul Veracruz. The second was someone like you, who'd spent a good deal of time down here—an American at home with the natives who was a brother to them. The third man was someone Dad knew."

"So you think it was someone from your office?"

"Yes, I do."

"How long is the list?" he asked.

She hadn't given it a lot of thought but off the top of her head she knew that it wouldn't be a very long one.

"Only a small number of people have worked with me, Raul and Dad."

"They wouldn't have to work with you directly, Jane. They could just be in your office."

"No. This is starting to feel personal. My gut says that it is someone I call friend."

"Why?"

"I haven't figured that out. I think that Raul is concerned about his family living on the Madre and he came down here to help them. I think that someone tipped off the government and they are in the middle of civilizing this country so they asked the men to keep it quiet. To do tests but not go public."

"And then…" Mac said.

"Dad realized what was going on and got me involved. Tell me if I sound paranoid," she said.

"Well, just a little bit. But a lot of what you're saying makes sense."

"I know. So what part do you play in this, Mac Coleman?"

"I told you that Yabidwa was killed by the disease."

"Yes, you did."

"What I didn't tell you was that he was the third man on the team that came to visit your father."

Chapter 15

Mac fell asleep as soon as they'd eaten dinner and bathed. The cabin they'd been given was only one room with a window in each wall. There were two cot-style beds draped with mosquito netting. The door was screened to allow a breeze to blow through the entire room. There were shelves built into the wall and Jane had unloaded the medicine she'd brought with her. The packs were holding but now that she was so close, sitting around and sleeping just wasn't something she could do.

Knowing Mac would be safe and that he needed sleep more than anything, she repacked her backpack with only the vials of medicine, leaving her spare clothing in the room. She jotted a quick note to Mac and told him not to worry. Then she set out to find Paulo.

Paulo was sitting outside their cabin when she emerged. He glanced up at her and then went back to the piece of wood in his hand. He was carving something.

She turned her focus to Mac. A lot of times there were local remedies for these kinds of injuries that were more effective than medicine brought from the outside.

"Paulo?"

"*Sì, señorita?*" he asked, without looking up.

"Mac was bitten by a spider…maybe a banana spider. His wound is taking a long time to heal. What would you use to treat it?"

He leaned back as if her words were hard for him to understand. And then she realized he understood her and he was trying to think of what they used. "There is a leaf that can be chewed to make a paste."

"Will you show me?"

He put down his piece of wood. "The leaf is this wide," he said, holding his hands about four inches apart. "There is a thick vein of red that runs down the back of it."

Jane followed him into the surrounding greenery as they searched the trees for the leaf. She found a red leaf with green veins and two different trees with vines that hung down them that had similar leaves, but Paulo only shook his head.

"Do you like living here, Paulo?" she asked as they moved through the jungle area searching all the trees.

"It's my home. My family is here," he said from under the awning of a large, waxy-leafed tree. He wore even less here than he had when she'd first met him on the trail. Now he had on some sort of shorts and though he carried the gun, he'd left off his ammo clips.

"Parents?" she asked. He looked young to her. As if he was in his late teens or early twenties.

"Yes, and a wife, Marcella. She is expecting our second child." A smile broke over his face and she saw his pride. And his fear, the fear new fathers everywhere shared because pregnancy and birth were things women did and men sometimes didn't fully understand.

Jane found another leaf, one that met his description. She held it up to him. "Wonderful. Congratulations. Soon?"

He shook his head at the leaf. "Yes, my wife will deliver soon. According to the doctor, only a few more weeks."

"Is she in the healthy camp?" Jane asked. She felt powerless knowing that she could probably help them but that they didn't welcome her help.

It wasn't the first time she'd encountered this, but to be honest it was the first time that she'd felt it all the way down to her soul. She was stuck in some sort of static state and couldn't help feeling…impotent.

Paulo nodded in answer. "But my mother is not," he said. Then he turned on his heel and walked to a tree a few feet from them. "This one."

Jane helped him cultivate the leaves they needed and they made their way back to camp. Jane and Paulo worked together on creating a paste for Mac's arm. And then Paulo handed her a leaf she did recognize. The coca leaf. From the plant used to make cocaine and crack. But she knew in this part of the world that many people used it to make tea and in many healing remedies. It could be chewed raw, kind of like chewing tobacco.

"This will help with pain," Paulo said.

"Thank you," Jane said. She went into the cabin. Mac was sleeping fitfully but his color looked better. She applied the salve to his arm. He sat up and his eyes opened. She noticed the pupils were of normal size and that he didn't seem to be running a fever.

"What's that?"

"A local cure."

"I'm sorry I've been sleeping. I know you wanted to get to the camp."

"I still do. I'm going to talk to Paulo some more."

"Don't leave me here, Jane."

"Why not?"

"Because I need to go, too. And you can't treat everyone on your own before reinforcements arrive."

She left the cabin without saying a word. He was right. And she didn't want to use Paulo, but she had a feeling he and his family might be the key to getting what she needed.

Paulo was nowhere to be seen when Jane stepped back out of the cabin. Instead, Ernesto sat by the fire. He glanced up when he saw her. "*Hola,* Jane."

"*Hola,* Ernesto. Did you come with good news?"

"Of a sort. You may visit your father but that is all. The council want no more of your kind of medicine."

"My kind of medicine? I haven't even been here before."

"That's the deal."

"Okay, I'll take it, but can I try to convince them—"

"Heal your father. That will speak more loudly than any words."

She nodded, already thinking of what needed to be done. "Do you have any sort of generator in the village?"

"Yes, two of them. One is in your father's lab."

"Dad has a lab?" she asked. That must be how he'd prepared the samples he'd sent. She had a hundred more questions and not one of them could be answered right now.

"Yes. Are you ready to leave?" Ernesto asked.

"Let me get my gear and go tell Mac."

"He's better?"

"A little. He's been sleeping and Paulo helped me make a salve that should help his arm."

Ernesto stared at her for a minute. "Why would you use our remedies?"

"Why wouldn't I? You know this area a lot better than I do. In fact, I used the bark and leaves my father sent me to come up with my treatment for this illness."

Ernesto said nothing more. For a minute she was afraid he was going to grab her shoulders and stare into her eyes again. But he didn't.

She hurried into the tent to find Mac packing up his gear. "I overheard your conversation."

"Are you feeling better?"

He didn't answer her, but shrugged into his pack and walked outside. She gathered the rest of her stuff and joined the others. Ernesto set off at a good clip and Jane found that she had no trouble at all keeping up.

She was anxious to see her dad, to assess his condition—and to be there for him. She also needed to check out his lab and see if he had any notes. She wanted to compare them with hers.

"Did you know my dad has a lab here?" she asked Mac. The trail between their cabin and the village was well traveled. Jane could hear the river flowing nearby.

"Rebel Virology supplied a lot of the equipment. Yabidwa, my blood brother, asked me to supply them and I did."

"You could have mentioned this earlier," she snapped. Knowing they had an equipped lab made her feel better. They could follow the progress of the treatment she'd brought and alter it as they went along.

"Jane, I didn't trust you."

"And now?" she asked, but she knew he did. She wasn't sure if she could trust him or not, knowing that he'd held back so much and could still have more secrets. But that didn't matter right now. She needed him to be her assistant.

"You know I do."

"Do you know who the other person was on the original team with Yabidwa and Raul?" Jane asked. Her suspicions that it was someone in her office were making her gut churn.

"No. We lost communication with Yabidwa after he arrived here with the lab equipment."

"Is the lab equipped to handle this?"

"Yes, I think the lab is well equipped. Yabidwa was very thorough. The lab should be able to accommodate anything we need it to."

"That's good. What happened to Yabidwa's body?"

"He was returned to his family three weeks after he arrived here with the lab equipment. I'm certain now that he was infected. I…uh, took the liberty of reading some of your notes. The symptoms match."

"Okay, I'll ignore the fact that you snooped through

my notes. What did they find in the autopsy?" she asked.

"The brain had hemorrhaged and there was some decaying of internal organs."

"Which ones?"

"Heart and liver."

"I don't know if that's consistent. I've never seen anyone who's died of the disease. I hope we can stop anyone else from dying."

Mac gave her a hard look and Jane realized he knew she was talking about her father. "I'm sure your dad..."

Jane stopped in the path. "We both know there's no assurance about him."

"Are you close?"

"No. We never were. He spent most of my childhood traveling and working in hot spots."

"You resented him," Mac said.

"Yeah, and then when he was ready to try to build a relationship, I wasn't."

"Jane, you can't blame yourself."

She hated seeing that look on his face. It was the first time he seemed to realize she was human. She wore her emotions about her father on her sleeve. She turned away from Mac. How could she have told him that?

She took several deep breaths. She needed to be very careful about what she revealed from now on.

She couldn't allow her emotions to interfere. She needed to be the virus hunter. Scientifically minded, focused solely on the virus and stopping it.

Jane hesitated in the doorway of the cabin that was her father's. She heard the labored sound of his breathing through the screened door.

Mac had gone to check out the lab and Jane wished for a minute she wasn't alone. Facing…hell, her worst fear. She closed her eyes and then pictured her father as she'd last seen him. Full of life, ready for a fight and willing her to believe in him. She wished she could go back in time and say she did.

Say whatever he needed to hear so that he would have stayed in the States, well away from the Yura and the Amazon strain.

The cabin her father lived in was raised off the ground, she suspected to let floodwater under it. She stepped up and pushed open the door. The room was shadowy in the late afternoon. The canopy of the dense forest around them let through dappled sunlight, but none of it was streaming in through the windows— someone had covered them with a light cotton fabric. The room was hot, almost stifling. Jane took a step forward, scarcely able to breathe.

Her father's bed was draped with mosquito netting. The floorboards creaked with each step she took but he didn't stir or move. On his bedside table was a pitcher of water and a picture. As she moved closer, she saw it was one of the two of them, taken when she'd graduated from college.

Tears stung the back of her eyes. She reached through the netting and took her father's hand in her own. His skin was warm to the touch, but not hot. His eyes were closed and the skin around them sunken and sallow. She rubbed her hand over his forehead.

She'd never seen her dad like this. Kneeling by the bed, she leaned her head down on his chest, listening to his heart beating.

She knew the Amazon strain wasn't an airborne virus so she felt no fear for herself from touching him like this. His heartbeat was a little erratic. She pushed to her feet, brushed her lips across his forehead and left the cabin.

She met Mac in the lab area. The refrigerator was an old one and noisy. It was the first thing she heard when she came in. It was dusty from disuse but was apparently working, as was the centrifuge machine that was spinning in the corner.

"How's your dad?" Mac asked as she entered.

He was bent over a microscope in the corner, checking out a slide. His hair was so long he'd tied it at the back of his neck.

"Not good. I want to give him the treatment and start round the clock monitoring," she said. Going to the long counter that ran along one wall, she started to gather the supplies she'd need to give her father his first treatment.

Since she'd never tested it outside the lab, she wasn't sure what to expect. But she was confident in her abilities and in her research.

"I'll help out. I'm checking my bug bite. That salve you put on seems to be doing the trick."

"Paulo knew exactly how to treat it," Jane said. "I'll take the first shift with my dad."

"Do you know how this is spread?" he asked.

She'd been able to determine that it was not an airborne virus and that some sort of secretion had to be used to spread it. But she hadn't really spent a lot of time on it. "No, I concentrated on isolating the virus and finding a treatment to stop its distribution. My father sent a wasp that could be the carrier, but I didn't confirm that."

"I'll start working on that," Mac said.

There was a change in his body language and she realized he was getting into work mode. A part of her wanted to stay here and watch him in action. But there wasn't time now.

"We can rule out water as a way the virus is passed because the CDC already did that research. Did you find any of Dad's notes?" she asked. Her father was meticulous in his research. She had two storage units at home that were full of his duplicate notes. Stuff that the CDC didn't have room to store but that Jane had never been able to throw out. Not even when she'd suspected her father of doing the unthinkable. Of causing a health scare to further his own career and make his name bigger in the virology community.

Mac pushed a small laptop computer, her dad's old Mac, toward the edge of the desk. It was scratched and had seen better days. "I found this, but all of his notes are in some sort of code."

Jane leaned over Mac's shoulder and saw the combination of numbers and letters. She'd seen it the first time when she was twelve and she'd sent her father a report she'd done on the code breakers of World War II. On his next visit home, they'd made this one up and had communicated by code until she turned fifteen.

"I know it," she said.

"Then I'll take the first shift monitoring your father while you read this. We need to know what he found."

Jane was reluctant to let anyone else, even Mac, sit with her dad. She knew that she had a vested interest in keeping him here on this earth and, although it was silly, she felt she could will him awake if need be. Her medicine would do the work and her spirit and determination would keep him going until the medicine could stop the virus in his system.

"How about if I tell you Dad's code?" Jane asked.

Mac gave her a look that was unreadable, but she sensed he'd misinterpreted her and thought she didn't trust him. She didn't know how to explain it without revealing to him things she didn't want to. She needed to be with her dad.

"I'm not going to harm your dad," Mac said, turning back to the microscope.

Jane crossed to him and put her hand on his shoulder. He didn't turn around. She seemed to always say the wrong thing around him. "It's not that I think you might. I just need to sit with him."

She hated how vulnerable she felt inside. Hiding that weakness from the world had never been a problem before, but now she found herself wanting to confide in Mac. Wanting to share her burden with him—and she didn't like that.

Mac nodded. "Okay. We lost the contents of one entire Styrofoam pack to defrosting so we're down on the treatment. But we can duplicate it here if Ernesto's people allow us to treat them."

"I'm not sure how to convince him," Jane said. Ernesto wanted something from her that she wasn't sure she'd ever be able to give him. He wanted to see something in her soul that she doubted she had. Though she believed her determination to heal her dad was going to help him, she didn't believe in a lot of spiritual things.

And Ernesto—well, the more she thought about it, Ernesto seemed to want spiritual awareness from her.

"I have a few ideas. I'm going to talk to them while you're with your dad," Mac said.

Mac had a rapport with the Yura tribesmen that Jane knew she didn't. And she never really could. She was an outsider to them and she didn't understand them the way that Mac, who'd spent most of his adult life living and working in this part of the world, did.

"Sounds good. I'll bring the computer with me and work on the code."

Mac left quietly and Jane took a few minutes to review her notes. She prepared the treatment for her father, grabbed her notebook and the laptop and left the lab. Several of the Yura who were nearby watched her as she made her way to her father's cabin. Jane had never felt more at home inside herself and more out of place with her world than she did at that moment. She forced herself to keep her head up and just walk.

The fact that these people had been betrayed by modern scientists made her job that much harder. The fact that she was one of the best virologists in the world made her confident she'd succeed anyway. Somehow she'd save her dad and convince the Yura to trust in her medicine.

Despite all the obstacles she'd faced getting here, she knew this one would be the toughest.

Chapter 16

Jane set up an intravenous drip of treatment for her father. She noted his vitals and the exact time she started the drip. She saw no immediate change in his breathing or skin temperature. Sitting down cross-legged on the floor, she opened his ancient laptop and powered it up.

Her cell phone had minimal reception here so she checked her e-mail on the laptop. Nothing new except one from Meredith that simply said, *The cat's out of the bag.* Tom had sent her a joke e-mail. She didn't open it because he always seemed to know when she had opened his messages.

She noticed that her GPS unit was flashing and wondered if she should turn off the transponder. She didn't want to unknowingly give away their location.

Was Meredith trying to warn her? Jane put the phone aside. Now that she was here it would take an act of God to get her out of the jungle and away from her father.

Jane opened the file that Mac had found and started working on the code. It was painfully simple and she was sure if any real code breakers got hold of it they'd figure it out in no time at all. It was based on their birthdays. Jane's was March 24, so the number *3* stood for the letter *A*. The rest of the alphabet played out that way. The letter *W* stood for the number *25*.

The process was slow and she worked at it methodically for almost two hours, stopping every thirty minutes to test her father. His breathing was steadier now and his skin cooler. Too cool?

She found that her father had concluded that the disease might be spread by the stinging wasp he'd sent to her. He'd managed to get the Yura to protect themselves against it but it was too late for some of the tribe.

His notes included a brief mention of going to the CDC office in La Paz. He said that he'd gotten nowhere with them because of his reputation. But that he'd learned that Raul Veracruz, his old protégé, was working in Lima.

Jane read her father's notes and could hear his voice.

I took samples from the infected group and packaged them as best I could. It took me a day and a half to get to Lima. Raul was surprised to see me, and I was surprised to see how well he was doing. I know that he played a part in what happened at the CDC and am still amazed that he wasn't affected by the fallout.

"*Hola,* Jane."

Ernesto stood in the doorway. In his arms he held a woman who was breathing hard, like her father. Laboring for each bit of air.

"Bring her inside," Jane said.

There wasn't a second bed in the room. But Jane grabbed some blankets from the table in the corner and made a pallet for her. "How long has she been like this?"

"She was fine when I left."

The woman was younger than her father, closer to Jane's age. Her skin was naturally tan and her eyes were sunken. Jane put her hand on the woman's forehead.

"What's her name?" Jane asked. She brushed the hair from the woman's forehead. She needed to get a cool compress on her. She monitored her pulse with her free hand, keeping an eye on the clock mounted on the wall.

"Selena. She's my wife."

Jane felt a weight press down on her. Always the reality of infectious diseases was so hard to take. This was the face of the Amazon strain. Not just her father, who was an anomaly here. Selena was part of the greater whole that was infected.

Jane put her stethoscope on and listened to Selena's heartbeat, which was more erratic than her father's had been. Selena was running a fever and Jane noticed some dried blood under her nose. Was it too late for this woman? The variables she'd tested in the lab were all so different from what she was doing here.

Did she dare delay treating Selena to run her blood through the machine?

"I haven't tested the treatment on people yet, only in a lab, and my father has taken one shot," Jane said carefully. The Yura were already reluctant to have her here—she didn't want to harm one of them by rushing too easily to the treatment.

"I'm losing her. I can't wait for you to be certain," Ernesto said. His large, dark eyes were fathomless pools.

Jane stood up and took her stethoscope from around her neck. She walked back to her father's bed and looked down at him. "Just as long as you understand the risk."

She heard him move behind her and then felt his hand on her arm. "I've looked into your soul, Jane Miller. You aren't going to try to kill my wife."

Jane turned away. That didn't mean she wouldn't. She thought about her father and about Mac. And other virologists like them who'd started out to save lives but sometimes ended up taking them, because viruses were by nature wily opponents that would do anything to survive.

She glanced at Ernesto and saw in his eyes what she felt when she looked at her dad. A desperation that was tinged by reality. Ernesto realized she wasn't promising him a miracle, but he was hoping for one just the same.

"Let's get a bed in here for her. I'll go get the supplies I need."

Ernesto left and Jane walked slowly back to the lab. He'd looked into her soul? She wanted to know what he'd seen, because she'd never really been too certain of herself on a personal level.

Mac was in the lab when she returned. It was still noisy and she was grateful for the funds the CDC had that enabled her to work with state-of-the-art equipment back home. "What's up?" Mac asked.

"Ernesto wants us to treat his wife. She's worse than Dad. I…"

"Jane, I've studied your work. You've covered everything."

She shrugged. What could she say? There was always an unknown factor. Treatments didn't work for everyone. And she liked Ernesto. "I'm afraid."

"We all are," he said.

He crossed the room and hesitated, then put his arms around her and hugged her close. She'd never really been hugged by anyone but her parents. She didn't know what to do. Mac just held her. "Share this with me. Don't take it all on yourself."

"I wish it were that easy."

"It can be if you let it," he said, his hands rubbing up and down her back.

"I'm not sure I can," she said, pushing out of his arms and picking up a vial of treatment before walking out the door.

Jane stopped in the doorway as she heard the sound of a low-flying helicopter. Mac was at her side in an instant. "Who the hell is that?"

"Don't be paranoid. They might get visitors all the time," she said.

"Doubtful."

"Yeah, Reynaldo did say that the Yura were more trouble than they were worth to trade with."

"This bites," Mac said.

Jane had to smile. "Thanks for your professional opinion."

"I just want a day—one day—where I can relax and focus on virology instead of having to fight with Veracruz and his posse like some sort of third-world bandito."

"What makes you sure it's Veracruz?"

"Don't you think it's him?" Mac snapped.

"I'm not sure. It could be someone from your organization." The more she thought about it, the odder it seemed that Raul would suddenly have a helicopter. She doubted that Thompson-Marks had them available for their R&D guys to use.

"Wouldn't I know they were coming?" he said sarcastically.

"How would you? Do you have some heretofore unmentioned gift of telepathy?"

"I like you like this," he said with a quick smile. For the first time in days she realized what an attractive man he could be. "Feisty."

"Don't get cute." Liking him was dangerous mainly because she wasn't sure she liked herself right now. And she really couldn't deal with anything else emotionally. Ernesto had placed his wife into her care, her father was waning quickly and then the entire Yura people, whom she hoped to help, didn't trust her. She didn't have time for Mac and his bedroom eyes and sexy voice.

"Okay, so it could be Maria. But she would have dipped low and made a second pass," Mac said.

"Let's wait and see." One of the things she liked about him was that he really listened to her. Gave her thoughts and opinions weight and consideration. She was used to that in the lab, but, outside, most men—hell, most people—didn't take the time to listen to anyone.

They waited a tense five minutes but the chopper didn't return. "I guess that rules out Maria."

"Yeah, it does. But you were right, it could be anyone. Maybe the government is doing sweeps here. I'm going to find Ernesto," Mac said.

Her watch beeped, signaling it was time to take another round of readings from her dad. She still had the vials of medicine and the IV drip bag for Selena. "I'm going to stay with my dad and Selena. I need to get her treatment started."

"Do you want my gun?" he asked.

"No. I've got my knife if I need it," she said. But hoped she wouldn't. She knew she could protect herself, but she didn't want to have to do it anymore. She wanted to concentrate on making her father and Selena well.

"Be careful, Jane."

"Why do you always say that to me?" she asked.

"Because you're always focused on everyone else," he said. He took her arm in his hand and held her still. She glanced up at him.

"I like taking care of others," she said. It made her feel as though she had some value outside of her own little community. It was something she'd always prided herself on.

"Who takes care of Jane?" he asked so softly she had to strain to hear him.

"I do." She pulled her arm free. Hadn't she proven time and again that she knew how to take care of herself? Dammit, she'd gotten them both here through some rather harrowing escapades.

"You put yourself last. Don't do that this time. I want you to be around when we get out of the jungle."

She didn't understand what he meant at first but he continued watching her with those intense blue eyes of his. She shivered a little with an awareness that had nothing to do with what they were talking about.

He wanted her as a woman. She didn't understand it. But she knew it with the same kind of bone-deep certainty that she knew she'd found the right cure for the Amazon strain.

"Why?" she asked.

"You're smart, figure it out," he said, pulling her toward him. He tipped her head back and kissed her as if there was no tomorrow and no yesterday. She tunneled her fingers into his hair and angled his head to take control of the embrace. His tongue brushed hers and she felt a shiver of awareness down her spine.

Why this man? Why now? She swept her hands up his back and felt the restrained strength in him. Felt the power with which he held her and realized in that moment that he could easily have overpowered her because she wasn't a big woman. But he hadn't.

She pulled away from him. He rubbed his thumb across her bottom lip.

"Think about it," he said, and walked away. She watched him go.

Jane realized she was staring and shook her head. She had work to do.

As soon as she got back to her dad's cabin she took his signs. His heart rate was evening out and his fever had completely gone. She bathed his head and fed him some ionized water. Most of it trickled down onto his bedding but a good amount got into his mouth.

Jane set up the IV for Selena and started jotting notes about her. She'd continue to observe Selena as she was her father.

She noted everything about her patients and then went to stand in the doorway. There was no breeze, just the straight falling of raindrops spattering on the roof.

In the middle of the night Jane woke to a scream. She sat bolt upright in the cot she'd found in the lab and brought to the cabin. Her father was still sleeping, but Selena moaned and rolled fitfully on her pallet. Jane got to her feet and went to the woman's side. Her skin was hot to the touch. Jane realized that Selena was getting worse.

Jane didn't know what to do. While she'd been with her father, Ernesto had gone off to seek a vision. To do a shaman's journey that would enable him to tell his people if they should trust Jane's medicine. She only hoped that his vision didn't involve taking dangerous hallucinogenic plants. What if something happened to Selena while he was on his spiritual journey?

Jane bathed Selena in cool water and gave her a dose of fever reducer. She jotted down all of the reactions that the other woman had and was careful to make sure that she missed nothing. Selena's tongue was swollen and there was more blood coming from her nose.

Jane took a swab of the blood and put it on a plate. She needed to check the virus and see how it was progressing. This was a variable she hadn't encountered in the lab.

The cabin door opened and Mac walked inside. "What's up?"

"Where were you?" she asked. She'd felt safe sleeping because Mac had been keeping watch over their two patients. Tired though she may become, she knew she wouldn't leave him in charge again.

"I had to take a leak."

She couldn't fault him there. She rubbed the back of her neck, feeling a tension headache starting.

"What's up?" he asked again. Brushing her hands aside, he massaged her neck. "You've got to relax."

"I know. Something's wrong with Selena. She should be improving by now."

"Give her time. You know that each of us reacts differently to medication."

She nodded. "I wish I knew more about how this started."

"Did you get anywhere with your dad's notes?"

"Yes, but there's still a lot more to go through. He thought originally that the disease was spread via insects like the stinging wasp. But then he ruled it out." She was glad she hadn't spent precious time researching the wasp when she'd received it.

"Did he make any further conclusions?"

"Yes. He was leaning toward the lemurs we saw the kids playing with. He thought they might have been carrying a parasite."

"Why?" Mac asked.

"They first noticed the disease in the children and the women. A few children have died. Dad only contracted it after prolonged interaction with both. He continued working with the families until he found small tick bites on everyone who'd contracted it."

"Ernesto said something about that. They've been vigilant in bathing and preventing tick bites since then."

"That's good. So we may know how the virus is spread, but these monkeys are all over the place. We really need to get the word out to the Brazilian government. And I'm not sure that the Peruvians really know what's going on here."

"I'll ask Ernesto to send someone to Puerto Maldonado in the morning to bring back a government official."

"That would be best."

Jane touched Selena's forehead as the woman moaned again. "She's burning up. I just took a sample of the blood from her nose and need to go look at it in the lab. Will you stay with them?"

"Yes. When do you monitor their stats again?"

Jane took her watch off and handed it to Mac. "It's set for every thirty minutes. Keep this so that the timing is accurate."

"I'll try to keep her cool."

"I'll be back as quickly as I can. I think I'm going to risk a call to the lab. Tom helped me with this treatment and he may have noted an anomaly that I missed."

"Doubtful. I can't imagine you missing anything."

"I make mistakes," she said.

"Yes, but then you fix them," Mac said quietly.

His quiet confidence in her meant more than she could say. He was right, she did know how to fix this. A few more hours in the lab were all she needed. She took a sample of Selena's blood with her and quietly left the room.

Walking through the moonlit village to the lab, she heard the rustle of wind in the trees. Though the cooking fire had died to only embers, the scent of the wood smoke still hung in the air.

Jane's mind was buzzing with all the different facts that she couldn't get straight. Something was happening with Selena that wasn't right. There was something Jane was missing. Was Selena infected with something other than the Amazon strain?

Jane reviewed Selena's symptoms and knew the woman had the same disease as her father. Selena's reaction might mean she was further along in the infection than Jane's dad had been. Or maybe the virus affected women differently than men.

She entered the lab and went straight to the microscope, examining the blood. The medicine seemed to have had very little effect on the disease in Selena's blood. She checked the sample of her father's that she'd taken earlier. He was improving slowly.

What had she missed?

Was this what had stymied Raul? For a moment she wished he was here so that she could question him. So that she could find out what had happened with the men he'd taken and tested.

Sometimes, looking at failure yielded a solution that seemed elusive. Jane grabbed her phone and logged on to her e-mail.

There was one waiting from her friend Sophia and two advertising sales from her favorite retailers. But nothing from the CDC. The silence spoke loudly to Jane and she knew that Angie had been right when she said Jane was on her own.

For a minute she wasn't sure what to do. She needed some outside help. She needed more than Mac working on the Amazon strain with her.

Knowing it was a big risk, she addressed an e-mail to Tom and Meredith. One of them had betrayed her. One of them was working against her. But one of them was still on her side and she really needed some help.

I'm at the Yura camp and my research is correct. They are infected with a lethal virus—the Amazon strain. Many are sick, but they are reluctant to trust me as some outsiders attempted to cure some of them and instead killed them three months ago. Meredith, I need you to find out what happened. We are going to notify government officials of the spread tomorrow. According to Dad's notes, the disease is spread by a parasitic tick that is carried by the lemurs of this area. The danger of spread is real and more people may be infected than we originally thought.

Tom, one woman is having an adverse reaction to the treatment. Were there any anomalies you saw when we were in the lab? Thanks, Jane.

Jane closed her eyes and prayed for time to speed quickly by, but she knew that when she wanted it to fly by, it never did. Instead, the hours and minutes would creep past and she'd be forced to sit and watch her own failure unfold.

Suddenly she opened her eyes and got to her feet. She wouldn't accept defeat. If her research was incorrect, she'd figure out the problem the way she always had. She was Dr. Jane Miller, level 4 virus hunter. A force to be reckoned with in the world of infectious diseases.

And nothing—not even Jane's own doubts—was going to stand in her way.

Chapter 17

Ernesto summoned her in the middle of the next night. Only the moon lit her way as she followed the path away from the village. She heard the steady beating of a drum, the same rhythm that had echoed through her body as she'd run through the forest with Tambo.

She hesitated when she smelled the smoke of the night fire and heard the sounds of dancing. The drum continued to beat and she felt called forward. Jane stood just to the side of the clearing, watching the Yura who were present. She couldn't identify any of them. They all wore red-and-blue paint on their face and only a loincloth. The women danced with their breasts free and swirled around the men, who sat on the ground in front of the fire.

Jane took another step closer and then stopped.

Though part of this ceremony called her to join in, the part of herself that she was more familiar with warned her to stay back. She hesitated another second and then turned to leave.

She got as far as a fallen log and brushed aside some vines to sit down. A few minutes later a man appeared on the path. He came up to her and sat down next to her.

She saw at once that it was Ernesto and she wondered what he'd wanted from her. "I can't—"

"Don't explain. You fear what is inside you."

"There's nothing inside me that I fear. I know myself too well for that."

"Then why did you leave?"

"I was uncomfortable."

"Because?"

He had her. No way was she going to lie to the shaman of the Yura while she waited to tend his people. While he held power over the one thing she really needed to do. "Okay. There is a part of myself that I don't want to confront. Happy?"

"Of course not. Perhaps you don't know what you lack."

"Courage," she said.

He shook his head. "Your courage is like a herald that runs in front of you and lets everyone know what you are."

She didn't understand him. Was afraid to believe what he said, because many of her actions had been motivated by not letting anyone see her fears. That wasn't courage, she thought. That was bravado.

"You can't see it, which is why you need to find the missing part of yourself."

"How can I find what I don't know I lack?"

"You'll have to seek it through your friends."

"I'm not sure I have any here."

"You carry them with you. Your friendships take the place of the family you've never had." She thought of Angie and Tom—were they her friends? Then her mind shifted to Sophia…and Mac.

It was embarrassing to hear him speak of these things. She knew she'd always been searching but she didn't want the world to know this. "I—"

"Now isn't the time to talk. It is your time to listen. While I was on my vision quest, your spirit animal came to me."

Jane was afraid to ask. Though she was open to many different beliefs and belief systems, she didn't want to think that something she lacked in her spirit was out there waiting for her.

"I can't. I'm sorry, Ernesto. I'm just not ready for this."

She tried to get up but he held her fast with an iron grip on her arm. "Look at me."

She turned to face him and he put his hands on her face, caged her head within his hold. She stared into his ebony eyes and saw something she couldn't really define.

Something that made her realize how small she was in the large chasm of time and space. How small her petty worries were when compared to ignoring the calling that this life had for her. How small her fears were compared to living her life without her spirit guide.

"Tell me," she said.

"You are a jaguar, but you've always run from it.

Hidden behind the work in your lab where you can safely close yourself off from people. But you are meant to heal, Jane. Not just find cures. And only when you acknowledge and carry the jaguar in your heart will that happen."

"I don't know if I can."

"Yes, you can. You saw it in my eyes. And now I see it in yours."

He let go of her face and Jane closed her eyes for a second. When she opened them she was alone. She wondered if she'd dreamed the entire thing, but felt a piece of leather around her neck. She reached up to touch it. There was a charm dangling there.

She didn't have to look down to realize it was a tiny jaguar. She pushed to her feet and walked back to the camp.

The new knowledge of herself swirled within her but she didn't understand it or how to tap into it. She only wished she did.

The sound of heavy rain woke Jane just before dawn. She was lying on her side on the cot and a blanket had been pulled over her. She blinked open her eyes and scanned the room. Mac sat on a chair next to her father. Both men were speaking in quiet voices.

"Then what happened?"

"Jane came out of the jungle surrounded by four warriors. She took complete control of the situation."

"That's my girl. She doesn't know how to let anyone else sit in the driver's seat." There was a subtle pride in her father's voice.

Jane felt tears burn the back of her eyes. For so many

years she'd felt as if she'd been a disappointment to her
dad. As if she didn't measure up to his expectations of
a daughter or a virologist. But listening to him now…
well, she realized a few things that she'd never noticed
before. She wiped her eyes on the sheet.

"She's hardheaded as hell but she knows her stuff,"
Mac said.

Jane sat up in the bed before either of them said
anything else. "Hello, pot, it's the kettle calling."

Mac threw his head back and laughed. And for the
first time since she left Atlanta, Jane felt truly good.
Deep inside, where the fear for her father and her fear
of the Amazon strain had lain. But this morning the sun
streamed through the windows and her dad was sitting
up watching her.

His hazel eyes were clear and calm. He was still too
thin, but his gaze was alert and his skin color wasn't
gray anymore. His light brown hair was long, hanging
around his shoulders, and she noticed he had a new tattoo on his left shoulder. It was similar to the one that
Ernesto had on his arm.

"Good morning, Jane," he said.

"Morning, Dad," she said. Emotion overwhelmed
her. There were so many things she wanted to say to
him. So many questions she wanted to ask. So many
words and yet none of them would come easily to her.
Not now.

"When did he wake up?" Jane asked Mac. It had
been a little less than twenty-four hours since she'd
started the medication drip. Jane ran that number
through her mind. It fit with what she'd found in the lab.

"About three hours ago. I documented everything,"

Mac said softly. She noticed he had a notepad in his hands—her notepad.

"Why didn't you wake me?" she asked.

"I tried. You were exhausted," he said.

She reached up and touched the jaguar charm around her neck. It was still there. She didn't remember moving to the cot or covering herself up last night. She'd been sitting between the two beds and just trying to will both of her patients to respond to the treatment.

"Can't your old man get a hug, kid?"

She hurried to his side and leaned down to hug him. His arms felt a little weak and he shook as he hugged her, but there was strength in his arms that reassured her. She closed her eyes and rested her head against his shoulder, feeling something she'd never experienced before—the impulse to let her dad help her carry this burden. To lean on him.

But she couldn't. She kissed him on the cheek and stood back up. Mac was watching her with his unreadable light blue eyes. "What about Selena?"

"She's like your dad was about six hours ago."

"Not out of the woods yet? What about her breathing? And the bleeding?"

"She had a small bleed from her nose about two hours ago but her breathing has evened out."

"Where's Ernesto?" Jane asked. She hoped that now he'd let her treat the village. Her father's recovery should aid in making that happen. But how was she going to convince him that she had the jaguar in her soul?

"He's still on his spirit quest," Mac said.

Mac didn't know that Ernesto had been successful. Or had she dreamed that whole thing last night?

"I sent an e-mail to Meredith and Tom last night asking for some further information on the disease. I'm worried about Selena. Dad, do you think Ernesto would allow us to move her to a hospital in Lima or La Paz?"

"Maybe. He'd have to believe there was no other way."

"We're not to that point yet," Mac said. "Are we?"

"No. We're not," Jane said. She looked down at Selena, brushing her hand over the woman's forehead. She wished there were easy answers. But science, though exacting and supported by research, always had variables that sometimes couldn't be controlled.

Mac pulled a second chair up to her father's cot and gestured for Jane to sit down. "We have some questions."

"I figured you would," Jane's father said.

"Did you bring Raul here?"

"No, he came to me. I think he was surprised to find me living here."

"Who was with him?"

"Tom Macmillan and Yabidwa Rodriguez."

Mac's blood brother. And...Tom. She didn't want to think about the fact that Tom had been here with Raul. That meant she'd been betrayed not once but twice by men she'd trusted.

Jane stood up and walked away from her father and Mac. She tried to remember what she'd said to Tom. He'd come to her. Offered his help—and then what? He couldn't have sent any of her research to Raul, because there simply hadn't been time. Or had there? She'd left him in her lab. Trusted him, because they'd been friends.

"Jane?" Mac took a step toward her, but it was too much. She needed to get away.

She shook her head and walked out of the cabin. She needed time to think.

She almost wished she could keep walking into the jungle and never have to deal with any men again. Not her father, whom she'd never trusted to stay and be there for her, and not Mac, whom she was coming to trust because he was always there even when she expected him not to be.

Jane found Paulo with a group of warriors and pulled him aside. "Would you do me a favor?"

"What do you need?"

"I think the governments of Peru and Brazil need to be aware of what's going on here. This disease is being spread via the animals in the jungle and we need to quarantine the area."

"The last time the government was here, men died."

"I'm aware of that. But my father is recovering and I hope that Selena will be by the end of the day. It's time to work together."

Paulo nodded. "I'll talk to the men and let you know our decision."

He started to walk away but Jane stopped him by grabbing his arm. "Paulo, time is the enemy here. If it spreads beyond the Amazon basin, there will be more deaths and more outsiders here."

He put his hand over hers and looked into her eyes, saying nothing. She did her best to look earnest and not panicked, because she was beginning to believe that unless they got more people here and quickly the disease would spread rampantly. "I'll do my best."

She nodded and pulled her hand free of his. He walked away and she could only watch him go.

She rubbed the back of her neck, feeling as though someone was watching her. She glanced around and saw Mac standing in the doorway of her father's cabin. The intensity of his gaze as he watched her was almost physical.

He confused her more than most men. There was something elusive about him and the way he never quite revealed his own agenda. Yet at the same time he'd always been completely honest with her. He'd admitted he didn't trust her, but at least she knew where she stood with him.

Overcome by everything that had happened in the last few days, Jane spun on her heel and stalked away. She needed to regain her perspective. She needed to find that strength deep inside herself. Ironically it was the same well she'd drawn from when her father had been disgraced at the CDC. She'd always been able to move on. This time it was important to make sure that no one saw the chinks in her armor.

Her ex-lover and a man she considered a friend were working together against her. Jane hardly noticed the path she took. Just went deeper into the dense jungle surrounding the village. The plants and trees around her were healthy and alive. She found a quiet spot, checked for insects and sat down in the middle of the jungle. The rain forest made her feel small and very aware of the fragility of human life.

Betrayal was something she should be used to. Her

business could be very cutthroat. The fact that she'd thought she'd worked in a group where everyone was working for the greater good didn't mean everyone really was. She'd left herself open for duplicity. And she wouldn't again.

She heard footsteps and turned to see Mac standing there. He didn't say anything.

"Is Dad okay? Selena?"

"Everyone's fine. It's you I'm worried about."

"Don't," she said.

"Don't worry about you?"

"Yes. I can take care of myself."

"I know that. But I have to worry about you."

"Why?" she asked, knowing she didn't really want to hear his answer but unable to stop herself.

"Because I care about you."

"I can't do this right now, Mac. I just can't. I'm not sure I'll ever be able to believe anyone again."

He closed the distance between them and sank to the ground, pulling her into his arms. Jane struggled. She was vulnerable and she didn't want Mac to know it. She knew how men thought. Knew that in their minds, vulnerability equaled weakness and she was determined he would never see her as weak.

But Mac wouldn't let her resist. He pulled her forward, wrapping her in a hug that left no doubt of his strength. She closed her eyes, pretending for a moment that no one could see this. That Mac didn't realize that she needed his strength. It wasn't a physical thing—it was the emotional strength she needed.

"Where'd you get this necklace?" he asked, brushing a hand against the charm.

"From Ernesto."

His shoulders were hard and muscled and for the first time ever she was glad of his power, glad that it outmatched her own, because it gave her the freedom to just lie there.

His hands roamed up and down her back. She knew he meant the embrace to be comforting, but when he tipped her chin up toward his face, she felt the timbre change. She knew this was her chance to change this notion of her vulnerability.

"Does it mean something?" he asked.

"No, nothing," she said, not wanting to talk about Ernesto and the jaguar. Leaning up she traced the seam of his lips with her tongue. He groaned deep in his throat and opened his mouth for her. Jane took her time teasing him. She loved his taste. Deeply, inherently masculine, he was like a sweet addiction that she couldn't get enough of. She pushed her tongue slowly into his mouth.

He tilted his head. His hands moved up her back, holding the back of her neck. The languid strokes of her tongue were met with slow thrusts of his.

Every nerve ending in her body came alert. She pushed on his shoulders and he fell backward. Jane moved over him, straddling his body. He watched her with that enigmatic gaze of his. A part of her knew that this wasn't the wisest course of action, but she was tired of denying herself. Tired of waiting for answers that seemed elusive. Tired of not taking what she wanted when it was right here in front of her.

She unbuttoned his shirt and brushed it aside, scraping her hands over his chest. He was lean with a light dusting of hair. She tangled her fingers in the thatch and tugged. Mac's hands tightened on her body, drawing her down toward him. Leaning up until his mouth met hers.

"I knew you'd be fire in my arms," he said.

"I didn't realize you were thinking about me," she said, nibbling against his jaw. She traced a path to the base of his neck and bit him carefully.

He groaned her name. His hips thrust upward against her thigh. She felt his hardening erection and knew the time for conversation and for teasing was over.

She didn't stop to think. Too much had happened in the last few days and she needed to just let go. So she did, letting her instincts take over.

Each pull of his mouth on hers drew her deeper into the sexual abyss that had beckoned since they'd first met. Deception, doubt and desire combined in a potent cocktail that left no room for anything but total surrender to each other.

He tasted of the mint gum he always chewed and something that she associated only with him. It was indefinable. She closed her eyes and let the jungle rhythm fill her from the inside out.

His mouth on hers was hot and his kiss deep and carnal. He pulled deeply on her lips as if trying to meld them together forever.

She undulated against him, enjoying the feel of his erection against her softness. His cock was hard, thick and hot even through the fabric of his pants. She slid her hands down his legs and cupped him. He wrapped his arms around her body and rolled until she was underneath him.

"Every time you issued an order, I thought of having you like this beneath me," he said.

"This isn't about power," she said quickly.

The ground was hard and a root dug into her back but his mouth on hers and his hands on her body blurred that. The only thing that mattered was the feelings that they generated together. Her entire body was on fire and blood flowed heavy in her veins, pooling in her center. She arched up into him rubbing against him and trying to find some relief from the delicious ache that grew more intense with each brush of his body against hers.

"God, woman," he muttered. He pulled her T-shirt off and then pushed her bra out of his way and stared down at her. "Yes, it is. It's about the kind of power neither of us is in control of."

There was a look in his eyes that she'd never seen before. His words echoed in her mind and she knew—just knew—that she'd lost something to him that she really hadn't been ready to give him.

She shivered as he caressed her breasts with sure hands. Rubbing his palm over her flesh, cupping and molding her. She arched upward again and he froze for a minute. Then supporting her back, lifted her until he could suckle at her breast.

He scraped his teeth over her nipple once, twice and then when she thought she'd die if he didn't do more, he finally placed his lips around her aroused flesh and suckled strongly. Her womb contacted as he brought her to the edge of orgasm with his mouth on her breasts. She clawed at his back, realizing that she was totally at his mercy.

No, she thought. She pushed and shoved at his shoulders until he rolled over. She was back on top of him at once and realized that this man would always be stronger than her. But that he'd always let her take control. The jaguar charm at her neck burned with her body heat.

Reaching between their bodies she unfastened his pants and shoved them out of the way. His cock sprang free from his boxers. Thick, hard and red...ready for her. She encircled him with her hand and wished she had more time for him. But the need inside her was too urgent. She unfastened her pants with one hand. Shoved them out of her way. They caught on her boots and Mac pushed her legs apart at the knees. It was an awkward pose but it worked.

She fumbled, pushing him toward her center. She was wet and he slid in easily. She braced her hands on his shoulders and looked straight into his eyes as she took him into her body. Again that emotion flickered across his face, but it was gone before she could identify it. He slid his hands up and down her body. Caressing her breasts, lingering to tease her belly button and then skimming over her mound.

His touch was butterfly-light and he kept it that way, teasing her as she thrust her hips, bringing him tightly inside her sheath and then letting him slip almost all the way out.

"You're toying with me," he said.

She liked it. She'd never been in charge before. She always demanded satisfaction from her lovers because she didn't see the point in doing this otherwise. But with Mac she wanted to linger and tease and find out what he liked.

"I thought you said it was mutual power."

He gripped her hips and held her still for his thrusts. They were stronger than hers had been. She was impaled by him as he went deeper than he had before. She started to tremble, felt the waves of his possession slowly spreading outward until there wasn't a part of her body that he wasn't reaching with each of those thrusts.

"Give me your breast," he grunted. The words were barely audible, so harsh and gritty was his voice. Shivers spread down her body at his tone. God, he was one sexy man.

She leaned forward and his mouth closed over one breast, sucking her deeply. She gasped and held his head to her. Tightening her body around him until she felt the first tingles of orgasm deep inside her. She rocked harder against him.

He bit her lightly and she cried his name as all sensation coalesced and she came. He thrust up into her, then she felt the moist heat of his seed as he came inside her.

He fell backward on the ground, pulling her down on top of him. She lay there, her knees sore and a little raw from the ground. Her breath sawed in and out of her lungs as if she'd just been running. Her heart beat so hard she knew he could hear it.

He rubbed his hands up and down her back, soothing her now that their passion was spent. She closed her eyes and didn't feel regret. She'd needed what he'd offered but she knew she'd let things change between them. Not just for Mac but for her. And it bothered her because she'd never slept with a man like Mac. She'd never let a man like him close to her.

Jane shifted off Mac and got awkwardly to her feet. She tugged her shirt down over her breasts and then pulled her pants up. She turned her back on him to fasten them. God, she had no idea what to say.

"Don't," he said, gruffly.

"What?" she asked, refusing to play along with him. She needed to get away. She needed to find her footing again because being with him had rocked her.

He came closer. She heard his footsteps and his body heat a second before he put his hand on her shoulder. "Put up barriers. It's too late for that."

"I wasn't…" She couldn't do this. The man-woman thing was the one place where she wasn't sure of herself. Give her a life-and-death situation. Give her a lethal disease that was spreading out of control. Those things she could handle and if they were hard or a challenge at least she knew she was up for it. But this…she never had been good at building relationships and she doubted she'd changed all that much in the two days they'd been with the Yura.

"Yes, you were. I wasn't expecting this, either. We'll figure it out later."

She couldn't believe he called her on it. That told her more than anything else how seriously Mac treated her and what had happened between them.

"Much later," she said, taking two steps away from him. She turned around so that he didn't think she was hiding from him. He stood a few feet from her and she noticed he'd fixed his clothes, as well.

The clothing didn't matter. She realized she could still smell him on her skin. Feel him in the wetness between her legs. Taste him on her lips and tongue. Her breasts were still so sensitive that her bra was a painful abrasion, making her long for the softness of his tongue and mouth again.

And that was what bothered Jane the most. She longed for no man because she'd decided long ago that men were only temporary and wanting one hurt a lot more than living without one. She stalked past him and walked back to the village, stopping abruptly when she saw Raul standing in the middle of the clearing with a gun trained on her.

Chapter 18

"Hello, Jane," he said.

She noticed the four men standing behind him all holding assault rifles loosely in their arms. She recognized Carl from their first encounter in the jungle. He had a bandage on his arm where she'd wounded him. His skin was ashen and his eyes seemed hollow with dark bags underneath them. Raul wasn't taking care of his men.

She still didn't completely understand what was going on. But she knew better than to question him now. The village clearing, which had been filled with the Yura going about their business earlier, was now empty.

"Raul. What are you doing here?" she asked, trying to seem nonchalant. Dammit, she'd gone complacent. So thrown by Tom's betrayal she hadn't even taken a weapon with her when she'd left her father's cabin. She had no weapon but she knew that it'd take more than Raul Veracruz had to capture her.

"What I was called to do," he said. He took her arm and led her to the lab. Once inside he closed the door. She saw his men continue to stay in position monitoring all entrances to the camp.

His calling? That was rich. Since when did making money for a big drug company count as a calling? "I don't understand what's going on. You've been following us, right?"

He nodded. "Yes, I have. Why did you run from me, Jane?"

"You set fire to my camp, Raul. I decided not to wait around and chat with you."

He shrugged. "It no longer matters. I have what I need now."

He gestured to the lab she'd been using. Anger began to build slowly, spreading throughout her body. She'd endured more than she wanted to recall to get here. And now Raul thought she was going to turn her research, her work, her results over to him? He had to be out of his mind.

"Why were you following me?" she asked at last. Though deep inside she knew the answer. Raul was good at working in the lab, but he had never learned to think outside the box. He'd never learned to look for new patterns, something she and Tom had never had any problem doing. She wondered if Tom realized that he'd probably become roadkill under the tires of Raul's ambition to find his big outbreak and treatment.

"Because I needed the treatment for the virus," he said.

Jane knew she had to keep him talking. She sensed that Mac was out there waiting for the right moment to make his move. Between the two of them they should be able to make some kind of stand. She knew she'd have to be ready to move when he did. "I know you were here before. I know about the men who died."

"Your father is better, I take it?" Raul asked. Jane thought she heard genuine concern in his voice. Which puzzled her, because keeping this disease quiet had put her father's life in jeopardy.

"Yes, he is much improved. I haven't been able to treat many of the Yura, though. They distrust us," she said.

"That's my fault. But I think that will change when they see the remarkable improvement in your father's condition," Raul said simply. Again she was struck by the caring in his voice. He did want to heal others and she wondered if that wasn't what motivated him to do this. Because the emotions were suddenly becoming clear to her.

"You tried to heal them before," she said out loud.

"You're damn right I did. My family lives just downriver from the Yura. I didn't want them to become infected."

"How'd you hear about it?"

"Why do you want to know?" Raul asked.

"Because I'm not sure how the disease is spread," she said. "We've never worked together, Raul. Let's do it now. Let's figure this out together."

"We can't, Jane."

"Why not?" she asked, but in her gut she already knew why.

"Because you are going to be responsible for the outbreak. You've been trying to hog the glory of the find, but you waited too long."

"You don't have to do this, Raul. Let's work together here," she said.

"You don't understand. It's too late for that," he said. "There's nothing left for you to do but wait for the Peruvian government to come and arrest you. I'm afraid the name Miller isn't really that reliable."

The anger that had been burning inside her almost exploded. She had to clench her fists to keep from beating the crap out of him. She waited only because she needed more answers. She wanted information that only two people had—Raul, and Tom. She needed to know what went wrong with the Yura tribesmen they'd taken. She needed that information because Selena wasn't responding to the medication as well as Jane would like.

"I'm not going to lie about this. I'm not going down without a fight," she said, warning him.

"I've always admired your spirit, Jane."

"Was that what you admired? I thought it was my ass."

He threw his head back and laughed. "God, I've missed you. You always were so feisty."

"Tell me what's going on here. Why didn't you come clean in Lima when we were at the hotel?"

"I wasn't sure what you had found. I have a contact at the CDC who's been keeping me posted."

Tom, she thought. She clenched her fists. Where was Mac? How long had Raul been in the village?

Would he know that she'd sent Paulo for the authorities? "When did you arrive?"

"A few minutes ago. I asked to speak to Ernesto."

"I'm not sure he's available," Jane said.

"He is to me."

"Why?"

"Because we are cousins. He trusts me."

"I don't think so," Jane said. She knew better than to believe Raul. She knew Ernesto no longer trusted the men who'd come into his village, taken his sick brothers and never returned them.

"I know so. Just like I know that, when they check the medicine you brought with you, they'll find that it's actually the disease and instead of treating Selena you've been making her sicker."

"What?"

"I paid Paulo to slip inside and exchange the IV drip last night while you were sleeping."

No longer able to control her rage, she doubled her fist and punched him right in the jaw. His head snapped backward and blood spurted from his nose. He advanced on her but Jane stood her ground, ready to kick his ass and then try to save Selena.

Outside the sound of gunfire echoed in the afternoon silence. Raul turned on her, slashing out with his left hand in a chopping motion toward her neck. She ducked out of his way but he still connected with her shoulder and it hurt.

She remembered the first time they'd made love and how sweet he'd been. The man standing before her now would kill to get what he wanted. "I'm not your enemy."

He sneered at her. "You always have been."

"I don't understand," she said, trying to ease away

from him. But he attacked her again, this time kicking her in the side.

She groaned and pivoted out of his way. She hit him hard with a kick that connected solidly with his groin. He staggered backward, muttering words in Spanish that she couldn't understand.

"Yes, you do. Your father was always holding you up as some sort of prodigy that the rest of us couldn't compete with."

No one had ever indicated that her father thought of her as anything other than a disappointment. She'd known when he'd finally settled in Atlanta at the CDC that he wanted to have some sort of relationship with her, but she'd never realized that he might have been proud of her work. "That's not true. Dad never thought I cut muster."

"Yes, he did. And the rest of us—I wasn't good enough to be his assistant."

"Then why did you date me?" she asked. Because that long-ago affair seemed to be taking on a new meaning. She'd thought… What a fool she'd been…she'd actually thought that Raul had been interested in her because they had so much in common.

"To twist the knife. To show your father that his second-rate assistant was sleeping with his precious daughter."

"You are wrong. He didn't care about that. Every time I talked to him he told me how brilliant you were," she said, though the words weren't true. Raul had always been a fair to middling scientist. Not bad, but not really that great.

"It doesn't matter. He knew I was screwing you and he hated that."

Jane hesitated. She'd let herself be used by this man. How could she have been so blind? Raul punched her hard in the stomach and Jane dropped to her knees. God, that hurt. Oh, God, she couldn't breathe. She struggled back to her feet to face Raul. Tears of pain blurred her eyes and he laughed.

"That's right. Daddy's little girl, and you shut him out. Even told me how you weren't sure you could ever forgive him for leaving you when you were a kid."

She tuned him out. Raul knew things about her that she thought she'd hidden not only from him but the world. She stopped thinking and just reacted. Her ears were buzzing, no doubt from the lack of air, but breathing slowly became easier and she attacked him again. This time from a more rational place.

She remembered the moves from her kickboxing class and executed them with as much precision as her battered body could produce. Her final side kick connected with his solar plexus. Jane felt a thrill of victory when he groaned and grabbed his side.

"Bitch."

"Aw, thanks!"

But she kept moving toward him, hoping to corner him. And then what? She glanced around the lab and saw her discarded camp shirt. She'd use that to bind his arms. If she could overpower him.

There was a lunacy in Raul's eyes that she'd never noticed before. She wondered if she could talk him out of whatever rage he was building up to. She needed him to calm down because fighting a madman was draining her.

"I'm not your enemy."

"You said that before. You can't change my mind, Jane. I've set myself on a path that I can't turn back from."

"Oh, Raul. There's always a way back."

"Not this time. I helped spread this disease. It wasn't the lemurs. They weren't infected until we fed them the disease."

"Why would you do that?"

"There was no other way. Thompson-Marks hired me to find a new breakthrough."

"In infectious diseases?" she asked. That made no sense. Thompson-Marks was in the business of selling drugs, not in finding new illnesses.

"No, in cancer drugs. But I couldn't. No matter how I searched the rain forest there was nothing…but then I found something that I could work with. I mutated a strain of Lassa fever."

"Except once you mutated it, you didn't know how to treat it," she said.

"Yes. And time was running out. People started dying and I went to my bosses, mentioning this new disease."

"How did you keep the Peruvian government from issuing an alert?"

"My boss did that. I worked long hours in the lab with that mutated strain but the treatment for Lassa didn't work even when I mutated it. When I heard the Yura were infected I came here immediately. But when I saw your father…"

"Things got worse," Jane supplied. She stepped closer to Raul. But he turned in fighting stance.

"Keep your distance, Jane. The next time I hit you, you won't get back up."

He advanced on her and she knew she'd made a mistake. Keeping him talking would have been better. She edged around the long table in the middle where she'd set up her computer. Searching the top for a weapon she found nothing. Dammit.

Then she realized that Raul was confident of his bigger body frame and his skills. Taking a deep breath she tried to remember what her instructor had taught her about using an attacker's momentum against him.

Raul swung his leg up in an extended side kick and Jane moved closer to counter with a punch to his stomach. She grabbed his ankle and his arm and then brought her left foot up to trip him to the floor.

Using her grip on his shoulder she pushed him down and then straightened, still holding one of his legs, and brought the heel of her foot down hard on his groin. He curled into a ball and lay on the floor. Jane reached for the shirt in the corner and quickly bound his arms together. Then she used the laces from his boots to bind his feet.

She climbed to her feet and took another vial of the treatment from the refrigerator, knowing that Raul had poisoned Selena and that he wouldn't hesitate to keep infecting the Yura until he reached his goal of discrediting her.

The village had been turned into a battlefield. Shots were fired in that rapid-fire tattoo that echoed in her head.

Guilt weighed heavily on her shoulders. She was responsible for this. Raul had fixated on her and her father, and then on these people, trying to prove he was something he could never be. It was a lesson that Jane had learned in childhood when she'd struggled to be a better athlete than she was. There were limits on what could be accomplished and no amount of desire to be better could change that sometimes.

Raul's men fired at anyone who moved. But someone was challenging them from the rain forest and she'd bet her last dollar that it was Mac. She hoped it was Mac. Because if it wasn't, he was probably dead. And she wasn't ready to lose him yet.

Jane hurried back into the lab and found her knife and Mac's spare gun. Raul screamed obscenities at her until she shoved a roll of gauze into his mouth. Then she pinched his carotid artery until his eyes rolled back in his head.

Jane's body ached from the hits she'd received. Her heart beat so fast she had to pause in the doorway before stepping out into the village again. She didn't know where the village warriors were, but she hoped many of them had bonded with Mac.

Jane eased the door open. She saw several Yura warriors starting to line the perimeter of the village. Raul's men were outnumbered but they weren't giving up. Carl saw her standing in the doorway. She saw the instant of recognition on his face before he fired directly at her. She fell to the ground, trying to stay as low as possible. There was little to use for cover and Jane wondered if she'd made a fatal mistake.

She lifted her head and saw Carl striding toward her, aiming at her point-blank. But before he fired someone shot him. He fell to the ground in front of her, dead, his eyes open and still filled with hatred. She reached out and closed his eyes.

Jane moved cautiously forward on her belly. Just staying low seemed to be the key to staying alive. She moved forward, aware that each second was a second out of Selena's life.

She paused as the firefight began to die out. She rolled into the hanging vines that surrounded the village proper. Crouching, she half walked, half ran toward the cabin. Standing, she leaned back against the walls. She heard movement inside the building. She hoped she wasn't too late.

Choosing each step carefully, she eased around to the front of the building. She couldn't crawl up the steps. She'd be exposed for about twenty seconds. And that was all the time it took to die.

She uttered a quick prayer and then ran, bounding up the steps in one leap. The air around her face stirred as a bullet whizzed past her. She tucked and rolled through the screen door. Her side ached, but she pushed up to her feet.

Her father was propped in his bed, his old Colt .45 revolver in his hands. "What the hell is going on?"

Tears burned the back of her eyes as she saw him alive. She'd feared that Raul had maybe taken the time to kill his old mentor before seeking her out. "You don't want to know, Dad," Jane said. There were bullet holes in the wall.

"The hell I don't," he said. Though he wasn't at full strength physically she felt the force of his will and his determination. Rob Miller was no weakling waiting to die.

Bending low, she brushed her lips against his cheek. "I love you."

"I love you, too, sweetheart."

"Raul's here. I think you and I may be responsible for all of this. I can't talk about it now, but I wanted you to know that people we thought are friends might not be."

"I already figured that part out. What's wrong with Selena?" he asked.

"Raul reinfected her last night to make the Yura distrust me."

"Can you save her?" her dad asked.

That was the one thing she wasn't really sure of. Two days ago she'd been cocky in her own faith in herself. She'd known she could save the world or if not the world then the Yura. But now...she just wasn't sure anymore.

"I don't know, Dad. God, I hope so." She didn't say anything else because if she did, she'd talk herself out of doing what she knew she had to. Giving Selena two treatments back-to-back wasn't something that Jane had calculated in her research. She'd never figured that someone would deliberately infect a recovering person with the same disease their body had just battled.

"If anyone can do it you can."

The quiet confidence in his voice made her feel better. She felt a pulse leap in her neck and the jaguar charm was hot again. She heard the drums again in her mind. This time they seemed to be beating out the word "heal." It kept repeating over and over and she knew she had to try.

She left his side and went to Selena's. She removed the drip bag from the IV tube and put it aside. She took a new bag, put the treatment in it and then hung it up.

As she watched, the medicine slowly dripped down the line. Into the back of Selena's hand. Slowly entering her system.

Jane hoped it wasn't too late. She took Selena's pulse. Felt the moment the medication entered her bloodstream because her body jolted. Was it too much? She wished they had more time to counteract the spreading virus. Wished she was in a real medical facility where she'd have state-of-the-art equipment and more doctors with second opinions.

Instead she had to rely on her gut. And for the first time in her life all of her research and connections weren't there. Jane realized in that moment that she stood by her decision. That she'd made the right choice—the only choice she could make and whatever the outcome, she'd know she'd done everything in her power to save this young woman's life.

Chapter 19

The gunfire stopped. Jane got up to check on the outcome. She had Mac's gun shoved in the back of her pants. Her dad kept the Colt ready and both of them were cautious.

"What's going on?" her dad asked.

"Nothing. There are several men down. Not all of them are Raul's. We need to set up a triage unit to start helping the wounded." Her mind was reeling and she didn't really know who to trust. Her dad, because he was clearly on the side of those wanting to stop the disease. Mac, if he was still alive. God, there was a part of her that wanted to rush outside and go find him. She wanted to see him come striding into the village with his easy grace and know-it-all smile.

Jane gathered things in her father's cabin. He had a

good-size first-aid kit that included sutures and needles for stitching up wounds. She found bandages and a drip bag with morphine.

"Where did this come from?" she asked. He was outfitted like a MASH unit would be. And the dates on the medicines were current, not years old as they'd have to be if he'd brought them with him when he first came to the Yura.

"I always come prepared," he said with a wink.

Her old man was a charmer. It was a side to him that she'd never seen before. "So do I. But I didn't think to bring this much medicine."

"Well, Bob was dropping supplies for me every thirty days," he explained.

Bob. She remembered Angie saying that her father's old buddy had volunteered to bring her to him. "Someone messed with his plane. We almost didn't make it here. Bob is…" She couldn't say it.

"I know. Mac told me about it while you were sleeping."

Her father drew her into his arms and held her. She turned her head into his shoulder, blinking to hide tears she didn't want him to see. She'd never realized how much she'd missed him until this moment.

"God, girl, I missed you."

"Me, too," she said, realizing that she meant more than just the last few years since he'd left the CDC. She'd missed him forever. Finally she knew how much she had in common with the man who'd shaped her life by always being gone. And she knew that she was following in his path. Would she be alone in the jungle, dying of an infectious disease some day? Because the way her relationship skills were shaping up, she didn't see a man in her future.

Though Mac was stubborn and she doubted he'd leave at first. Did she want him to stay?

"They really need assistance out there," she said, uncomfortable with the direction of her own thoughts.

"Go ahead. I'll watch Selena."

Jane hesitated.

"Dammit, girl, you still can't trust me, can you?" he asked. She was surprised by the anger in his voice. But once she heard it, she realized she'd be the same way. It was hard to know that some actions in people's lives could never be outlived or outrun.

"No, Dad. It's not you." But a part of her acknowledged it was. Not because of anything he'd done in the past but because she couldn't let go of the control. If her father took over watching Selena and something happened, or if he misrecorded a detail, she wouldn't know how to trace the steps and figure out what happened.

"How can you say that? I'm here and I'm qualified to handle this."

"You're still recovering," she said. He was still pale, though he looked much healthier today than he had yesterday.

"Yes, but not from the disease. Funny that I could beat death but can't beat my rep. Don't worry, Jane, I'll make sure everyone knows you did your best in spite of having me as a dad."

"For God's sake, stop it. My problems aren't with you and your reputation. My problems are with control. And I think you're partially to blame for that, as well.

I don't like not knowing what's going on every second with a patient. I'd do the same thing if Meredith or any other virologist was standing here with me."

He narrowed his eyes, staring at her, and Jane knew she'd said too much. But it was too late to call the words back. She wouldn't, even if she could, because there was a part of her father that was going to have to make his own peace with his past. "Can you stand?" she asked him.

"Yes," he said, pushing to his feet. He swayed and she worried that he might fall over but she didn't rush to his side. The fierceness in his gaze warned her away.

"Good. Call me if you need me," she said, leaving the cabin before she did anything else she'd regret. She knew she had issues. She knew she should have left them in Atlanta, but they were so deeply ingrained. She knew that it would take way more than a few light moments to erase a lifetime of patterns.

And despite the recovery her father had made, despite having had sex with Mac in the jungle, she knew that she was still afraid to let anyone—any man—close to her.

She stepped out of the cabin and eased her way slowly into the clearing. She felt tense and unsure until she saw the first wounded man. His eyes were wide open and he stared at her with a pain that was palpable.

She hurried to his side and started examining him. In that moment she knew where her true strength lay and she didn't question it. She was meant to be here. In the field, helping those who might not live if she wasn't here. And that affected her very deeply and made her glad she'd decided to leave the safety of Atlanta to come to the Yura.

* * *

Two of the men on the ground were dead. She recognized them as Raul's. She applied pressure to the wound of another man at her feet. His eyes were glazed over and he was in shock. She knew that she'd need to get him into a bed. Where was Mac?

"Get up."

Jane turned to see Ernesto standing above her, his AK-47 held loosely in his arms. For the first time since they met he had that look that made her realize the shaman was also a warrior.

"What's the matter?" she asked, trying to stay calm, but it was hard. He could kill her with one careless flick of his finger and she no longer believed she'd glibly live to a ripe old age. The rain forest had changed something inside her. She knew that life and death were balanced on the same sword's edge. She'd seen it briefly in Selena's eyes. Seen it in the eyes of the man who'd died earlier.

"Two of my men think you deliberately poisoned our people," Ernesto said. In his eyes she saw his shaman power and felt the palpable force of his anger. Ernesto had led her into the midst of the Yura and if she was responsible for harming them he'd deal out retribution.

"I'd like to know the names of my accusers," she said, not feeling particularly brave at this moment because she still wasn't certain what Ernesto had wanted to find in her eyes. She'd come closer to understanding herself in the last few days but still the kind of self-knowledge she needed for the shaman eluded her.

"Paulo is one of them. He says you reinfected—"

Ernesto broke off and Jane reached out for him. Saw the tormented husband behind the village leader. Knew in her heart that if Selena didn't live that this man was going to be inconsolable. Who could blame him? Certainly not her, she understood his pain and though she had no lover she'd kill for, she did understand the depth of those emotions. "Ernesto, you know me. You looked into my soul and saw what I lacked. I've used that awakened part of myself for your people and your wife."

That lack in Jane was the very emotion that had kept her always moving on and never staying with one man very long in any relationship. Even her friendship with Sophia drew its longevity from the fact that they both were career women and lived on opposite coasts.

"I can't prove anything but I wouldn't do that. Paulo knows it isn't true. Ernesto, you looked into my soul. You know I'm not capable of doing something like that.

"I'm not giving up on Selena. And you shouldn't, either. She's fighting the double dose of the disease that's in her body. She's a woman you should be very proud to call your mate."

"I am," he said.

Jane got to her feet and looked at Ernesto. Willed him to find the answers he'd been seeking in her since they first met. Because she'd found answers that she'd never thought to find. Answers about her life that had eluded her—but no longer.

She now knew that she'd always had her father in heart and that was a kind of reassurance it wouldn't have been before. She also knew that she was damned good at her job. She'd found the answers to a lethal disease that a number of other virologists hadn't.

"Put the gun down, Ernesto."

Mac had come up behind them. He held his handgun on Ernesto. Jane felt deep inside that if she had to witness one more person die today, she'd break down.

"No. He's scared, Mac. His people are dying, and we said we were coming here to help them. Let us do that now, Ernesto."

She saw the battle in both men's eyes but Jane couldn't—wouldn't—allow any more men to die. "The only way I can prove you wrong is to treat your people. And that's what I'm going to do.

"Raul is tied up in the lab. I think he can answer your questions, but I'm not going to let any more time pass before I start the work I came here to do." She had no way of getting through to him. Her only options were to do what she came here to do before anyone else arrived to stop them. The back of Jane's neck tingled with some undefined emotion that felt like something unresolved. Despite having defeated Raul there was still something bothering her about this situation.

"Let's go question him," Ernesto said. He came abreast of her and took her arm, holding her still.

Jane felt the tension in him and shook deep inside where she hid all her fears. She looked him straight in the eye and saw a man torn between desire and duty and she knew that was a rough place to be.

"You have questions and so do I, but we need to treat the people first. I was wrong to wait for you to decide if I could or not."

"I'll look into his eyes and know the answers to my questions. Then you can treat my people."

Jane led the way back to the lab, where she'd left Raul bound and gagged. As soon as she stepped inside she knew he was gone. She scanned the interior and he was nowhere to be found. Dammit.

Ernesto said nothing. Mac was equally silent but he moved into the room and examined the long, low tables and the centrifuge machine. "These have been tampered with."

Jane realized what had been bugging her. The refrigerator wasn't working. When she'd been in the lab earlier it had been silent.

She ran across the room and opened the refrigerator door and found the treatment vials all melting. The medicine was becoming active and they'd have less than four hours to use it before it would no longer be effective.

"This is wanton destruction. Something's wrong with Raul. He's not the man I remember."

"How can we be sure it was Raul?" Ernesto asked.

"We can't. You can trust me and save your people or you can continue to trust the man who killed two of your tribesmen. The choice is yours." Her jaguar charm was red-hot at her neck. She couldn't believe that Ernesto didn't see the same truth that was so clear to Jane.

Mac dropped back and went to work trying to fix the freezer. Jane appreciated the fact that he didn't jump in to try to solve this problem for her.

Jane set everything she was carrying on the table. "Your people are dying, Ernesto. It's not from Mac or I but from people you've trusted in the past. We can understand that you are reluctant to put your faith in us. But time is slipping away. Time that could be the difference between life and death."

Mac got the refrigerator humming again. "I'm going to start replicating the treatment, Jane."

Jane looked at Ernesto. "Can I help those with gunshot wounds?"

Ernesto nodded. She left Mac in the lab and went around to each of the wounded, bandaging those who were still bleeding. Two of the Yura warriors were in desperate need of a hospital.

When she'd done all she could for them, she went back to the lab to help Mac. Jane worked into the night with Mac at her side. They made a good team. She didn't dwell on the fact that she'd made a good team with Raul and Tom, as well. Mac was different and she knew it in her heart.

Selena was finally making progress. Either Jane, her dad or Mac stayed with the woman at all times. It was tiring, and Jane was more than ready for a nap when the end of her shift came. But Ernesto was waiting at the door with a line of Yura infected with the virus. They had to make more treatment.

"Dad, can you handle this? I'm going back to the lab."

"Yes," he said. Though he seemed fatigued, as well, he was on his feet and she saw in his eyes what she felt in her soul—this was what they were called to do.

Mac put down the clipboard where he'd been making notes. "I'll come with you."

"Thanks, Mac," she said.

"Hey, babe, this is why I signed on," he said, grabbing the back of her neck and pulling her close for a kiss.

"Did you just call me *babe?*" she asked, pulling back. The man was too cocky for his own good.

"Yeah. So?"

"I don't think I like it," she said.

"Good. It'll keep you on your toes, *babe.*"

She shook her head and walked past him. The Yura didn't look very good. The ones who were infected were eager to try her cure. They were sick of the fever and pain that went with the disease. Seeing them suffering started a slow burning rage in her.

Jane's father medicated as many of the sick as they had medicine for, then sent the rest back to their homes to await treatment. Jane and Mac worked in the lab. Ernesto shadowed Jane as if afraid to trust her and afraid not to.

Finally they were ready. She and Mac split up to give treatment. Jane had never worked harder in all her days. Ernesto followed her from house to house with his weapon at the ready. She wasn't sure if he was guarding his people or warning her, reminding her that any death would be her responsibility. She half expected him to demand she return the jaguar charm. But then she emerged from a house and found Ernesto gone.

Mac met her outside the fifteenth house. He held more bags containing the treatment. "We're out of IV stands."

"I ran out two houses ago. I've been rigging them up the best I can."

"How many more houses?"

"Two."

"I'll take one of them."

"Thanks. Did you check in with Dad?"

"Yes. Selena's breathing is settled, and though she hasn't awakened all the signs point to recovery."

Jane muttered a silent prayer, fighting to keep her expression serene. "Good."

"Yes, it is. How are you holding up?"

"I'm fine. Don't coddle me, Mac. I can handle this without breaking a sweat."

"We both know that you can't."

"Don't," she said, softly. "I need to believe I'm indestructible at least for a few more hours."

He cursed under his breath. "Okay. Don't go back to the lab on your own," he said, walking away.

Jane took the remaining bags of medicine and went into the cabin on the left. It was built the same as the others she'd been in. Except this family was one of the larger ones. And four people were in the two beds. In one, a woman cradled a toddler in her arms. A teen and an older woman shared a second bed.

"*Hola.* I am Jane."

"I'm Marcella."

The toddler, a boy, was breathing heavily. And there were traces of blood under his nose. Jane leaned closer to the woman.

"I'm here to help you."

"Help my son," she said.

"I will. I'm going to have to put a shunt in this hand. It will hurt, but only a little. Then I'll do the same for you."

Jane put the IV into the boy. He didn't even flinch when she pricked his skin. She looked around the room and found some string which she looped over the exposed beam in the roof and then suspended the bag from it.

"How long have you been sick?" she asked the woman as she worked on her, setting up the IV and drip.

"Three days. But little Jamie has been sick longer. Same with my daughter, Emilia."

"My father, *el médico,* was sick but has fully recovered."

"*El médico* is a good man."

"Yes, he is," Jane said. "It takes about a day to start seeing results."

The place was dark and dank and smelled of sickness. Jane crossed to the windows and opened them. The water basin was empty, she wanted to refill that. And to make sure that everyone was sleeping comfortably. "Is there anyone who can sit with you?"

"My son—here he is now," she said.

Jane turned as Paulo walked into the room. She didn't know what to say to him. He'd betrayed not only her but his people. He'd almost cost her a patient. And the wife of a very powerful man. One who would not hesitate to bring retribution to anyone responsible.

"What are you doing here?" Paulo asked, distrust and fury in his tone and body language.

"Helping your family," she said quietly. She wasn't going to argue with him. She'd done her job and would continue to do it. "They need some cool water to bathe them. Will you fetch it while I finish this last drip? Then I will give you some directions on what to watch for and how to care for them."

Jane could see that he was torn. He knew she'd spoken to Raul. Either that, or his own guilt over what he'd done was weighing heavily on him.

She'd always believed that in the end everyone had to answer to themselves. She had no idea what Raul had promised Paulo, but seeing his suffering family, she could think of nothing that would be worth it.

The teenager opened her eyes when Jane adjusted the blanket over her. Jane muttered soft words in English, reassuring the girl in a way that she couldn't do in Spanish. Long-ago words from her mother came to her and she uttered them without thinking.

They were a mother's prayer for a peaceful night's sleep. The teen recognized them. Jane saw it in her eyes. She took Jane's hand, holding it with a desperation that needed no translation. It was the anguished fear that she might not live. But Jane knew this girl would live. And she promised herself that she'd heal the Yura with her last breath if need be.

Chapter 20

"I wonder where Raul went," Mac said as they walked back to the lab.

"I'm sure he'll be back. I want to check on Dad and then try to contact the CDC again," she said. She was tired of operating outside of the organization. They needed more help here in the Amazon basin and Meredith needed to send it.

"Why?" Mac asked.

He had that tone. The one he always got when she talked about the CDC. She shivered a little, feeling chilly despite the humidity in the jungle. She was tired. Tired of fighting with everyone to simply get this job done. And she knew that, despite the fact that the Yura had been treated, this wasn't over. Raul wasn't going to quietly disappear. He'd be back.

"Why what?" she asked. She turned on him, getting up in his face and making him take a step backward.

"Why the CDC? They haven't given you an ounce of support here."

She shook her head. Mac was talking sense but she wasn't ready to blow off her fifteen-year career. She knew that the circumstances of this case made things difficult for Meredith. Jane wasn't so sure of Tom. "Believe me, I haven't forgotten."

"I'm not trying to make you forget."

"Just to make me angry," she said, sensing it was a deliberate move on his part.

"Well, it's an improvement over that pale look on your face."

She gave him a halfhearted smile. She wanted to curl up next to him and forget about all the troubles surrounding them. She knew this wasn't the time but soon, when the Yura were healed and Raul was brought to justice, she thought she might give it a try. "Are you trying to be my hero?"

"I'm afraid my answer will incriminate me."

She had nothing to say to that. He put his arm around her and hugged her close. Closing her eyes she let the rain forest drop away. Let the worries and fears that had been her constant companions for the last seven days disappear. Pretended she was just a woman with her man.

Then she tipped her head back and looked up at him. They weren't Adam and Eve and no matter how lush, this wasn't the Garden of Eden. Though Raul bore a striking similarity to a snake.

"Whatever is going through that supercomputer brain of yours, don't worry about me and you," he said.

"I'm not." Really, she wasn't. But even to her it sounded like a lie. She was thinking about Mac. Her last serious relationship had been with Raul almost five years ago and look at the fallout from that.

"I'd be offended but your eyes say otherwise."

She wasn't sure she liked that he was so perceptive when it came to her emotions. She wasn't about to admit that he was coming to mean something to her.

"How did we get here?" she asked. She was letting him manipulate her. They needed to focus on Raul. On where the Amazon strain would hit next and how to stop its spread. This other stuff, this relationship stuff, could wait.

"I was gathering my courage," he said.

She slipped out of his arms and started walking again. She didn't understand him. A part of Mac was like all the other men who'd mattered in her life. He was very like her father who blended seamlessly into cultures and with other peoples. He was very like Raul—driven to succeed in the field of virology and determined that nothing would stand in his way. And yet, at the same time, he was just himself and a mystery to her. "To do what?"

He stopped walking. Jane turned to face him, unsure of what to say. What if he asked her to move to Europe with him? What if he asked her to give up the CDC because he couldn't be involved with a woman who worked for them?

What if…? Her heart actually beat a little faster. Not because of what he might ask but the fact that she wanted him to ask her for something that had nothing to do with science. Or work. She wanted him to ask her because she was the only woman he wanted.

"To ask you to join me," he said at last.

"For?"

"Work. What were you thinking?"

"I was thinking work, of course," she said, hoping she sounded blasé. But she doubted it. She was out of her league here. Operating on only a few hours sleep and juggling too many balls in the air. She needed to drop one of them. *Drop the relationship ball,* she thought.

But she didn't want to.

"I want you to quit working with the CDC and join us at Rebel Virology. Now that I've seen you in action I can safely say that you would be a perfect fit."

"I'm not sure... I can't resign without returning from my leave of absence. Plus, my life is in Atlanta."

"Your life is wherever you are, Jane. This is an easy thing to do. Call Meredith and say, 'Screw you, I quit.' Then you turn to me and say, 'Hey, babe, I'm yours.'"

"Mac, does any woman ever fall for your outdated lines?"

He waggled his eyebrows at her. "I don't know. You tell me."

"No. At least I don't. Listen, we need to work on making more of our treatment and finding out who else has been infected with the disease. You mentioned a tribe you'd been living with in Belize. Do you want to take a team to them and use the treatment?"

"Yes. I'm pretty sure that it's spread up and down the border. I've heard reports from the tribal men of the same type of sickness everywhere."

"Then we need to make a plan of action. I'm going to call Meredith and insist that CDC send some reinforcements. I think we should tap the WHO, as well. Do you have anyone at R.V. who's available? Is Maria still at Tambo's village?"

"Slow down, Jane. With Raul on the loose I think our first priority should be apprehending him."

"That's not what I'm here to do. I came here to save lives. That has to be my priority."

"Very well. Let me call Maria and find out if she can join us."

She tossed him her phone. "Thanks."

She turned away from him and walked into the village, very aware that nothing had been settled between the two of them. But she'd fallen back on virology. Infectious diseases were safe and predictable once she figured out the key. She wished Mac were as easy to unlock.

Jane walked into the lab, eager to type up her notes. She entered the room and noticed the centrifuge machine was running. Immediately, she glanced around. Mac was in the rain forest talking on the phone and her father was with Selena. Who else would know how to operate the machine?

She took her knife from her ankle sheath and dropped back into a defensive position. Had Raul returned?

There were several crates stacked along the wall that hadn't been there before. What the hell was going on?

"Hello, Jane."

Meredith sat on the floor in the back of the room, sorting through the cords to plug in a second centrifuge machine. Packing materials littered the floor around her. She had her hair pulled back in a ponytail and her clothing was rumpled.

"What are you doing here?" Jane asked, keeping the knife out. Meredith noticed the weapon and lifted her hands, showing that she wasn't armed.

Jane tucked the knife into her pants at the small of her back. "Sorry about that. The last time I was in the lab I was attacked."

"I'm the one who's sorry. I should have listened when you first came to me. I'm afraid I acted right into their hands when I heard your father's name."

"Why?" she asked. Years of friendship were gone, in Jane's mind. There was no reason why Meredith shouldn't have trusted her. Jane had worked long, hard hours to get where she was in the world of infectious diseases and not once had she taken a shortcut.

"Because I felt he'd betrayed me. Anyway, I finally got the go-ahead to back your project."

"Why now?"

"A separate report of a strange virus in the area. I apologize for not backing you. I knew you needed help and from the beginning my gut said to trust you."

Jane didn't buy that, but she wasn't going to argue. She needed another set of hands here. "We've just started treatment for the village and I'm ready to send other virologists to other camps in the region. How many others are coming?"

Meredith got to her feet. She looked sheepish. "No one. I came on my own. But now that I'm here...all I can say is that someone was feeding us the wrong information."

"Not me," Jane said. She wasn't ready to forgive and

forget. She'd had a rough time getting to her father and a little help from Meredith would have eased the way.

"No, not you. But someone close to you."

"Tom."

Meredith nodded. "How'd you know?"

"Dad. As soon as I got here he told me about the team who'd come from Lima." Meredith looked away from her and Jane wondered if Meredith had seen her father yet. It would be hard to face an ex-lover and man who you thought... Jane stopped, realizing she and Meredith had things in common that neither of them wanted. They both had given themselves to men who'd do anything to further their careers. Jane was beginning to believe that her father had not deliberately set out to harm others.

But Raul was a different story. And a part of her was saddened by what had happened to him. Maybe if she'd been a different kind of woman, able to look outside herself and her career, she would have been able to help him.

"There's one man I wasn't familiar with," Meredith said.

"Yabidwa Rodriguez. He worked with Rebel Virology. He was doing a kind of internal investigation. Mac Coleman took up the task."

"Where is Yabidwa now?" Meredith asked.

"Dead. He was the first casualty of Raul's and Tom's greed." Jane watched her boss move around the lab, setting up equipment and straightening the place. She sensed that Meredith was nervous. Why?

"Tom is talking and I've brought in Interpol to find Raul," Meredith said at last. "The Peruvian government and Brazilian officials are working with us—well, the State Department—the WHO and each other to make sure that the virus doesn't leave this area."

"Good," Jane said.

She took her notes and jotted down a few things about the treatment of the village. "I need to start making rounds in about twenty minutes. I'm going to check on Dad. Want to come?"

"No. I'll help with your rounds, though," Meredith said. There was an aura of sadness around the other woman that Jane didn't wholly understand. She wondered what had really been the basis of the relationship between her father and Meredith.

And though she was still a little miffed at the way her boss had handled this entire outbreak, Jane couldn't ignore years of friendship. She wanted to comfort her friend.

"He's not like I remembered him, Mer. I think you'll see he's changed."

"I'm sure he has. I'm not sure I have. I'm still mad at him for throwing away…"

Jane understood. "If it helps, I was equally blind at the time to both Dad and Raul."

"Are you sure this is Raul's doing and not your father's?"

"Yes. He was here in the village just yesterday. He's crazy. He admitted to starting this whole outbreak himself. He needed to find something to save his job."

"By killing?"

"Yeah, struck me the same way. I'm not sure I can really explain it, but I think he wanted to have the kind of big find that hasn't been seen since AIDS."

Meredith shook her head. They saw it all the time. The search, the fruitless stops and starts that led nowhere. Virology grew and changed, but it was still just a science and subject to the whims of Mother Nature.

"Has he changed his mind?" Meredith asked.

"I don't know. I just hope he's caught before he does any more damage."

Jane headed for her father's cabin, eager to check on both him and Selena. Heavy humidity hung in the air and there was no breeze stirring around. It felt like the buildup before a heavy rain. She hoped it would hold off a few more hours so she could make her rounds at least once without getting wet but she knew that Mother Nature made her own decisions.

Selena's condition weighed heavily on her. She hadn't seen Ernesto, and she hoped he was with his wife. Hoped that they were now sharing some sort of time together that would reassure the shaman that she didn't mean him and his people any harm.

She heard footsteps behind her and glanced over her shoulder, then stopped in shock. Raul stood there—but not as she'd seen him before. He was unkempt, his hair standing out from his head and a wild look in his eyes.

She had seconds to decide if she should try to reason with him or just run. She turned and sprinted away. He caught her before she'd taken four steps and brought her down to the ground, holding her in an iron grip that allowed no movement.

Jane bucked and arched her back, trying to throw him off but he held her with a maniac's grip that couldn't be broken. He had a stranglehold on her neck.

Jane lifted both hands to her neck to try and free her throat but then she noticed the hypodermic needle in his other hand.

"What?" she managed to choke out.

"I want you to die for your find," he said, spittle dribbling from his mouth. "How tragic that will be."

He was enraged and there was nothing she could say to stop him. She tried to push his hand away and realized he had a kind of strength she couldn't beat.

Like hell.

She wasn't going down without a fight. She wasn't going to lie here while he injected her with a lethal virus just because he… She'd heard his reasons before but she still didn't understand what was going on.

Levering her feet under her body she pushed up from the ground and knocked Raul off balance. His grip on her throat tightened. She kept pushing until he rolled to his side. The tip of the needle brushed her arm and some of the liquid spilled out of the tip but he hadn't broken the skin.

A small panic stirred to life inside her. What if she was infected? She'd vaccinated herself, but with an untested vaccine…. She pushed the panic aside. Cool, calm reasoning was called for. The kind that she was famous for possessing.

Jane tried to get to her feet, but Raul tackled her in the back of the legs, bringing her down again. Rain started to fall, shockingly cold against her skin. She squirmed to get out of Raul's grip, but he held on.

She drew her leg back and kicked him in the chin. He groaned as the heel of her hiking boot connected solidly with his jaw. But he didn't let go. He slammed her hard into the ground. Jane's head snapped backward, connecting with the solid earth.

Stars danced in her eyes and she struggled to stay alert. Raul moved toward her. Jane didn't let her gaze leave the hypodermic in his hand. She tried to push to her feet but was too dizzy to stand.

Physically she didn't stand a chance against him. He was stronger than she was normally and his rage was adding to that strength. Jane swallowed and realized that she had to find a way to connect to the man he'd once been. The lover she'd known for a brief period in her life.

"Please, Raul. I don't want to die like this," she said, playing to his fears. He wanted her weak. Perhaps she could avoid being injected if she seemed to give up control.

He paused—for a second, she saw a bit of clear reasoning enter his gaze. "I don't want you to die, Jane."

He came closer to her. "Good. Let's work together, Raul. Isn't that what you wanted us to do?"

"Yes," he said. He dropped to his knees next to her and reached out, running one finger down the side of her face. "Together we can do great things."

She wasn't sure about that. But as long as together they both lived she'd figure the rest out later. She had to get the needle away from him. She levered herself up on her elbow.

"I know that there's a way to work this out. Why don't we find a place that's dry where we can talk?"

Raul shook his head. She saw him glance over her shoulder. His face tightened and the maniacal gleam was back.

Jane peeked over her shoulder. Mac moved toward them, looking like a man searching for vengeance. He had his gun drawn and an expression on his face that she'd never seen before.

Jane was caught between the two men. Her knife was digging into her back and she tried to reach it. But before she could pull the weapon, Raul moved.

He pushed to his feet. Reaching behind his back, he pulled a semiautomatic handgun and fired. He hit Mac in the chest and then the leg. Her ears rang from the sounds of the shots. She was helpless to do anything but watch the blood flow down Mac's chest as he fell to the ground.

Mac still fired two shots. One hit Raul's side—was it fatal? The other grazed Raul's temple. Raul dropped to his knees.

Raul's attention was on Mac and Jane pulled her knife from the small of her back and threw it hard at Raul.

She caught him in the shoulder of his gun hand. The hand spasmed and the gun dropped to the ground, firing one more time. The bullet grazed her thigh. God, it burned. She pressed her hand to the wound. But that only made it hurt more. She rolled to her feet.

Raul pulled the knife from his shoulder, then fell to the ground.

He turned toward her, blood seeping from his mouth. "You win."

But it didn't feel like victory as she stood in the cold pouring rain with two of her lovers lying on the ground, dying.

Chapter 21

Jane hurried to Mac's side, checking for a pulse. She found one and it was strong. He moaned as she unbuttoned his shirt and pushed it aside. She probed for the bullet but he brushed her hands away.

"I'm fine," he rasped.

She closed her eyes and leaned down, resting her forehead against his. "You crazy man."

"Hey, I've got to do something to keep up with you."

She shook her head. He opened his eyes. "Don't do anything like that again. I thought he killed you."

"I was afraid for you, Jane. I don't like that feeling."

"I keep telling you I can take care of myself."

"I know it, but sometimes... Hell, woman, you aren't invincible."

Each word he spoke was thinner than the last and she

knew that though he was putting on a good show of being okay he wasn't. She inhaled deeply and was assailed with the coppery scent of blood. She sat up. "I can't tell if the bullet's still in there. I need to get you to a bed."

"Why do you say things like that when I'm weak?" he said, attempting to waggle his eyebrows at her. "Damn, I ache."

"Come on, tough guy. On your feet."

He groaned as she levered him up into a sitting position. She'd seen him looking worse with the bug bite and she knew that Mac had the kind of strength she'd always wanted to find in a man and rarely had.

And she also knew that he'd taken a bullet for her. That he'd stepped into the open with her known enemy to save her life.

"Can you stand?" she asked. She wished she had the strength to carry him but she didn't. She scanned the area around them. Most of the Yura were in their homes tending their own sick. The thunder must have covered the sounds of the gunshots, for no one had come to investigate.

"Yes," he said, his voice filled with gritty resolve.

"Here we go," Jane said. He cursed loudly as they both got to their feet. He swayed and Jane feared he was going to collapse. She knew she had to get him good and angry or at least determined in order to get him to a bed.

"You've looked better," she said, forcing the words to sound light. Her heart was breaking to see him like this.

"Hell, I've felt better. Babe, you're hell on me," he said.

"It's not me," she said, stepping under his arm and turning him toward her father's cabin. "Can you walk?"

He took a step forward but swayed and almost fell to his knees. "I don't think so. Dammit, Jane. Don't think I'm weak."

She held him up, taking all of his weight and wrapping her arms around his middle. "I know better, Mac. Thank you."

"For what?" he asked.

She cradled his face in her hands. He was pale and his breathing was shallow. "Being my hero."

"Don't play with me."

"I'm not."

Raul groaned on the ground. She saw his body convulsing and she knew she couldn't let him die like this. "This isn't over."

"I sure as hell hope not."

She saw Ernesto emerge from her father's cabin and move toward her with that effortless stride of his.

"Take them both to Dad. He'll know how to treat their wounds."

Ernesto gestured to his men.

Two Yura warriors each lifted up Raul and Mac and took them away. Meredith stood in the doorway, just watching. Tears ran down the older woman's face and Jane realized that she was in some kind of shock. Jane felt the same thing herself.

Meredith and Jane followed to help. The next hour was a blur of stopping blood flow and cleaning wounds. When they'd done all they could, Jane left the cabin to check on the villagers and found a pretty Hispanic woman and five men in the clearing.

"I'm Maria Cortez with Rebel Virology. This is my team. We're here to help the Yura."

Jane brought the other woman and her five-person team up to speed and sent them with Meredith to check on the infected people. Then she hurried back to her dad's cabin. When she entered she found her father and Ernesto playing a game of chess in the corner of the room. Selena slept peacefully. Raul groaned on the cot and Mac slept on her father's bed.

"Mac?" she asked her dad when he looked up.

"He'll live. The bullet passed through clean. I gave him some pain pills and antibiotics. But he should be fine."

Jane crossed the room and stood by her father. "Thanks, Dad."

"No. Thank you, Jane. For coming when I needed you despite what you thought of me."

"What did happen?" she asked. She never really understood what had gone wrong. "I really want to hear your side of the story."

"Raul was eager to please and wanted more responsibility so I kept giving it to him. Only years later did I realize that I should have been double-checking his work."

"Poor Raul. He always thought he had to have a big find to make a name for himself. He never realized you've made a career of just solid medicine." Jane thought a lot about men like her father and Mac and how Raul could have had a quiet career full of the kind of successes that no one ever wrote about in the *Journal of Medicine* or in *Science Times*.

"Neither did you," he said quietly.

Jane leaned down and gave her father a hug. There was a new acceptance deep inside her. She knew she wouldn't return to the CDC and lock herself away in her lab. "Thanks, Dad."

"For what?" he asked.

Jane suddenly was aware of Ernesto watching her and she felt…awkward, but there was a calm acceptance in his eyes and she knew that she'd found the missing part of her soul. The part she'd always been embarrassed by.

"Everything," she said at last.

"I know I've never been father-of-the-year—"

"I didn't let you. But I think we can make up for that now."

"I think so, too."

She left them to get back to their game and went to sit by Mac. She'd learned more about native medicine in the last twenty-four hours than she'd ever expected to. She looked down at Mac's sleeping face.

He still looked like a tough-ass bandit without a heart but she knew how deeply he cared and how important his work with infectious diseases was. He'd never leave her hanging the way Meredith had. Jane had made her decision last night and had spoken to Meredith about it. She wouldn't be returning to the CDC.

Jane packed the last box of her stuff and put it in the storage unit just outside of Atlanta. It had been three months since she'd left the Amazon basin. The Amazon strain was now under control, although they'd found it had spread throughout the area. Raul was looking at a long-term prison sentence and Tom was going to be serving one, as well.

Meredith had resigned her post with the CDC to join Rob Miller in the Amazon basin. Jane had been surprised by the move but then change seemed to be in the air.

"Hurry up or we'll miss our flight."

Jane turned to see Mac waiting for her, holding out his hand. He wore dark aviator-style shades and his beard was neatly trimmed. She'd taken him up on his job offer.

Jane was slowly getting used to having him in her life. They'd actually been living together. "What's your hurry?"

"The clock is ticking, babe. And we don't want this germ to get a leg up on us."

She shook her head. "With the virus hunters on the case I don't think any outbreak stands a chance."

She hopped in the Jeep and Mac steered them toward Hartsfield International Airport, where they'd board a flight for Ecuador. Jane found working for Rebel Virology was giving her a chance to really blend all parts of her life together.

There was just one thing she had to set straight, right now. "Mac?"

"Yeah?"

"Don't call me babe." His laugh echoed into her heart.

And she knew she was happier now than she'd ever imagined she could be.

* * * * *

Mills & Boon® Intrigue
brings you a sneak preview of…

Jessica Andersen's Meet Me at Midnight

Secret Service agent Ty Jones had only one lead
left to the madman who'd plunged Boston into
a blackout, ambushed his team-mates and
kidnapped the vice-president – Gabriella Solaro,
the computer hacker he's been keeping tabs on
with a fake online romance.

Yet when he meets her in person she casts doubt
on his suspicions. Drawn to her, he promises
to keep her safe. But when the time came, would
he follow his heart…or his duty?

Don't miss this thrilling new story,
available next month!

Meet Me at Midnight

by

Jessica Andersen

Dear CyberGabby:

I've never used a service like Webmatch.com before, so I apologize in advance if I mess up. I saw your picture and read your profile, and I think we have some things in common. My name is Ty, I'm thirty-five, divorced and relatively free of baggage. Like you, I enjoy classic cars and driving fast. I work as a body-guard because I also like traveling and staying on the move. It's not as exciting as it might sound, though. I work for a corporate type, so it's mostly standing outside boring meetings. Which, I suppose, is better than actually attending the meetings. Anyway, I'm looking forward to getting to know you better. I've posted my picture and profile (click here). If you're interested, shoot me a note and we can chat.

[Sent by TyJ; March 17, 1:03:13 a.m.]

9:58 p.m., August 2
7 Hours and 40 Minutes to Dawn

Ty Jones paused in the shadows beyond a small, cobbled courtyard in Boston's North End, breathing past the tension of battle readiness.

The light from a kerosene lantern broke the absolute darkness, casting warm shadows on the woman who waited for him in the hot, humid summer night. The lamplight should have been almost painfully romantic.

Instead, it was a necessity.

Boston had been in the grips of a widespread blackout for twenty-five hours now. Most of the city's inhabitants thought there had been a massive failure at Boston Power & Light, but Ty and his teammates knew the blackout had been no accident. It had been a cover. Under the cloak of darkness, a man they'd once trusted had kidnapped Grant Davis, Vice President of the United States.

Now, twenty-five hours later, with Davis's life hanging in the balance and his captor hinting that a bomb had been planted somewhere in the city, Ty and the others were out of time and options.

Which had brought him here, to a clandestine rendezvous with Internet bombshell Gabriella Solaro.

Ty's watch chimed softly. It was ten o'clock. Time to meet the one connection he had left, the one woman who could possibly lead them to Liam Shea, the man behind the blackout.

Taking a deep breath, Ty stepped out of concealment and swung open the ornate wrought iron gate that separated the North End courtyard from the narrow street. Pitching his voice low, he called, "Gabriella?"

The woman was facing away from him. At the sound of her name, she turned and lifted the lantern. "Ty?"

Her voice was soft and feminine, just as he'd imagined it during their online conversations, first in a chat room at Webmatch.com, then one-on-one via e-mail and instant messenger. But oddly, she looked nothing like he'd expected.

Her dark eyes complemented full, red-painted lips, and her features were sharp and exotic, but in the lantern light, her hair seemed darker than the fiery chestnut she'd mentioned, and her simple sundress made her figure seem more angular than her self-described curvy-bordering-on-plump.

She was lovely, but she wasn't anything like the picture in her profile. Then again, why should that surprise him? It was all too easy to bend the truth and become someone else on the Internet.

He should know.

Stepping forward into the circle of lantern light, Ty hesitated, wondering what she'd expect. Should he hug her? Kiss her? They'd met through an online dating service, which carried a certain expectation, and they'd e-chatted long into many nights, forming the illusion of intimacy. But none of it had been real, had it?

More important, their last few exchanges had been increasingly tense, as he'd pressed for a meeting and she'd resisted, which had solidified his suspicions even before Liam had made his move.

Now, though, Ty had a part to play. He leaned in and kissed her on the cheek. "It's nice to finally meet you in person."

If he hadn't been watching her face as he eased back, he would've missed the moment her eyes slid beyond him to a deeply shadowed corner where two brick-walled houses converged.

Instinct tightened the back of Ty's neck.

Someone was watching.

He forced himself not to react, instead smiling easily. "I'm surprised you agreed to meet me in the middle of this godawful blackout, especially with the curfew and all. Heck, I wasn't even sure my e-mail would get through, or that you'd have enough juice to read it."

With Liam's three accomplices, his sons Finn, Aidan and Colin, all out of action—one dead, one comatose, one not talking—Ty had known Gabby was perhaps their last hope for finding the mastermind. He'd broken into a stranger's car, plugged his handheld into the cigarette lighter and stolen enough charge to send the message. Then he'd waited in the darkness, listening to the sounds of growing violence nearby as the looting continued and the National Guard moved in to enforce the mayor's new curfew. The mob had almost reached him by the time she'd e-mailed back, arranging the meet.

As Ty had locked the car and slipped away for a quick radio convo with his boss, part of him had hoped she'd agreed to meet him out of curiosity, that the woman he'd gotten to know online was the real deal.

Now, as she glanced into the shadows a second time, conflicting emotions stirred within him—vicious satisfaction that he'd come to the right place and disappointment that she hadn't been the real deal, after all.

"I got your message on my Blackberry," she answered. "I was surprised you wanted to meet face-to-face, especially after that last e-mail I sent you, but I was…curious, I guess." She glanced at him, eyes dark and a little cool with an emotion that was either nerves or calculation. "You didn't have any problems getting here? Nobody stopped you?"

"I made it okay." His credentials had gotten him through the first two roadblocks, but he'd ended up ditching his car near the waterfront, where the Guard's bulldozers and tow trucks hadn't yet cleared the roadways. Numerous cars had wrecked right after the blackout, when the traffic lights went down, and even more vehicles had been abandoned later, when rumors of a terrorist attack had sent the city's residents fleeing in panic, only to have them wind up trapped in gridlock, frying in the hot summer sun.

Dull anger kindled in his gut at the thought of so much chaos created by a single ex-con and his sons, but he kept his voice light and friendly when he said, "How about you? No problems so far with the lights off?"

She shifted from one foot to the other, seeming uncomfortable—or was that just part of the act? After a hesitation so brief he wouldn't have noticed it if he hadn't been looking, she tipped her head, fluttered her eyelashes and said, "Would you like to sit down and talk for a little bit? There's a fountain and some benches in the next courtyard over. The neighbors won't mind."

She pointed to a secluded spot where the cobblestone path narrowed between two planted areas, no doubt near where her associate waited.

Keeping his weight evenly balanced on the balls of his feet, ready for a fight, Ty nodded. "The courtyard sounds perfect."

She set the lantern on the edge of a nearby stone planter before starting down the short path. Was it a signal? Ty didn't know, but he was tense with battle readiness as he followed in her wake.

They'd taken just three steps into the shadows when he heard a rustle and the faint indrawn breath that presaged attack.

"Freeze!" Ty palmed the revolver he wore at his hip and grabbed Gabriella in a single move, spinning her back against his body and clamping an arm across her throat.

She screamed and struggled to escape, her elbows digging into his ribs, her heels drumming against his shins. He could feel her heartbeat jackhammering beneath his forearm, mute evidence that she might be a liar, but she wasn't a trained operative.

"Be still." He cocked the revolver, and the click resonated on the humid air, freezing her in place.

He carried a semiautomatic with fifteen in the clip as his primary weapon, tucked into an underarm holster, but he'd long ago found that the six-shooter had the edge when it came to intimidation.

The click said he meant business. Right now his business was finding Grant Davis and locating the bomb that'd been planted somewhere in the city, and to do that, he had to get his hands on Liam Shea.

Adrenaline pounded through Ty's veins as he leaned close and spoke into his captive's delicate ear. "Tell him to toss his weapons and come out with his hands up."

If he was damn lucky, it would be Shea himself. If not, he hoped it was an underling he could lean on for the bastard's location.

Gabby whimpered in the back of her throat and jerked her head in some semblance of a nod. Tears streamed down her cheeks and she was shaking all over, almost enough to convince him she was for real.

A sliver of compassion twisted through Ty, along with snippets from the hundreds of notes they'd exchanged over the past five-plus months. She'd written about honesty, and about problems with her family, and, damn it, she'd seemed real enough that he'd responded in kind.

Maybe she really hadn't known what she was getting into, he rationalized. Maybe it had seemed like a game to her, or perhaps she was one of those bleeding hearts who believed in rehabilitation of hardened criminals.

If so, he could've told her not to bother. Liam had been a traitor eleven years earlier, and he was a traitor now.

One who damn well belonged back in jail.

When there was no motion from the bushes, Ty raised his voice. "Come out here. Now!" A breath of wind disturbed the hot, humid air, unfurling a nearby flag and making it snap. "You've got until three. One…two…"

The bushes moved and a figure stepped out onto the path, nearly lost in the darkness.

"Back up into the courtyard," he ordered, his pulse accelerating as he tried to assess the risks and control the scene.

"Go on. Easy now." He marched Gabby along the path in front of him, using her as a shield as the shadowy figure complied, backing into the courtyard with a hitching motion, as though feeling the way. Moments later, the figure stepped into the circle of lantern light, and the illumination chased away the anonymous shadows.

Ty froze.

It wasn't Liam Shea. It was a woman, and she sure as hell didn't look like anyone's hired gun.

STAYING ALIVE
by Debra Webb

Claire Grant had become a target for one of the most deadly men on earth. The FBI's ultrasexy agent Luke Krueger stepped in with a plan to take out the terrorists – using Claire as bait.

LAZLO'S LAST STAND
by Kathleen Creighton

Corbett Lazlo needs her to play his lover to lure the terrorists out of hiding – but his growing feelings for Lucia Cordez could be an even greater danger than the assassins on their trail.

BLOOD CALLS
by Caridad Piñeiro

Five centuries ago Diego had vowed never to turn another with the bite of the undead. The underworld of New York was no place for a human, yet his desire commanded that Ramona be his...

TAKEN BY THE SPY
by Cindy Dees

Kinsey Hollingsworth's tropical-getaway plans didn't include a speedboat chase with a tempting spy who'd commandeered her boat. The socialite would handle anything Mitch demanded – whether it meant going undercover or under the covers.

To marry a sheikh!

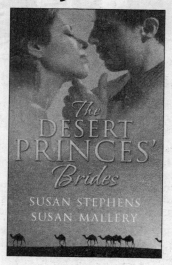

The Sheikh's Captive Bride by Susan Stephens

After one passionate night, Lucy is now the mother of
Sheikh Kahlil's son and Kahlil insists that Lucy must
marry him. She can't deny her desire to share his bed
again, but marriage should be forever.

The Sheikh & the Princess Bride by Susan Mallery

Even though beautiful flight instructor Billie Van Horn
was better than Prince Jefri of Bahania in the air,
he'd bet his fortune that he was her perfect match
in the bedroom!

Available 19th December 2008

FREE!

4 Books
and a surprise gift!

We would like to take this opportunity to thank you for reading this Mills & Boon® book by offering you the chance to take FOUR more specially selected titles from the Intrigue series absolutely FREE! We're also making this offer to introduce you to the benefits of the Mills & Boon® Book Club™—

- ★ **FREE home delivery**
- ★ **FREE gifts and competitions**
- ★ **FREE monthly Newsletter**
- ★ **Exclusive Mills & Boon Book Club offers**
- ★ **Books available before they're in the shops**

Accepting these FREE books and gift places you under no obligation to buy, you may cancel at any time, even after receiving your free shipment. Simply complete your details below and return the entire page to the address below. You don't even need a stamp!

YES! Please send me 4 free Intrigue books and a surprise gift. I understand that unless you hear from me, I will receive 6 superb new titles every month for just £3.15 each, postage and packing free. I am under no obligation to purchase any books and may cancel my subscription at any time. The free books and gift will be mine to keep in any case.

18ZEF

Ms/Mrs/Miss/Mr ....Initials.................................

BLOCK CAPITALS PLEASE

Surname...

Address...

....

....Postcode.........................

Send this whole page to:
UK: FREEPOST CN81, Croydon, CR9 3WZ

Offer valid in UK only and is not available to current Mills & Boon Book Club subscribers to this series. Overseas and Eire please write for details. We reserve the right to refuse an application and applicants must be aged 18 years or over. Only one application per household. Terms and prices subject to change without notice. Offer expires 28th February 2009. As a result of this application, you may receive offers from Harlequin Mills & Boon and other carefully selected companies. If you would prefer not to share in this opportunity please write to The Data Manager, PO Box 676, Richmond, TW9 1WU.

Mills & Boon® is a registered trademark owned by Harlequin Mills & Boon Limited.
The Mills & Boon® Book Club™ is being used as a trademark.